SISTERHOOD
of the
INFAMOUS

SISTERHOOD
of the INFAMOUS

a novel by
Jane Rosenberg LaForge

LIBRARY OF CONGRESS CATALOGING-IN-PUBLICATION DATA

Sisterhood of the Infamous
Authored by Jane Rosenberg LaForge

ISBN: 9781734383539
LCCN: 2020944149

For Eva

CONTENTS

PROLOGUE

A BODY ALWAYS BEGINS A STORY SUCH AS THIS. My body, her body; mine to be burned, hers razed by violent action; to be discovered along a remote trail of russet hills and yellow grass, beneath a rare, open sky. She will be laid in a cemetery that becomes a stop on a tourist bus or a destination undertaken on adolescent pilgrimages. I will be spread on the water, to sink to the bottom, or evaporated into the nether-history of the air.

My city is one of many bodies and many hillsides to receive them. Only a particular type of body found on a hillside, by a jogger or a group of stoned teenagers, inspires curiosity into its origins. Only a body that is female and clean, with neither venereal nor retroviral antibodies in the blood—without the scars of surgery, braces, medically sanctioned beatings—much like I wear now. But they are temporary; they too will be swallowed up by the fire. Her body will be remembered because of its face, recognizable and youthful or with the power to remind people of their youth. Mine reminds people not so much of age but the frustrations of aging: missed opportunities and squandered talents.

Some bodies are born to this punishment, like mine; others are drafted, like hers. Some are transformed by the brutality of other bodies to become grotesque discoveries. I think that is how I became this way. Not dead but dying.

1

Others do not seem capable of death, their resources of power and elegance planted among the masses so that there is always more to draw upon, more to be inspired by, more fodder for creation. When she dies in body, she will not in spirit; she will have a legacy and become a font for new traditions, a fountain of redemption. And people will bathe in it in her memory. They will consult it when they're blocked, or bored, or require an excuse to dispose of their responsibilities. I would have liked to participate in these rituals, but I will not. My body precludes me from such strenuous activities.

CHAPTER 1

I HANG ON THROUGH MY SISTER'S VISITS. She visits for many reasons, none of which have anything to do with me. She is visiting me now because she believes, with all of the best intentions, that this is the end for me, and she feels that she should be here, despite her feigned distaste for morbid events. She did not visit when our mother was dying, though that may have been because I did not let on what was happening. I didn't want her there, with her asking the doctors questions intended not for answers, but to make her look better. I didn't want her there swooping over the nurses, bandying about with directions that were meaningless. I suppose she was there for our father though. She likes to remind me. She relishes it. I was not there and proud of it.

But the mind wanders. My sister is now visiting. I don't know when she arrived, but I can guess it was difficult and dramatic. She lives in New York with her husband, the piano player, and daughter, who is still in elementary school and therefore requires inordinate amounts of attention. The daughter makes it a sacrifice for my sister to just contemplate coming. She cannot leave the daughter for a single moment unattended, as our parents often left us. The daughter makes it heroic for my sister to accomplish anything: getting dressed, paying her bills, carrying sufficient amounts of cash when she is dining out with friends or family. The daughter is my sister's career now that she does not have one.

But the mind wanders. It wandered during the chemotherapy, and the nurses called it "chemo brain." It wanders now, and there is no therapy. Only palliative care. Stopgap. Ad hoc. Answering the pain. Treating the symptoms. My sister is visiting, and she must have gotten in last night, because I heard something. The front door opening, as if the house had to take in a gulp of fresh air to steel itself for her visit. The delivery of luggage, the wheels against the slate floor before it reached the carpeting. The machinery of the blow-up bed, a sustained, almost nasal hum, as the oxygen was shoved inside of it. This morning, she was sitting here, by the bed, speaking her nonchalant nonsense, and then people came in. A herd of people I did not know; I could tell by the heaviness in their footsteps. They tried to be delicate about it, placing their feet on the floor as though they expected to fall through it. But their boots betrayed them.

They shouted: ma'am, miss, Ms. Ross. Hello, hello, can you hear us? They shouted some initials, and police! Police officers! They snapped their fingers in my face. I felt air expel from their middle fingers and thumbs, as if they wanted to pinch my cheeks. I felt more air, a wave across my face: a nurse, or nurses, shooing them away. All the nurses have accents. I think there are three nurses on the day shift. The Nina, the Pinta, and the Santa Maria. That should cover all the categories: Haitian-Jamaican-Mexican-African-Asian. I can no longer distinguish them or even what they're saying. But I know what accents do to people, men especially, policemen in particular. It makes them disinclined to listen.

I feel more air, as if a small piece of fabric is being unfurled, a washcloth, flickering at my forehead. This is how the nurses run interference; I've seen this before when the neighbors have come over, or the attorneys, or even some friends of my mother's. They scroll out these rags as if they were the bloody flag, fan me with them, send out a distress signal, limp warnings via a raggedy semaphore. This woman is in hospice. What part of "hospice" do you not understand? Does "cancer patient" mean anything to you? Do you really want to upset the cancer patient? Do you know what happens when she is upset, have you seen it? The flood of tears, the saliva wetting her chin? The mucus that invades the throat and sinuses, threatens to drown her breathing, and choke her off: do you really want to see that? A dying person cannot control her functions; once the mouth and sinuses go, you know what is next. You are making more work for us.

I can hear voices coming from somewhere, the living room or the kitchen. The bedrooms might as well be soundproofed; voices carry only from the living room or kitchen. I don't know if it's the distance or the angle, but I can't latch onto the content of what is being said. I'm getting the noise but no articulation, just the insistence and urgency that comes from hostile dialogue, one-sided discussions. There are eight types of noise, and twenty-six different ways to measure them, not including subcategories, colors, and noises that are concurrent with the signal that fails to unify both elements.

I can distinguish this noise by how it recollects previous sounds in this house, like the arguments my parents had once they put me and my sister to bed—arguments that taught me to hate my father's voice, its pace and fury. There was always some kind of rumble to it, as if he kept his anger on call, so that he could summon it on the spot, as he liked to for most any occasion. He also loved to talk, tell stories. They weren't really stories to me, more like lectures. The man could not shut up. Even when he was happy. Then it was as if a low-grade fever gripped the household, and any movement that was too fast, any comment that was the least bit bold or deviated from the script, might set the fever climbing to cataclysmic levels.

For now, the sound being carried throughout the house is lukewarm, gray but brightening at its edges, with a potential of snapping into orange. Something is stopping it, cooling it down. Like something that my mother used to try, without much success; once, she tried keeping the books for one of our father's so-called businesses, and he could not distinguish profits from losses. That's because they were indistinguishable. Or another time, something else about money. How much of it was real, how much had he imagined and borrowed too much against? At the time these situations were unraveling I knew nothing, though my sister might have had a better grip. Her bedroom was closer to the kitchen and living room. Her being older, though not by much, she might have been able to intuit variances in tone if not individual words and their connotations. Much, much later, when we were both failing as adults—I admit it, but my sister is far more self-deluding and reluctant to acknowledge it—our mother finally briefed us on all the scenarios that fueled these vocal workouts, which we in our youth had largely avoided.

Now I am in my mother's room at the back of the house, the master bedroom, the sanctum my sister and I were permitted to enter only on the direst of occasions: earthquakes and thunderstorms. And the school holidays when we were bored and defeated by the neighborhood and the other kids. Our mother would let us watch television here when our father was not home. He hated us in his bed, said we vandalized it with the muck we carried from the backyard, the street, the school, from childhood.

This must be where I was conceived. My parents were rather conventional in that way. Not like the other parents, the famous ones, musicians, actors, comedians, the down-and-out, and the up-and-coming. Their children were funneled through the school system like the rest of us, but their parents were special. They weren't married. Sometimes they were lovers. Sometimes best friends. Sometimes they did not speak to each other but were partners in a songwriting enterprise or a production company. Somehow they made their offspring differently because they were special too. Dazzling in the attention they demanded. Everything about them, their tastes and talent for leadership, seemed more vivid. They were like Jasmine, who almost got me out of this house. They were like Jasmine, raised to be famous. They were like Jasmine, rare and radiant. Those qualities made them not only desirable, but also hard to capture, hold onto, onto her, because they burned as they escaped your grip: more fireworks you weren't supposed to play with.

My father had a thing for these people. He spent hours in this bedroom, watching them on television. He said he did business with some of them: selling them clothes, campers, and Christmas trees and decorations, and catering deals and Fourth of July packages. I think he made up much of what he told us, how he had known this one or not, had gone to school with the other one, had a friend who went out with the last of them. He spoke of them not as gods, and not as characters in a soap opera, but somewhere in between; some place that was accessible and not, always above our heads, a place this family, his wife and daughters, should not try to breach.

My father was so attuned to how everything should be done. The gold couch was for grown-ups and guests; we could sit on the black chair with the ottoman. We carved lines into the leather piping with our thumbnails. The leather responded to us, opening itself up as if to expose its blood, a rawness compared to the polish of the rest of the ottoman. We had heard of "blood brothers" and "blood sisters," but my sister and I lacked the strength to poke through our skins. We were frightened by what might come out, the combination of liquids and pathogens. But leather could not make such complaints. We sliced into it wholeheartedly, as if we could wed ourselves to it. It made us into materialists.

When our mother discovered the marks, she simply turned the ottoman around, so the degraded piping no longer faced out into the world. Now it was a secret. Had our father stayed longer, I suspect, he might have discovered this act of concealment, a veritable conspiracy to defraud him on the household's conditions. He might have had a genuine fit over it, as he did over the handprints we embossed onto the walls of our bedroom, or when we came into the house from the backyard barefoot. It was not that he did not love us, our mother said once; it was that he did not like evidence of us, the trail of crumbs, the pebbles and gravel we excavated and collected, whatever tracked on the bottom of our naked heels and soiled fingers. When he caught my sister and her boyfriend, he said she'd wind up a prostitute; no decent man would ever marry her. When he saw me with Jasmine, he thought it was chic, European, for us to be holding hands, exchanging kisses on the cheek. This was her game, a way to be out while still being officially concealed. When he found out about what I was, he said I was like a virus, a carrier spreading diseases, and I should be dumped in the San Francisco Bay with the other AIDS victims.

This bed is not where my mother died; the honor for that was usurped by a hospital bed. Economy mattresses, I've heard them called, but I've tried not to think about that. My mother often said she didn't care how or where she died, or what happened to her body after death. She said she wasn't going to be around for it, so why should her opinion matter. This must be what my sister remembers, when she decides to drop in or out, atone for whatever sins she's imagined she's committed by donating her time away from her husband and daughter to be here, to witness this important life event. An important event in her life, I suppose. A new one, at least, to add to her recitation of important events that make her who she is, that person to be admired for her selflessness.

I wonder what kind of act my sister could possibly be putting on now, in the kitchen, for the benefit of the policemen. I've seen all of her acts, or I've heard her talk about them in some way. She is definitely talking to the policemen; I know that now. I've figured it out. Something having to do with their shoes: you can always tell a narc by his shoes, she told me once. I don't know how she knew this. She wasn't a juvenile delinquent or one of those stoner girls. She just liked to act as if she wanted to be. She wanted to be famous or famous for rebelling. She wanted to be like Jasmine, but she wouldn't admit it. Her rebellion was disingenuous, though: you can't rebel by copying, and that's what she always does.

One thing I do remember about the arguments my sister heard, and I didn't: she said she felt as though she were trapped in the bed as they happened. She wasn't trapped, really, but experienced the sensation of being in bed as if she were locked into a restraining device, a brace, almost. That is something I know about, but she doesn't; I was put into a brace every night when I was a toddler. This is also information gleaned from one of my mother's confessions. I was born pigeon-toed, so my legs were broken, set into casts, and my left shoe was put on my right foot, and my left foot was put into a right shoe. At night, the shoes were locked into a bar screwed into the rails on either side of the bed. I slept with what my sister called "a perfect turnout," a term left over, like her dancing mannerisms. Every lift of her arm, or step she takes forward, has a slow, considered affect about it, as though each is a great moment of lights twinkling and rainbows unfurling. When she moves, she might as well be in suspended animation, because of the care she gives to each stage of her performance, as if her walk or backward glances should be treasured. For her to say she feels trapped when she has never been immobilized like I was, like I am, is not some kind of a joke—it's the worst kind of insult: insensitive and malicious. It also confirms everything I know about her and also our relationship—that she doesn't have my mettle, my will power, my strength, and she's jealous.

My sister doesn't dance anymore; she hasn't danced since before her daughter was born, but she is still the dancer—afflicted and aggrieved, with her discipline and accomplishments still a part of her body. They rise close enough to the surface so that anyone might be able to identify them and recognize her as someone of a particular achievement. When she says she felt as though she were trapped in the bed, then, you understand what an odious, indeed, unnatural state for her to have been put in. I might be experiencing a sympathetic reaction right now to what she claims to have withstood, though I was the one who endured it, who had to live with the residual effects if you could call this living.

MY SISTER COMES BACK. I can tell by the sudden depression in the bed, a slope that has taken root in the mattress. Everything must slide toward my sister. She makes sure of it. My sister was a ballerina, but her impact upon any surface is more like an elephant's. She is tilting and shoving, if not at me then at the coils and mattress stuffing.

She wants to tell me something, she says, but isn't sure whether she should; whether it would be the right thing, under the circumstances, my condition being so fraught, so precarious. But if she doesn't tell me, and I should find out on my own, what would I think of her? Nothing worse than I think of her now, because nothing could be. She has a talent for manipulating the focus, drawing it exclusively onto herself, as though she were the only objectively interesting subject in any setting. The other details—the other people, their circumstances, what brought them into this orbit—are crushed and discarded in all of her scenarios. Even in the ones where I am dying, where I will be dust. She will stir me up with her broken, suffering toes, and I will be in the background of her life forever.

The mattress shifts downward toward where she has finally settled, and she is holding my hands. She used to have such a fetish about my hands—how small they were. Like an infant's, she said, almost as if I were underdeveloped. She must be in one of her most earnest poses now, because she says she has to tell me this: I have a right to know. Or more likely, she has a right to tell me. Her grip is mechanical. She has become a conduit, and through her all information must be imparted, no matter how impolitic, unnecessary, rude, or vulgar. She is the older sister, and the older sister knows, protects, instructs, defends, and escorts the baby sister into this life and now apparently out of it.

She is always doing this to me, this brandishing of information, the top secrets, the confidential, and the private. She does this because it is her only way of demonstrating that she is superior, in the only way that she is superior, in years. She is two years older, but she is still the stupid one, though I don't mean that in a mean or malicious way. This is purely factual. She is not particularly smart. That's why her life turned out the way that it did, and why my life was what it was, or why our lives turned out so differently. She had advantages I didn't have, though I'm sure she doesn't see it that way. She'd have to admit that she is stupid and that I was the only one with a mind.

Yes, I have a mind. And it wanders. She says she has something to tell me, but I might not like it. This hasn't stopped her before. Once, she told me that I hated my father so much because I am so much like him. Once, she said being a gay woman was no big deal and that I'd better find another cross on which to nail myself, especially since all of her men friends were dying of AIDS. Once, she said I should watch out for the nurses, especially the Filipina ones, because they'd steal everything, though she said she could tell me this only because her Filipino lawyer had said to give me his message.

This time, she says she's going to tell me anyway, and I know why; because I don't have much time left. She doesn't actually say this, but it's implicit, embedded in her distractedness, the fidgeting and stalling. Everything has to be a performance, a gala of excerpts, never the whole story, which might make her look tawdry and narcissistic, which she is.

She says Jasmine is dead.

The mind wanders.

CHAPTER 2

"YOUR SISTER IS A STALKER," the cop said, and I suppose it was true. But I'd never heard it put this way. It was a little shocking to think of my sister as dangerous, uncontrollable, criminal. My first instinct was to deny accusations and to protect her; she was my little sister, remember, who was younger and shorter. My daughter called her "Aunt Baby." But I had nothing to protect her with.

"We have witnesses," the cop went on, and I didn't doubt him. Nothing else could have tied Barbara to Jasmine except witnesses, people who knew about them, about Barbara, about what we didn't think was stalking, but instead was a harmless obsession—harmless to Jasmine, that is, not to Barbara.

"Jasmine's father, her brothers: they told us. They've seen your sister on multiple occasions."

"She didn't start out that way," I said, because this was also true.

"Then how did it start?" he asked.

"It's a long story," I said, because it was thirty years long, although there had been a few breaks in between. Like when Jasmine moved out of town or when Barbara was in college. Then when Barbara got sick, was on chemo and didn't have the strength to drive by Jasmine's house, let alone bike or run past it. If anything, the cancer broke her of a habit, I thought.

Cancer was an incomplete blessing. But that was only a small part of the story. I wasn't ready to begin the whole thing.

"It always is," the cop said, nodding. He was trying to commiserate, act sympathetic, draw me out, and obtain my confession. But I hadn't done anything, and it should have been obvious to him that Barbara was incapable of doing anything.

"I couldn't tell you much," I admitted. "I was gone for most of it."

"'It'?" he insisted.

"They," I answered, but only because he had asked me directly. "They happened. My sister and Jasmine."

"Oh, I see," he said, though I knew this was an act; he was acting. Shocked, scandalized: he'd never heard of such a thing, two girls going together in high school. Like I had offended his sensibilities. After all, he was an older man, or he walked and sat as an older man would, like he was trying to balance the great bulk of his stomach on a tired body. Or maybe that was also part of his act, to present himself as harmless and at the end of his career, serving time until his retirement.

"I moved to New York after I graduated," I said. "It all happened when I wasn't here."

"Do you still live in New York?" he asked, but I could see he didn't care about where I lived. He'd gotten what he came for—a salacious detail or its confirmation. He must have already known since he had already talked to Jasmine's family. He asked a few more questions he probably already had the answers to—what year did Barbara and Jasmine graduate, when was the last time Barbara saw Jasmine—and maybe some he didn't, like when did I graduate, when did Barbara get sick. He must have thought the questions made him look genuinely interested in Barbara even though she had turned out to be a dead end. I was used to answering questions like this about my sister and the cancer, sometimes about what happened to my career. People ask not because they need this information but because they don't want to seem arrogant, or preoccupied. Maybe they even want people to think they're sincere.

"How long are you going to be here?" the other cop asked. I didn't get his name—it was spelled W-Y-R-E-C-K-A, and I couldn't imagine how to pronounce it—and the older cop, the one playing "good," I suppose, shot him a look that made me wonder whether I was really supposed to answer.

"He didn't mean that," the good cop said. His name was Simpson. I called him "Officer" when he came to the door, but he was a detective-sergeant, he informed me. He handed me his card and one from his partner: Homicide Special Section, the cards said. I could have asked why this was "special," but quickly thought better of it.

"I'm very sorry about your sister," Detective-Sergeant Simpson said, though moments before he had demanded to see her. He didn't believe me when I told her she was unable to come to the door or the kitchen; he didn't believe me when I said she was so sick and couldn't deal with visitors. He didn't start to believe me until I led him into the back bedroom. But still he had to snap his fingers in her face and shout out her name, probably to make certain she wasn't faking.

"My condolences, ma'am," the other cop said. I nodded even though it wasn't clear why he was offering them: for my sister? For Jasmine? But if I nodded, I knew he'd just go away. And there'd be another suspect knocked off his list. My sister. Like the guy who killed John Lennon. Except Lennon's killer was able-bodied, walking and talking when he did what he did. My sister was dying of cancer.

IN THE SICK ROOM, it was always night, timeless. The hospice nurses kept it dark, the shutters locked against the picture windows, like they were concealing a secret: how to die young, who will help you do it. Though the lights were off, the television was on: it was how the nurses told time, by the schedule of shows on one of the local channels. Everything was set to happen in half-hour slots or the length of syndicated sitcoms.

The nurses took Barbara out of her room, which had a twin mattress on the floor, and put her into this big bed when they moved her to hospice. This was our mother's bed or, more precisely, our mother's bed frame; we finally got rid of the original mattress when Helen got sick with pancreatic cancer and the strokes that followed. She was on that new mattress for about four months, and then she was gone. The bed stayed empty until Barbara needed it. So I guess she won. As kids we competed to see who could get the big bed, who could stay in it with our parents, and finally with only our mother until she said we were too old to be doing things like that. Grown girls do not sleep with their mothers, she said. But still, Barbara did on occasion. My daughter ended our rivalry, because in Helen's eyes, the granddaughter took all the prizes.

"What did the police want?" Ionie, one of the nurses, asked.

I shook my head, because I did not want to announce to the room that the love of Barbara's life was not only dead, but murdered. I didn't want Barbara to wake up to that. I wanted her to hear it gently at first. Then, if necessary, at a respectful volume. Not shouted across the bed. I got Ionie to follow me into the hall leading up to the master bathroom and explained I wanted to be alone with my sister once she was awake.

"The police wanted to tell her something," I said to Ionie, "about a friend of hers."

"Police came here to tell her something about a friend?" Ionie asked, but she had a way of asking questions without having her voice rise. Her questions became statements, truths, or her comment on how impossible were the truths she repeated back to you.

"The friend died," I said, apologetically. Ionie was the head nurse—self-appointed, I believe, over two other day nurses, but the head nurse nevertheless. And I didn't want her to think this was trivial. "I've got to tell her," I said.

"Police came here to tell her that her friend died?" Ionie said.

"Worse than that," I said, because I realized in that room with the television always going, she could just as well find out from some news bulletin and the nurses chattering on about it. "Now I've got to tell her."

"Is it going to change anything, telling her the friend died?" Ionie said. "Is it going to make her feel better?"

"'Better' is not how I'd put it, but she has to know," I said. "It was a special friend."

"Why does she have to know, so you can have her upset and then crying and then the choking and the congestion?" Ionie said.

She had a point. But as I considered the alternatives, like not telling her and having her finding out on her own, I thought no. Things happen between sisters, and this was going to be one of them. I had to tell Barbara because this was my job, as the older sister. I was the one who had to tell Barbara she'd lost too much weight and was probably anorexic; that the diagnosis for our mother was pancreatic cancer. I had to tell her whenever our father, Irv, had miraculously reemerged onto the scene and later that he died and left a nightmare for us to clean up. I was the perpetual bearer of bad news: the end of playtime, the end of fantasy. It was not a fantasy that Jasmine and Barbara had been an item, that they were in love and had gone steady. People gossiped; they speculated about what Jasmine saw in Barbara, though never the other way around. People talked and then they stopped talking, because it was over. Everyone moved on. Everyone except Barbara.

"This is personal, okay?" It was my turn to make declarations and make a decision. "When she wakes up, give me a minute with her."

We watched the television when we weren't watching Barbara. The nurses had already woken her up as they did each morning, but she had fallen back into unconsciousness. All the sleeping could have been a sign that death was closer, or it could have been proof the morphine they squirted onto her tongue every few hours was working. The drug was mint flavored, and she told me she liked it once she finally agreed to start taking it. For weeks she denied it to herself because morphine is a sign the patient has given up, released her reins on life, all the usual claptrap. Barbara was afraid that everyone would say she died an addict, like she was some kind of wastrel rock star. But she wasn't. She was a mathematician. Technically, she was a software engineer, but math is how she did it, what she studied, what she couldn't escape. She wanted to be a rock star, but she didn't want to die like one. Barb soldiered on without morphine for 21 long days after the nurses suggested it and then gave in to the sensations hammering away at her—like something blooming in her bones, she said. It tore through the marrow and proteins to make room for whatever was so determined to grow in them.

I knew the nurses would have to wake her again around noon to check on her pain patch, her diaper, her limbs so that they could be moved and therefore not slip out of her skin. The nurses were obsessed with bedsores. Not because they meant infection but because they might signal neglect, lack of due diligence. The nurses were diligent in meeting their schedules for changing the sheets, administering the morphine, feeding, and bathing Barbara. They did not miss a step in this routine while I sat there, reduced to observing them. I wanted to urge them on, get them to wake Barb up before the 12 o'clock news break, when there would have to be some sort of notice about Jasmine, the rock star, found dead that morning. Jasmine, found murdered. Jasmine, the mystery that had sucked so much life out of my sister. Why not have her suck out just a little bit more, whatever was left, before she was gone too, though without all the notice and hoopla.

"She had a tough night last night," Ionie said. The other nurses, Maria and Rubylyn, were strictly on the day shift, nine to six, so presumably they knew nothing about it. Yet they nodded in agreement. Ionie had said the same thing to the cops when I brought them in, and now she was repeating it for my benefit. "Why such a long night, waking up, not sleeping, complaining?" Ionie shuffled around the room, running a dust rag over the furniture and opening a shutter to take a look out on the street through the picture window. But there was nothing to see. There rarely was.

"How is it so," Ionie muttered, "that there is so much pain in such a small body?" She didn't wait for an answer.

My sister had always been little, and always in some kind of pain. She never reached that adult plateau of five feet, or sixty even inches, and when she was born, she was pigeon-toed. The tortures that were devised to turn her feet out, set her legs straight. At the end of her life, Helen said she still felt guilty about it and wondered if the trauma of that treatment was responsible for all of Barb's subsequent ailments. When she was in junior high, she had some sort of bladder problem; there were operations, exploratory and corrective, and at the end of high school, there was the anorexia saga, which may have stunted her growth, we couldn't be sure. We were both on some sort of slow growth plan, having descended from a long line of short people, as Helen put it. The anorexia ensured she would stay short, although she presumably recovered. It was the cancer that carved away whatever was left on her bones. She was down to about a bag of sticks. Whenever the nurses pulled off the blanket to reveal her limbs, I was always shocked by how much of her had been consumed. And yet the disease still hadn't finished.

I used to make a big deal of my sister's smallness. Her hands were puffy like a baby's, dainty and plush. When we were younger, I used to stroke Barb's hands and call her "Little Hands" as we lay in the big bed. By the time we were in junior high, that was all over. But her hands seemed to stay sweet and petite even though she stretched them past their limits, taking piano lessons, modeling and refinishing skateboards, and teaching herself guitar. Maybe there were callouses and cramping but I don't know. But it was as if her size was immovable. I grew taller—though not by much—or maybe the dancing raised me up; that's what Helen always said. Dancing gave me a decent body. I didn't know how decent it was once I was finished dancing, but dancing stretched me out and taught me how to hold myself so I could hold my own in the *corps* or a chorus line. Barbara stayed small not only in size but in how she saw her stature in the world, her conception of herself as a bereaved child.

So we were opposites, and it was going to end that way. She would die and I'd remain alive. I had a sudden need, then, to hold Barb's hand to prove to myself there was at least that much of her left: the precious little fingers and palms like a doll's, pristine in their tininess. "Little Hands, Little Hands," I said quietly, so the nurses wouldn't hear it. "Come out to play."

I didn't get a smile out of her. But her face filled with color and her lips parted like she was going to laugh, but it was an involuntary reaction.

"You awake?" I asked, and she shook her head no.

"I've got to tell you something. Some real bad news," I said, and she shook her head no.

"Why are you always pestering your sister?" Ionie admonished.

"She's going to find out anyway if you don't turn off the television," I said.

Ionie took a step toward the TV, and I thought I saw some real panic dash through Ionie and Rubylyn, their eyes switching between Barb and the screen and between each other's faces. I must have been a monster to them, first robbing them of the TV, then with this news. I didn't want to think of all the other ways I must have seemed monstrous: whatever Barb and her friends had told them about me or the instructions Barb gave to the hospice before she was on morphine and was still able to speak coherently.

"I need to be alone with my sister," I said, monster be damned for the moment. "Just for a minute. Then you can do whatever all of you want."

The nurses conferred in their silence and expressions. All three of them withdrew. When I was sure they were out of earshot, I climbed into the bed on the other side of Barbara, picked up one of her hands, and stroked it.

"What's happening?" Barbara said. Her mouth seemed to catch the words like they were floating by. "Am I going to die today?"

"Nope," I said, because I knew this routine. "Not today. Sorry."

"I thought I was supposed to die today," Barbara declared.

"All the dying's done for today. It's over. Finished. Guess you missed the boat."

"I missed the boat?"

"It was somebody else's turn today," I began, but then I took a moment to make sure that I wanted it to come out this way, something normal in the course of human events, like our mother said—no big deal, not of earth-shattering importance.

"I don't want to die," she said.

"I don't want you to die either."

"Everybody dies," she said, which was something her doctor has evidently taught her to say. She said it when she called us in New York and told my husband that the cancer had spread to her bones, but she didn't want to talk to me about it. She said it whenever I told her somebody died—a celebrity or someone who went to school with us. She said it when she called to tell us that she was going into hospice, but she didn't want me to visit.

"You're going to die too," Barbara said.

"So we'll be even. Okay?"

"Never soon enough," Barbara acknowledged. "So who died today?" Barbara asked.

There were no more ways for me to stall, so I exhaled: "Jasmine."

Barb opened her eyes and kept them open. Her mouth opened too, like she wanted to say something, but her throat couldn't grasp the sounds, her mouth the words. She looked like I had just forced something down her throat—a drug to revive her, a shot of oxygen, a squirt of morphine, and she was undecided whether it would work or if she would let it. I've seen Barb tied to a hospital bed; I've seen her starving. But this was like confronting the rawest part of her, if not the cancer itself, because Jasmine had been her one and only, all consuming passion.

She turned her head toward me and said, "Jasmine?"

I could only nod.

Barbara was as still as glass—as death, I thought, except for the blue pulse in her forehead. A vein I had never noticed before, running from her eyebrow and into her hair, which was strawberry blonde. One of my friends once called her Peppermint Patty. When Irv revealed himself to us all those years after he left our mother and heard that Barbara was still living in the house, he said he knew she'd never grow up. My daughter seemed to confirm this when she could not say "Aunt Barbara" and instead called her "Aunt Baby." But Barb must have grown up that minute when she heard the love of her life—the only love in her life—was dead and had died before her. Because there was none of the screaming and the tears released in blinding frustration that usually came when she was delivered bad news, awful news, the most hideous. There was no seizure-like fit, no temper tantrum, or vocal wrath. Only a question.

"What happened?" Barbara asked plainly.

"I don't know," I said, although by now I had my suspicions. The police had only implied the possibilities, but I had grown up here, and I knew how these things usually went: sordid, tawdry, graphic.

"The police were here, they wanted to talk to you, but you were out of it," I said. "I talked to them, but they didn't say much. They gave me their card, told me to call if there was anything—"

"The police," Barbara said slowly. She was not drifting back into unconsciousness. She might have been trying out a prayer, an affirmation, almost, meant to sustain her through the following hours. "The police wanted to talk to me about Jasmine."

"Yes, they did," I agreed, because this fact was somehow soothing to Barb, like it was leading her into a comfortable trance, diverting her from whatever pain all the narcotics could not kill inside her. I had been right to tell her: score one for me. Big deal.

CHAPTER 3

I DIGRESS SO OFTEN BECAUSE MY FATHER DID. He did it because it is deceptive. Not because it distracts or delays but because it provides an illusion about your focus. People are confused, thrown off, as to the source of your problem. If you digress, your obsessions seem manageable and normal. They are loose and free to wander, to be relieved occasionally, and to be forgotten completely, and you were just interested or had an enthusiasm. And you got over it. But all roads really do lead back to that animating luminance. You can guess what mine is. Jasmine.

In my father's case, the obsession was Los Angeles. Its history and lore, show business, and scandal. When we were little girls and dressed in matching outfits, he drove us to an empty lot where he said the body of a famous starlet was discovered. The Black Dahlia. And then he took photographs. He was obsessed, but I think what really obsessed him was the sound of his own voice, telling or embellishing these stories. He could not relax unless his voice penetrated whatever setting it might find itself in. Of my father at least I can say that he never ran out of material. Not so the settings: Helen got rid of him for my sake and my sister's, as soon as she was able to get a grip on the finances. In the meantime, he had plenty of opportunities to distract us with his charm and his penchant for tangents.

But there was something my father, our father, didn't understand about this city. Or perhaps it was more about time—the era of his childhood versus the Age of Aquarius, when my sister and I grew up. He couldn't fathom the difference between years, generations, and epochs. To him Los Angeles would always be a small town. Everybody knew everyone. Therefore, everyone was equal. If not in wealth and status, then in access to that wealth and status. Of course, there were hierarchies, dynasties, in-groups, and exiles. The Hollywood Ten and the blacklisting of suspected Communist Party members: these were among my father's favorite sagas. Interminably, at dinner. He said he wanted me and my sister to learn something. But Hollywood, as he spoke of it, seemed much smaller, always within reach and just next door, than what my sister and I knew of it. In his imagination it occupied perhaps a few square miles that began down the street or behind a house with an open-door policy. For me, and possibly for my sister, Hollywood was a far vaster and wide locale, with sinister overtones and conspiratorial politics. Who was in it and who wasn't infested our arrangements in classrooms, the politics of the playground, and the invite list of every child's birthday party. To my father, Hollywood was nostalgia and romance. To us—or to me—it became confusing and malicious. Because my sister and I lived so much closer than he ever did to the scorching white nerve center of animosity and status.

But of course I am trailing off, forgetting my subject here. Is it Jasmine—or the machinery that created, nurtured, packaged, and launched her so directly into my line of vision—that I could never quite be rid of? Though she certainly got rid of me. I have discovered while dying that all thoughts and memories are a digression, a detour to avoid the inevitable.

This should be obvious for someone in my position. But like anyone else, I also forget. My sister knows the names of all the ancestors, the cousins, and shirttail relatives; where they live and where they went to college; and the highest degree they obtained upon matriculation. Why she knows this when she has barely been to college herself is both digression and explanation; perhaps she does this to reassure herself. They made it through so she can too. But life doesn't work that way. Or maybe it does. It will for me, if not for her, and I am jealous.

I will be the first untimely death in my family. I will die from a disease we have no history in, though we should because we are Eastern European Jews, and statistically 1 in 40 Ashkenazi women develops the BRCA (breast cancer) gene mutation. In other words, I was sentenced before I was ever convicted. My fate has always been laid out for me like a dare or a warning. My father said I would never amount to anything because I didn't finish the second semester of high school physics. I was already in college then. Junior college. I was trying to get some of the cheap credits out of the way the semester before I enrolled in the university of his choosing. At least that was what, at the time, I was telling him. I don't want to say what I really thought, what I really believed, because it is embarrassing now to think of it. Just as it is embarrassing to think of Jasmine.

I think of Jasmine and I think of someone who was unmarked, unlike me and my sister. My sister and I were born ugly; she in the face, me in the body. Or me in the body and the mind, since it was my need to be around beauty, to always be as close to it as I am enamored of it, that made me so ugly. That is what my friends or, as they are better known, my associates would tell you. The police asked my sister who my associates were, and she told them that I don't have associates; in this she was wrong. She is correct that I am not some kind of fla-grantly cruel business executive who knows people she only bumps up against for purposes of carrying out underhanded enterprises. But she is wrong in believing or in repeating to the police that I have "friends"—people whose experiences and passions have dovetailed with my own to the point that they continue to care about me and the new experiences and passions I might collect. I know people whose experiences and passions for a time impeded, if not outright collided with, my own to the point that they consider me a mass of ugly impulses and emotions that I never hesitate to act upon. I would say that I am candid and honest to a fault. My associates would say that such are my greatest faults, and with faults like those, no others are relevant.

But to appearances, which are paramount: my sister was born hideous, with a deviated septum, thin lips, and a chin that disappeared into her neck, as if she had been punched and strangled in utero. In fairness, I can't say she always appeared like this. Her baby pictures—our baby pictures—are requisitely cute and diminutive. But I also can't say when her face began to stretch out like a horse's and when the bridge of her nose emerged at such an aggressive rate it bypassed all ratios of politeness. There's no record of how or when her matura-tion turned freakish. Knowing what I know, I'd guess all this began to transpire when she was in second or third grade, as her adult teeth were budding out beyond her gums and her smile became garish and awkward. She was relentlessly teased, and she responded with relentless tears, so that she was often called a "cry baby" or overly sensitive, depending on who was doing the name-calling or "labeling" for purposes of the educational bureaucracy.

This is the ugliness in which I was raised, the curse of my inheritance. I was gorgeous, with my red hair and freckles. My proportions were reasonable: my brows thin, eyes big, and eyelashes long, and I had an ample mouth for the teeth I harbored. I did not require any of the gear for my head or neck, nor metal for my teeth, to which my sister was sentenced. As an infant I was admired by movie stars my mother encountered on elevators; in elementary school I was invited to play games with boys on the playground. My sister has often reminded me of my youthful adorability, particularly as it has been preserved in photographs. And yet, as I was sent on to each new grade and classroom every September, I was immediately recognized by teachers as the younger sibling of the girl who cried too much but then again, why shouldn't she, saddled with the face of an old maid in the making.

I was made ugly by association, which is not a bad way of putting it, since my sister and I were never quite friends. Competitors (I was and still am smarter than she is), rivals (if not in romance, then in professional success and the emotional resources of our parents), or outright enemies (the battle over my mother's estate was epic), we are united by blood if not by loyalty or wistfulness for our childhoods. But my sister and I know each other too well to say that we are estranged or lost to each other. We continue to argue although I'm no longer capable of voicing my distaste for most of her actions and opinions. She is using me now as she always has in ways she probably could only have fantasized about when we were younger.

She wants to be my representative to the world. Legally, she is not, but her face, the slight and easily serviceable decay of her body, and her sense of justice and fairness might make a play for it. She has a need to appear as the most dedicated, beleaguered, and brave sibling on the entire planet. She thinks she is being my advocate. She is clearing the way. She is running interference. She asks whether I want to cry—to get it all out, whatever feelings I have left for Jasmine. She asks whether I'd like to turn on the television, see the news coverage, or call somebody, anybody I used to know, to come over and commiserate over Jasmine. She asks my permission to explain to the nurses who Jasmine is or was; she switches her verbs indiscriminately, because she is confused as to both the relativity of time and to the etiquette of speaking of the dead.

"My sister and Jasmine," I hear her begin. She doesn't have to say Jasmine's last name because she no longer has one. She is a star like Cher, Madonna, or the rappers with their symbols and abbreviations. Or now that Jasmine is dead, her name is a brand, for that is how people talk about stars now, in the coldly efficient language of commercialism. There will be a Jasmine memorial T-shirt and tribute albums on CD. Benefit concerts will be held for Jasmine's favorite charity; if she did not have one, one will be provided in her memory. It will have to be an acceptable charity, perhaps something that straddles both music and children and avoids thorny questions about their poverty or sexuality. Something that will purchase instruments for public school music departments, I'd bet, provided that no instrument goes to an LGBTQ individual.

"They were friends in high school," I hear my sister say. I can open my eyes just long enough to see my sister's face gauging the reaction of the nurses. My sister's brand is nonconfrontational, going along to get along, don't ask and don't tell, though telling is obviously required here. "Kind of like girlfriend and boyfriend in high school. Kind of like a couple. Like—"

Someone says something; it is accented or perhaps muffled. One of the nurses, though I can't much tell one from another now. They are all small and dark, except for those who are giants, with the strength to lift me up and keep me suspended in midair while the sheets are changed or I am bathed or my limbs are rearranged, to take the pressure off the joints and extremities. I wonder whether my sister stopped speaking because the nurses called her on her attitude; whether they asked her to cease addressing them as if they were idiots. That is just another corollary of my sister's brand, hip, world-weary, and far better informed than all the rubes and peasants.

The conversation is over. I imagine my sister interrupted whatever the nurses tried to interject. They don't need to know about me and Jasmine. They don't care about my past. I am their patient. They must take me whatever my condition. Their brand is fairness. Perhaps they are the only people in all of my life who have done this: approached me without judgment. Without regard to my size, my appearance, and the ugliness that for years has been growing within me. They say it takes years, decades, for a cancer to make itself known once it commandeers a chromosome or two, insinuating itself into the master code. There it rests, awaiting the most opportune moment to expose itself. For leukemia that is usually when the immune system is compromised, such as when the body is recovering from streptococcus. For breast cancer, it is always time for cancer to announce itself. Weight, the abuse of alcohol, childbearing, or menopausal age: none matter. What matters is where it's caught until it does not matter anymore—into the fatty tissues and ducts, lobes and lymph nodes, across the walls and into the muscle. It always finds a way.

But the nurses don't care about that. They don't care as my sister attempts to convince them of my extenuating circumstances. Never married, never moved out of my mother's house. Never again fell in love once Jasmine was finished with me. Never again, not even the slightest bit interested. She is leaving some things out, the inclinations and morbidities that should have protected me from cancer, this final, dark, and fluid ugliness. They don't care that I was able to hold my breath for years after Jasmine threw me over and that only now am I drowning in my broken heartedness. They only care that none of it gets on them and into their nodes and sympathetic nerve systems. That is why they have always worn surgical gloves and why they are obsessed with cleanliness. Because this kind of ugliness just might be contagious.

The nurses agree to switch on the television. They don't care what's on it, whether it's Jasmine or some other news tragedy. They don't care about the soap opera I used to watch with my mother or the sitcoms that come on afterward. They steal equally from all their patients; they are professional in that way, practically magnanimous. They can steal whether the television is on or if it's not.

The nurse who was here before the hospice, when I still could get out of bed, walk with some assistance, and talk as much as ever, took thousands from me. No one quite knows how much; my sister wanted the police involved, but everyone else said it was too much trouble given the odds that I'd be able to recover it. I was vulnerable, my sister said, because I was so sick, but I think I was vulnerable because that nurse recognized what is ugliest in me, perhaps my guilt and the need to be purged of it. She must have had that same need, that urgent wish not to be forgotten or discarded. I told her, this nurse, I wasn't afraid to die but to have been considered irrelevant or unimportant. This nurse told me she was sick and needed money so she wouldn't have to ask her children for it. I suppose I gave it to her because I understood how she didn't want to be a burden to her children, only for them to love her for her strength and independence.

But nurses are not supposed to care about how they are regarded. They're not supposed to care whether the patients and their families think they are brutal or compassionate. They just have a job to do, a schedule to keep you on, and an agenda that holds them harmless against liability and lawsuits. So no matter what my sister says, or how the television might drone on about the beauty and talent that Jasmine was, the loss that her death represents, another hit to an industry in swift decline, with so few stars of her character, the nurses will not be deterred from their tasks. My body must be bathed and manipulated. The sheets on the bed must be changed; the dosage of morphine refreshed. Someone has shooed my sister away from the side of the bed where she had been trying to command my attention. I feel arms under my neck and at my ankles, a sudden absence at my back where the mattress and sheets had been.

I'm being turned onto my right side. I have to be turned onto my right side, because the left is where the cancer began. The cancer began in my left breast, specifically, and when it broached my skeleton, it was the left hip that first surrendered. There's speculation now that cancer is more than uncontrolled growth, but also the readiness, or willingness, of cells to accept that growth. They are prone in some way to abdicate their responsibility to fight off the invader. If the nurses rolled me onto my left side, what a blast of pain I'd get, as if someone or something had taken a knife directly to my pelvis. That person or thing would simply wheedle away, as if drilling with a dull bit. I thought I was healthy after the two rounds of chemo, the surgery, and the radiation. I was running again when I felt an intrusion into my left hip. It was a pinch that ricocheted down my leg with each step. Now it's a well that's being dug, a full-scale public works project. Morphine dampens the sensation, but it is always there, like a bug in your ear, threatening to feast if you fail to pay attention.

These are the mechanics of cancer. It is wily and unstable, but it does exhibit patterns, which is all we've really studied. The hip is one of two favored places for breast cancer to take refuge. The other is the brain, as though it's not enough for the cancer to attack your biological identity. It also wants the one you've constructed. Or once it's done with what makes you, in part, female, it has to go for the rest of you, your humanity. I know one other woman, a friend of my sister's, who fought her last battle against breast cancer in her liver. What kind of comment is that, I wondered? Perhaps payback for all that processing of narcotics and alcohol. My sister's friends are all addicts, I'm pretty certain. That's what happens to dancers, my sister said, with all their aches and pains. They should know how this feels in this cloud meant to muffle sensation.

I'm certain, though, that the cancer has not reached my brain yet. I can still process what is happening around me. The protocols and procedures, the time of day they take place, and the change in the nurses' shifts. I know what day it is. Wednesday: they're saying so on the television. They want to have a public memorial service for Jasmine by the weekend. There are no specifics, but they need to do something because the scenes outside her house, outside the label she founded with her mentor, and at the few remaining record stores in Los Angeles might get ugly. The fans must be satisfied, their grief given a healthy outlet. I wonder, how will they be satisfied? Jasmine is not coming back. No one does. That is what I have learned, subsisting through this ugliness.

CHAPTER 4

THE FIRST THING MY SISTER DID when she was diagnosed with breast cancer—no, it wasn't the first thing, because when she found the first lump, she knew what it was and what it meant. She diagnosed herself. And she did nothing. It was days, weeks before she said anything to anybody, and by the time she mentioned it to Helen, it was too late. There were three lumps by then; she hadn't seen or felt the other two, but they showed up on the tests.

Barb didn't wait for the test results. She diagnosed herself again after the biopsy, before the results came in. She saw the blood jumping back into the syringe during the biopsy and knew that meant cancer. She did not tell our mother, but she told me in a brief telephone call so that it would "sink in," she said. When the results came back as Stage III, she set out to find Jasmine. It would be the first time they had spoken in years.

I wasn't there. I don't know what happened. At first Barb would give me only the most cryptic bits and pieces: the setting (Jasmine's neighborhood), how Jasmine looked (gorgeous), the sound of her voice (seductive); things I already knew because Barb had been wallowing in these excruciating details all of her adult life and never let me forget it. I don't know whether Barb was trying a kind of desperate, "would you love me if I told you I was dying" trick. I only know what

Barb told me: Jasmine was unimpressed. She said nothing. Or maybe she said something about how sorry she was but there was nothing she could do about it. I only know what Barb told me, and over the course of her treatment she revised this story into distinct versions. In one Jasmine was sympathetic; in another she was angry and threatened to call the police; in another, Jasmine asked Barb how she "could have let this disease into her life." On Helen's advice, I did not push for a definitive retelling that would reconcile all the previous renditions. It was bad enough that she had seen Jasmine with the usual disastrous outcome.

I also did not tell the cops about this meeting. I did not tell them for several reasons beyond the obvious. I did not tell them because at that moment, in those five seconds when she and Jasmine might have made eye contact, or those five minutes when they might have spoken, Barbara wasn't just another stalker. She was an equal to Jasmine. They had a shared past, and Jasmine was acknowledging it. Jasmine may have buried that past, but it was alive that day. It couldn't be avoided.

As my husband said once, the Barb-Jasmine thing was like opera, though to me it was more like ballet. He sees things in those kinds of musical terms, I guess, while I see them like stories: a lover wronged yet compelled to yearn for the one who wronged her. It could only end one way, but I never said anything to Barb about how these things went in ballet. She was living it and could find out the rest for herself. Besides, everyone knew about Barbara and Jasmine; everyone who went to our high school, who worked with my sister, or whoever she could tackle at a concert or a bar, as if Barb had a plan in mind. She wanted the gossip to get back to Jasmine. She wanted to put Jasmine on the spot and force her to admit that they had once been together; that it wasn't some hoax or fantasy on Barb's part; and that Barb had been there, present when nobody else was. I think that's what my sister wanted. Acknowledgment.

"This Jasmine, did she have a fan club?" Ionie wondered. We were watching television. All the channels were all Jasmine, all the time. Special Reports, no game shows or reruns or anything syndicated. This was a sad day for Los Angeles, and the television was letting us know it. Barb was "resting comfortably," as the nurses liked to put it, passed out on her afternoon morphine ration.

"Maybe that's who did it," observed Rubylyn, who sat at the edge of the bed.

"You mean like Selena?" Maria asked.

Selena: someone I knew. Because Jennifer Lopez made a movie about her. Jennifer Lopez, the former dancer; on the Great Chain of Being a Dancer, she's at the bottom or the top, depending on your point of view or where you're standing at any given moment.

"Lord, let it not be so," Rubylyn said.

"At my sister's wedding, for the first dance, my sister and her husband, they danced to Jasmine," Maria said.

Jasmine had penetrated the cultural ether so deeply that even someone as out of it as I was had heard her song, "First Dance." It had become traditional at weddings. After the happy couple danced to the first verse everyone would sing the chorus. Of course Barb hated that song. She hated all the hits. She hated all of Jasmine's fans too and did not consider herself among them. Fans were ciphers. Obsequious. Vacuous. I suppose she had a point, though what would I know about fans. We didn't exactly have them in my line of show business. We did have patrons, benefactors, sponsors, and donors: all the people who subsidized the company or were able to get their businesses and employees to subsidize it, because there weren't enough genuine fans whose ticket purchases were able to keep the company going. Those who subsidized it had their reasons for giving money—some because of public relations, *noblesse oblige*, politics, keeping their hand in the arts scene should they ever need recognition. In other words, they were fans with benefits, with some fans getting more benefits than others, depending on what went down at the annual gala or some other event. Barb called these fans "groupies" and held a special dislike for them where Jasmine was concerned. She said they were fame whores.

"Do you know anyone who didn't have that song at their wedding?" Ionie said, and she smoothed a spot in the blanket so she could sit next to Rubylyn. They blocked my view of the television.

"Wow," Maria said. The commentator was describing gatherings of people at Jasmine's stars on Hollywood Boulevard—she had two. They were leaving teddy bears, flowers, and prayer candles on the sidewalk. Some of them howled; others stood by and contemplated. The mayor might issue a proclamation, a citywide day of mourning.

"Can you believe this girl knew Jasmine?" Ionie said, and I could have swatted her for saying so. But Ionie had put her hand on a rise in the blanket where Barbara's feet may have been. I didn't want to disturb the delicate quiet—such as it was—wake Barb up, and have the nurses fuss over her for no reason.

"You don't say," Rubylyn said.

"Your sister knew Jasmine?" Maria said, and Ionie looked back at me, like she was daring me; she obviously hadn't believed me. As head nurse, she had to out my lie, like she was going to discredit my status as the only next of kin.

"In high school," I said.

"Did you know her?" Rubylyn asked, and she sounded like she was scandalized.

"Barely," I assured her. "She and Barb were two years behind me. Plus they were in a special program."

"Special program," Rubylyn repeated. She too was unconvinced, or maybe she thought I was speaking ill of the dead, and the dying.

"You know, for geniuses," I said, and this she could believe. Because Jasmine was a musical genius. Everyone on television was saying so. She knew how to make hits. She could make a hit for anyone. She knew when to hold back on a song too, give it to another artist, because she knew it wasn't right for herself. Jasmine was a very accessible genius, the people said on television. My sister's kind of genius was apparently not as accessible. She worked with numbers and science, populations and probabilities; sometimes I'd try to describe how she put all this into new computer languages, but people's eyes would glaze over. They'd feel inferior, like they were missing something. Or they'd feel like I was acting superior, going on about her doctorate and pretending to know something about it.

"Do the police go around and notify everyone in that special program?" Ionie said.

"It was a small program," I offered.

"One genius dies, do all the other geniuses need to be notified?" Ionie said.

"I guess," I said, like I didn't know what she was getting at. Who gets called in the event of a suspicious death: family, friends, and suspects? Ionie was bursting to announce which category Barb fell in. "That special program: they were a tight group," I suggested.

"Your sister is a genius?" Maria asked but Ionie silenced her with a look and her finger raised to her lips. It must not do well to know too much about the dying person whose death you are in charge of.

On the television, Jasmine was being praised and hailed for all she did, for other artists, and for Los Angeles. She wasn't a Madonna or a Cher, but a native of Hollywood. She lived in the same neighborhood she grew up in, raised money for music in the schools, and opened a conservatory for low-income children. A woman was crying on screen; the announcer asked her what she was holding. A framed picture of Jasmine because of the influence Jasmine exercised over her life and work. She was a hairdresser, a personal trainer, and a holistic nutritionist, but mostly she was a singer. There were other testimonials, from those healed in body and soul by Jasmine's words and music to those who found new purpose, new courage in the arc of Jasmine's career.

Rubylyn and Ionie still weren't letting me see the screen. I had to listen carefully to get at what the broadcast was saying. Jasmine was a role model. I could not see the loop of pictures of Jasmine in various settings rolling across the screen. But I could easily envision her face, as I had seen it so many times earlier in the day. I always thought she was a pretty, even a beautiful girl: dark eyes that matched dark hair, flawless features. No matter how you looked at her, whether she was done-up or photographed candidly, she was stunning. The angle of the shot never mattered. In this way, she had a kind of blank look, like she could be anything to anybody. People could pour their assumptions into her, whether she was an artist or a savior or a female CEO for the new world, and they'd pop right back out, confirmed. For businesswomen, aspiring entertainers, down-on-their-luck fashion designers, runaways, and suicidal teenagers. Another mourner told the cameras how she was going to kill herself because she was alone in Georgia and a lesbian. But Jasmine's music showed her there was hope.

"Did I already know this?" Ionie said.

"Know what?" I said, because I had to say something, and it had to be nonoffensive. A little dumb, maybe, or neutral. Something that may not stop the speculation, but to slow it down, stretch out the big reveal, since I could see there was no hope for canceling it entirely.

"Don't I always know these things?" Ionie said.

"So does the rest of the world," said Maria, who was sitting beside me but had a better angle for seeing the screen and Ionie and Rubylyn's expressions.

"Did your sister know?" Ionie said, but she did not turn to face Maria or me. She was addressing strictly the television and the newscasters, like she had some kind of bulletin for them and they'd get it if they listened for it hard enough.

"Now's not the time to talk about this," Maria said.

"Your sister's—" Rubylyn began.

"Yes, because all lesbians know each other," I said, because I was angry. I wasn't even close to gay, as Barb liked to remind me; I was heteronormative, straight, insignificant, and ordinary. If I said any particular woman was beautiful, Barb would go into a rage and say I was raiding her territory. But this was my territory, this hospice arrangement. I didn't set it up and I wasn't paying for it. The nurses had reduced me to an observer; I couldn't touch my sister without their say-so. But I knew this house, how to get to the market, what to buy, who should be asked to come over. I was doing whatever I could, which wasn't much, but I was pretty sure I didn't want to go looking for new nurses because of religious objections or fear of AIDS or some other excuse the head nurse and her minion were cooking up. I could see it as they turned to face me with shock in their expressions.

"Why was this not disclosed?" Ionie said.

"Because whatever 'this' is, is none of your business," I said.

"Call the office," Rubylyn said. "They're supposed to screen for this."

"You want to quit?" I asked.

"No, no, no one's quitting," Maria said. "You want the compliance officer out here?"

"I don't have a problem," Rubylyn volunteered.

"Good," I said, "because I was wondering: what year is this?" I could have asked whether these women called themselves Christians—but thought better of it, since the answer, like my response, was obvious.

"We're all good here," Maria assured me, and she squeezed my arm like that would make her declaration all the more convincing.

Rubylyn had returned her attention to the television screen, but Ionie continued staring at me, at Barb, at Maria, like she was trying to decide who was the most evil, which one of us needed to be removed, and to keep the world safe for her sensibilities and prejudices.

"Ionie, we're fine, right?" Maria asserted.

"I don't have a problem," Rubylyn repeated.

"Someone has a problem?" Ionie asked: I could hear her voice climb just so slightly. Or maybe she wanted us to think that we had heard it, like she was reserving her options—for the rest of my sister's natural life.

CHAPTER 5

AUTHENTIC MEMORY IS THE CONTRABAND OF LOS ANGELES. It has to be. Otherwise, Hollywood would lack its powers of monopoly. The monopoly serves many purposes, including the illusion of democracy. The machine is disorganized and cacophonous but ultimately it is a machine that digests, grinding away at the sharp and unsightly edges and polishing the dull places in the national epic. When Hollywood is finished with any particular scene or chapter, the discordant or ugly features have been persuaded to take their usual place in the background, and the diversions that raised too many thorny questions have been dispatched. Hollywood produces not so much nostalgia as it smooths, coats, and digests the messy business of becoming an overnight success, a national hero, or going from rags to riches. It provides a template for these trajectories that is both misleading and inspiring, and by doing so, Hollywood gives us something to fight for. Hollywood makes us a nation. You too can make it big in your profession, chase your dream, and find a reason for living, all while you keep going to movies and concerts. You can pay off that debt. New vaccinations are coming: one for cancer, any minute.

My sister tells me the news crews and cameras are here. I wonder whether this is what they have come looking for: my authentic memories of Jasmine. They're outside at the doorstep wanting a statement, my sister says. No one is willing to open the door for them; so they are just out there waiting on the steps where my sister and I used to crush bugs and throw stones into the neighbor's side yard—the steps where we splatter-painted and pooped and peed in our diapers on the broiling days when our mother couldn't stand to be in the house with us for another minute. Such history in those steps, though to the news crews it is irrelevant. We are not famous as Jasmine was, as so many of the kids we grew up with. But that ends today. After today, we will be infamous.

I knew something was happening when I heard shouting in unison. The nurses and my sister did not so much say the same thing simultaneously as they took in the same gust of breath, registered their shock at the same volume, agreed that some event carried the same degree of freakishness for all of them. I don't know what that event was, but after they made that sound, one of the nurses tugged at my big toe. Apparently it is the only digit that still registers contact. I am deteriorating from the inside out. I am crumbling backwards. I opened my eyes to see everyone pointing at the television screen as though it had said the unmentionable and offended their sensibilities. I don't know what was on the screen beyond the blur of black and white patches I could make out, seemingly arranged in the shape of my house and the driveway.

My sister no longer knows the names and faces of the local newscasters, but she does recognize their equipment. The microphones and cameras she knows because she is preternaturally attracted to their powers: magnification, amplification, exaggeration, and transmission. She was always that dancer who made the mistake of dancing to the camera, rather than to her partner or the other dancers; that's my estimation. She's said there are many reasons why she wasn't more successful in her career and why she couldn't get beyond the rank of soloist in her company, but there's no way she can explain it to me because I haven't lived her life. But my father explained it to me, no problem. Just after he rose from whatever substrata had been harboring him after my niece was born. He said he wanted to be a family man again. This time he'd get it right, and if he didn't, he had the real parents—my sister and her husband—to cushion the negative impact on the children— or, in this case, his one grandchild. Not for a second did he ask about me but instead lectured me on how my sister's dancing career was much like that of a politician's. Walter Mondale's, he said. He just might have beat Reagan if only he had more time. If the election had been a week or two later. But it wasn't. You've got to get these things done on the deadline. My sister's body had a deadline, and she blew right through it. She did the next best thing after that and became a mother.

I quit being a musician after high school, and my only motivation was fame and money, while hers was the love and perpetuation of an art always on the precipice of disappearing. But my sister is, first and foremost, my sister, and I know the desperation and desires she must harbor that live openly on her face and are there for anyone to recognize, like the slope of her nose or her eyes set too close together. My desires lived in my throat, my vocal cords, and the high whine of my voice; the unrequited pangs and frustrations that would overflow from my mouth if I were to speak, sing, or part my lips. It is amazing that I have not drowned myself yet, though the cancer is probably doing that for me.

When we were young, our father insisted on watching only one network for both local and national news, and we came to recognize Jerry Dunphy and Walter Cronkite as if they were our grandparents. There was a boy in my class in elementary school, a boy who couldn't read when he was called on. He was late to school practically every day, and after school he drove his minibike on the playground. He ran into trash cans, scattering the garbage, and broke up baseball and basketball games no one would let him play in. He chased after girls too, just to see their underwear, a glimpse of something else he was afraid he'd never have, unless he just reached out and grabbed it, even as it bucked and twisted out of his hands. He graduated though, with all the rest of us, because his stepfather was one of those TV anchormen. He wasn't on our channel, but you might see him in the advertisements in the newspaper. Or when we tried changing the channel, or when our father demanded that we change it back. The stepfather didn't share a last name with his stepson, and they didn't look alike, of course, but everyone knew which one was his stepfather because it was in the air like electricity, like the water in the school water fountain. It was in that pissy little taste that made you thirsty all over again, so you couldn't get enough of it. I don't know what became of that boy, but in junior high and high school there were other children and stepchildren of anchormen to replace him.

When I asked my sister about what she thought of Jasmine, she said, "She's pretty," as if that were the only thing that mattered to her. I asked her why she said that, and she answered, "That's all I know about her." When I told her about me and Jasmine, she said, "Congratulations," as if this were some sort of monumental breakthrough. I had blown a hole through an impenetrable wall, taken the gates, and toppled the barbarians. Girls like me weren't supposed to know Jasmine.

My sister said she didn't know Jasmine, but this she knew: that I was meant only to watch her from a distance. I wasn't supposed to get close to a person of Jasmine's stature. I wasn't supposed to have that kind of access. To smell the salt at the back of her neck, taste the ridges in her lips, feel the slope of her cheeks and nose against my face. Jasmine was off-limits to all that I was. I was what she wasn't: obscure, simpering, insignificant. My parents were nobodies, peons, uptight, and out-of-date disciplinarians. I could play my music only after I had studied for my tests and completed, to their satisfaction, my homework. I had an electric guitar, but it came from Sears. I was too embarrassed to audition for the talent show, besides which, my bandmates said it would have been mortifying to play on our own school stage. Jasmine, meanwhile, was already famous.

Jasmine was born to fame. This is not the same as inheriting it. Of course she did inherit it: her parents were studio musicians. No one knew which instruments they played, whether they were stylists or technicians or classically trained. But we knew they were the Partridge Family, Bobby Sherman, and Leif Garrett. We studied the liner notes on their albums, but we could not quite confirm Jasmine's parents' names. Her mother didn't use her married name and her father used several monikers. It was too risky for them to come out and own their fame. They wanted to keep Jasmine, all their children, anonymous. They failed, somewhat: word got around somehow. They were besieged by requests for autographs; eight-by-ten photos; the off chance to be introduced to David, Bobby, and Leif; and anyone else they impersonated: Scott Baio? Shaun Cassidy? I don't know. At a certain age, you stop keeping track of these things. But again, I'm having trouble concentrating.

What I should make clear is that what Jasmine had, what she was born into, was far better than some inheritance. I dare not say "fate," because that would make it all sound too easy. Only one person, or entity—God or a group of gods—is involved in "fate." Many disparate individuals were involved with Jasmine, the making of Jasmine, and her progress through life. All the teachers at her schools, counselors at her summer camps; all the babysitters, nannies, and pediatricians who must have taken care of her as her parents took her from one location to the next. All the boys at her schools who watched her develop faster than the other girls; and all the girls who watched her too, because they wanted to be just like her, be close to her, or be inside a body and a face that was just like hers—so they had to absorb every minute of her eminence. It was as though Jasmine were conceived under the most fortuitous conditions—the most proper alignment of stars and planets. All these people made certain her days were graced with beauty, acclaim, and splendor. Jasmine arrived for high school immersed in a swirl of intrigue, curiosity, and speculation. With that face and that body, how could she still be a virgin or not have a boyfriend? With those parents, who knew the rich, the powerful, and the prominent, how could she be just a girl, unsigned and un-agented in the entertainment-industrial complex?

In other words, wherever Jasmine arrived, she arrived with an audience. She came equipped with one. That's what I was to her: a piece of equipment. Something she might use to increase the effect; press me against her ear, so that the deepest secrets might be better communicated to her; press me against her eyes, so that the phenomenal colors residing within them might be better seen. Press me against her mouth, so that the width and softness of her lips might be better known. Press me against her chest to amplify the already quickened pace of her heartbeat. Press me anywhere against her body; I would take any part of it. Press me against the places that are not supposed to be pressed; I was young and innocent, which is what she thought, and so if she pressed there, it would be confusing and queer, but it wouldn't make that much of a difference. How could it?

I am skipping over so much, because it is so complicated. Jasmine did not need to die to sell more records. She did not need to be murdered to sell more T-shirts, outtakes, or side projects. But she will. Now with wall-to-wall coverage, breaking news, exclusives, improved graphics, and the full attention of the viewing audience, she will be the most talked-about, most analyzed, most imitated, and significant artist in real time. We are present for the creation. Out of a brutal murder a legend has been born, and we are the witnesses. Especially at my house, I in my deathbed, party to this live resurrection in high definition. It's something I'll take with me to my grave, though I don't want a grave. I've told everyone. It's in my will. I want to be burned, reduced to something unidentifiable; so finally I'll be able to blend in and not be such a spectacle.

Right now, my house is the spectacle: the front door that no one will answer. Through the haze of my painkillers, I can recognize it on the television. The two heavy brass door handles. My mother hated them. My father picked them out—they looked like a pair of prison bars topped with the heads of generic birds. He said he liked them because they reminded him of mansions—all the pretensions of old Hollywood and Art Deco—the architecture of his childhood. My mother relented. My sister and I invested a good deal of our childhood trying to liberate them from the door. We attached strings to our bicycles, tied the strings around the birds' heads, and then attempted to pedal away. Obviously, we didn't get far. We had the neighbor boys try. We tugged. We lit firecrackers. We charred the beak of one bird, the eye of another. We kicked at those door handles and tried to chisel them off with our dinner knives. But they would never give. After the divorce my mother tried to have them removed, but the contractors said she'd have to replace the entire door, the frame, and the gutter that took the rain away. It was something about the dimensions and the materials, how they became obsolete, impossible to match. The one status symbol my family had, and you couldn't give it away.

The stairs leading up to the door—pebbles and cement my sister and I used to draw on, paint, scrub out with soap and water—are crowded with cameras and sound equipment. Suddenly I taste mint on my tongue, the mint of morphine driblets. It's either time for my regular dose or someone has decided to shut me up, put me down, take the edge off the next few hours, because whatever happens next cannot be good. I am in hospice, I am on opioids, and my sister wants to go outside and talk for the cameras, telling the world about me and my freshly murdered high school girlfriend.

This is why I didn't want to go on morphine. Morphine takes away all control. Morphine isn't like the patch on my back, or the antihistamines and steroids they once poured into my chest. It is not like the antinausea or antianxiety medications meant to make the chemo go down, spread out, that much easier. Morphine is the end. It is the last consent you'll ever give. Once you're on it, you cannot go off it. You are its prisoner. It masters your appetite, your digestion, your tolerance to pain, your need for relief from the pain; it compresses everything. Cravings, constipation, your endurance between doses. I did not want to go on morphine, but here I am, sinking and submerged into it.

Before you go on morphine, you can still measure in whole numbers: days, hours, minutes. Once you are on morphine, there is no more measuring. You may have weeks left; you may have only days. But you can no longer measure time. Time becomes rubbery and subjective. I could swear that I decided to go on morphine the last time my sister was here. It was May, maybe June. Now it is summer, and morphine absolves me of all time. I can't remember how long I have felt this way, only that I've always sought numbness in one way or another, and what follows numbness is more numbness.

Numbness is my preferred condition. I told the nurses, my friends, the doctors, and social workers; I even told my sister. Don't put me on morphine. I don't want to die addicted. I've been addicted to so much in my life. I want to die clean, without provisos and without exceptions. I was addicted to alcohol, to being famous, and to people who hated me. I've been addicted to hate; so I would not be addicted to love. I've been addicted to Jasmine, I admit it; I've been addicted to starvation. I've been addicted to attention. I've always wanted people to help me. I couldn't swear off any of these addictions, but I thought morphine could be one I didn't surrender to. I thought I could be stronger.

Everyone told me I was being ludicrous. They did not say, "This is the end of your life, so go for it," but that's what they meant. That's what they meant when they said how much simpler it would be if I went on morphine. They didn't say that it was a matter of it being simpler for them. They did not say, "This is the end of your life, enjoy it when you can." They said without the pain, I could relax and be less anxious; I wouldn't have to be afraid of everything the nurses did, because I wouldn't have to feel anything. No more lifting and stretching, bathing and diaper changing. It will all become one fluid motion, unlike the ordeal it had become. Every single touch, every movement, sent me into cascades of pain. I wanted to scream. I wanted to vomit. I wanted to fight back and slap the nurses away. I wanted to slug them. But I was also preoccupied with the sensations I had, tracking their reach and variety. I thought I could calculate, by degrees, how much more resistance I had in myself. Eventually I got lost somewhere in parts per billion in my blood, and on my chest and joints, absolute tonnage.

Once I started on morphine, I lost all my needs. If I had known that I would feel this way, I might have started on morphine a lot sooner, and this is what I was afraid of. I did not want to live without Jasmine after what happened with her, with me, with the "us" that we were, until she decided we were no longer an "us," though I was still me and she was still Jasmine. But during our relationship I had changed, she said. I was no longer acceptable or presentable; I was too much of a responsibility, one she couldn't handle. This is one of the versions of what happened, something I heard somewhere in retrospect. The point is that I changed, somehow, out of my control or notice. She had the power to see it, sense it, reject it, even, while I was clueless. I couldn't even change back when she told me about it. She said she was looking for someone who wouldn't get lost as she took off to the top of the entertainment-industrial complex. It was what her talent deserved; her looks could take advantage of. There was nothing I could do with my looks, my talent, my attitude, the clothes I wore, or the timbre of my voice. All my qualities, habits, and characteristics were wrong, wrong, wrong for that kind of life. I would never fit in. I would never make it. So I was abandoned, rendered into irrelevance. I had fallen off the bike, the horse, what would have been the ride of anyone's life. And I never got back up again. I have remained where I fell in the dirt that turned out to be toxic.

I used to watch Jasmine—on television specials, in movies, in magazines, in advertisements, in newspaper reviews, in gossip columns and in deep explorations into the savage heart of the music business—and I wonder, how does she do it? How does she walk away from someone and never think of her again? Never shows any outward signs of having been affected by someone as though that person never existed? I see Jasmine in the news, in photo spreads, and on the covers of albums and concert programs, and I understand how completely I have been erased. I am neither a before, nor an after, nor an addendum, and yet I can account for days, nights, weekends, years that took place before all this. I am a reliquary of censored events. Should I be opened, pried apart like a rusted entrance or a door warped and rattling against the defeated timbers? All that time and truth escaping? It would knock the universe off its axis.

Morphine does not knock the universe off its axis. It does not inspire me or elevate me above the bed or beyond my sick organs. It does not flood me with a vague sense of well-being or a specific sense that I can beat this disease, finally. But the numbness and lightness infused into my system—the act of subtraction that morphine performs—make anything and everything possible. Anything and everything without having to be famous to do it: escape the room with its crushing protocols. The feeling of snapping and scraping returns to my bones, my limbs distended, and my breathing undaunted. I might climb mountains or topple off their peaks; grow a set of wings or slam into a cliff after jumping, so that I shatter and separate into a million pieces. I would have the courage, the prowess, the genius to restore myself, even if I were nothing more than a fan, a poseur, an amateur, a quitter. A rock 'n' roll failure, a star-fucking groupie, anorexic, compulsive. I was a prodigy in mathematics. I was my family's last, best hope for a doctor or a professorship. I had my symmetry, all my lymph glands, and both of my breasts. My lungs were clear and my liver voluble, if overtaxed. I had my endorphins. I was healthy, once, before all this.

My sister and the nurses are dragging out the telephone. I can hear it as they transfer it from lap to lap to lap. The bell goes off, as if the ring were dieseling. Maybe they should call my attorney or my conservator—my legal representative— the man who pays all of my bills, since I certainly can't trust my sister to do it. I had to hire someone to act as though he were my family. Because all that I am to my sister is money; it's all I am to anyone. Money to buy them dinner, concert tickets, or airplane rides. Money to help with their bills, so much more burdensome on them than they could be on anyone else, especially myself, because I am single, unattached, and without any obligations whatsoever. I know the people who look at me helpless in this bed, especially my sister, are waiting for that moment when I lose my grip, so they can snatch at everything I have. But they have the telephone in their lap now. It registers whose body harbors the most poison, whether it be radiation or an abundance of concern over my condition: perhaps they are the same at this point. I can hear my sister emoting; she doesn't understand why it always ends like this for us: our family. If you can call what we had a "family," if you could call it that.

Like for all my ancestors, my death is turning out to be feverish. I don't even know which ancestors my sister is talking about—great aunts I never met, great uncles I didn't know existed, great grandparents I have rarely heard mentioned. My sister knows all their names and which side they hail from, a thoroughly cursed bunch. But how can I be cursed if I never knew who was who—if I never participated in "family," its gatherings and rituals? I am feverish in my own right, like all my dreams, and the strategizing I've done to get close to Jasmine again.

My life will dissolve and dissipate, spike like influenza, when this is done. When a fever breaks, there is a sense of relief, of freedom from whatever pain there was. But my fever will not break this way. I intend for people to go on feeling and to have them ruminate and experience anguish and to torture themselves over what they did or did not do in my name. I will have a broken death, one that will come at them like a swat, a thwack, or a steel beam thrown under the axel of a truck—the axis of the universe thrown on its head. I should feel something for how Jasmine has died—has been murdered. It has to be worse, going that way. But I can't feel for someone who never felt for me or who pretended never to feel for me, because there were those days, I remember them, when she felt for me most intensely.

The nurses and my sister are scared. The nurses are scared for themselves, whether they'll be able to make it home after their shift. All that traffic with the news vans, the road closures, and the hastily fashioned detours. It'll be a nightmare. Perhaps they will be trapped here; the night nurses prevented from reaching the house and relieving the day shift. They worry over their offspring, their spouses, the meals they will not be able to fix for them, the decent night's sleep they will have to sacrifice just when they need it most, so they might face yet another day they hadn't anticipated with their dying patient. Shouldn't she be dead by now, they must wonder, although of course they say nothing that might betray their disgust and dread. But I can sense it, this spike in their anxiety at the prospect of another 12-hour shift. It rolls off them like sulfur, having no place to wash their sweaty bras, to loosen their waist bands, to separate themselves from the discharge that accrues in their underpants. My sister is scared for an entirely different set of reasons, almost more legitimate; the nurses may desert her, and she will have to take care of my needs by herself. Obviously, she is not equipped to do this and realizes she will either have to be more solicitous of the nurses or pay better attention to their techniques. The nurses and my sister talk, they make calls, and they brace for the siege ahead.

The telephone rings. My sister is overly efficient in answering it. We used to fight about this. She relied on the telephone far too much, our mother said. She was always waiting for a call from a friend, a boyfriend, a casting director, or a scout from ballet company X or Y. She should get her own line or an answering service. My mother and I were not secretaries. We were not paid to take her messages. I tried charging her once: I made a chart and invoices for hundreds of dollars. My mother told me not to be preposterous. Still, it makes sense to me that when threatened with a real responsibility, my sister would reach for the telephone for help to find someone who could help her avoid it entirely.

She sounds smarter than she is as she speaks to each caller; she is convincing as a sympathetic figure. At least she knows the vocabulary. Perhaps the cops who were here earlier—this morning? yesterday?—should be "dispatched" to the house, to provide "crowd control" for all the "media." "What are they waiting for, the perp walk from a dying woman?" she asks; I could not help fully comprehending that one—about either my impending death or my status as a suspect in a murder. "This is what you want, a passion play?" Her voice rises to the occasion. "You want to intentionally inflict emotional distress—that's actionable, you know. See you in court, then."

Six years ago—before the chemo and radiation, before the surgery that was followed by more chemo and more radiation, all the treatment that didn't really matter as it failed to capture the few errant cells that escaped from my chest and into my hip and therefore my entire skeletal system—six years ago, I found Jasmine. I found her in her neighborhood café where we used to hang out and drown our coffee in milk and sugar so we could keep drinking it and keep our table. I found her there, or perhaps she walked in as I sat in a booth with my beverage and took my time with it. I was running out of time then, and I had to make her know what was happening to me. What was happening to my body, how it was happening, beyond my control. There was no body-mind connection involved. This was random, something I had deliberately tried to avoid.

I did not ask for cancer. I did not seek it out. I did not stalk it and force it into the most fetid and vulnerable part of my body where it was sure to multiply and set out on a savage mission to infest and distort my entire musculoskeletal system. But six years ago, in the beginning, when remission seemed possible, if not permanent, the cancer did make me feel special. Inscrutable. No one could tell that I had this secret, a biological mystery, inside of me, commanding me. I had to have Jasmine know this—that I was unidentifiable at a glance. That what went on within me was individual, truly individual; I could no longer be classified solely through my appearance. The proof was there in the oncologist's report— the distinguishing features of my special cancer and the unique mix of poisons that would have to be concocted for my case. For once there was something unknowable about me. I was defying my stereotype.

I needed Jasmine to see this. To see me without knowing a thing about me. To see that she could be deceived. I did not necessarily want this deception to be public. But the neighborhood café was the only place where she could be found reliably. I went to the neighborhood café where all the people from her neighborhood go, and there she was in a booth with some other woman. This woman did not look like a lesbian, but neither did Jasmine. They were sitting in the booth and I told Jasmine about the cancer, and she said, "Interesting," as though cancer were a new drug, the name of a gig, or the label you'd put on any proposition that would enrich her, specifically; as if cancer were my final plea to her, and she could take it or leave it.

"What did you think was going to happen when you told her?" my sister said when I told her this story. "Did you think she was going to lay her hands on you, heal you?" No, I did not expect that. I didn't even want to be healed, at least in that sense. I wanted something less from Jasmine, though it would have taken something more from her to give it to me. I wanted acknowledgment. I wanted to matter to her, and for that, I would have had to be her equal. I could have been her road manager, her money manager, or anyone in charge of wrangling, cajoling, organizing, and giving orders. I could sort through Jasmine's acolytes, separating the poseurs from the righteous. I could patrol her entourage. I could get rid of mooches and hangers-on, elevating the deserving. I could banish all the drug dealers, or I could have found her a truly loyal connection. I could have done drugs for her. I could have kept drinking. I could have monitored her alcohol in-take, the chemicals in her makeup, whether she was getting enough vegetables. I could have appointed a security detail, running background checks on all comers. I could have lined up babysitters for her son. I could have made her doctor's appointments, researched diets, rearranged her closets. I could have done anything had I the chance to demonstrate my competence; to prove I had also done it, this growing up thing, becoming an adult. I did not have her life, but I did have a life, with a title and income, a reputation that I coveted: I was dedicated to my work. I was diligent and caring. I had everything she had, though I was better educated.

"Why do you even bother?" my sister asked, after I told her what happened. "She's impressed with only herself. She has no idea who you are. Did you think she'd suddenly wake up, and remember? I mean, did you think that after all this time, you'd finally get through to her?" No, I did not expect that. But I wanted it. I deserved it. I certainly deserved an apology. I wanted her to be sorry I was dying. I wanted to have my suffering declared worthy. I wanted my suffering to make me human in her eyes, as human as she was. I wanted her to know that I also had a story to my life and that soon my story would be ending.

What I did not expect her to do was to say, "Interesting," and then go back to her salad or hamburger or whatever the café knew in advance to have prepared for her because she'd been eating there since before she hit it big; before she could hire a personal chef and an entire domestic staff and afford the more opulent dining options available from the best caterers and restaurants. I did not expect her to say, "Interesting," as though she couldn't bear to make even small talk with me; so she just muttered whatever syllables would randomly fill the space between us until I left. I didn't think she'd say, "Interesting," to block out the time until the next subject came up, when she could be her charming and witty self because she wasn't inhibited by the peril and awkwardness I presented. I did not expect her to say, "Interesting," when she was not the slightest bit interested, intrigued, or sentient, and have her lie to me again, like she always did. Because "interesting" is not ever how she thought of me, my life, or my problems. The problem was that I was never interesting enough, though I now hear I am a "person of interest," someone the police want to talk to, to find out what I know about Jasmine and her habits.

I'll tell you what I know. I'll tell you all about Jasmine. She invited me into herself, but I was the one consumed—my emotions, my anatomy, and the way I saw myself among women, musicians, and even men I wanted nothing to do with. She invited me into her mouth and her hair, and yet I was the one who got engulfed in all the slick romance and the undertow of her famousness. She said she could get me a shot and get me and my band noticed. I'd have to ride in her wake but so what? Lots of people get their break that way. This was my one and only chance at being someone other than who I was: small and star struck, emotionally unstable, and in way over my head. Jasmine invited me into herself, and I drowned there in her face and music; I was never able to right myself afterwards.

That was why she broke it off with me. She said she couldn't give me what I wanted. What I wanted was too much; I was too much of a responsibility. She couldn't deal with it. So she cut it off before it got dangerous. In another version I heard from someone, she said she broke it off because she was more interested in one of my friends, one of the girls in my band. The girl I used to play hopscotch with in elementary school; we discovered together that we were lesbians. We didn't really understand how lesbians could be a "them," because there was only us. In junior high, there were even more lesbians. But when this lesbian was fooling around with Jasmine and I found out, it was over between me and Jasmine. I was the big girl in this situation. I was the adult. I would not stand for this betrayal. I was saving myself from further humiliation when the truth would become public. And it would go public, because one of us would make sure of it. That girl, the hopscotcher, the one who swore us to secrecy, who made the boys swear, too: she was the one who told everyone, because being with Jasmine, and betraying me, made her look good.

"You should stay away from her. That girl is like toxic for you," my sister said after I told her about running into Jasmine. "She's like poison." But my sister does not know that poison is essentially what they give to cancer patients. The agents, antibiotics, inhibitors, and antimetabolites are poisons that harden cell walls, interfere with DNA, prohibit natural cell division and renewal, and shut down the immune system. Some are dangerous to the heart. Others could result in more cancer or leukemia. But poison was the only chance I had.

CHAPTER 6

THE NEXT DAY, RUBYLYN WAS GONE. The hospice office called to say she wasn't coming in; there'd be a replacement as soon as they could manage it. Maria told me we didn't have to replace Rubylyn. Instead we could have Ionie stop dusting and start doing some real nursing. It wasn't clear whose decision it was, and we had more urgent matters. From the picture window parallel to the sick bed, we had seen the news vans down below, lining up on the street. Their crews spilled out of the sliding doors with tons of equipment. We assumed they were pooling around the front steps of the house, but the three of us were afraid to walk up to the window and be ensnared by the cameras.

The three of us—four, if including Barbara, who passed out after her morning routine—monitored what we could on television. The screen flashed images of the front door, the sidewalls, the white plaster, and the blue paint I had grown up in, and it made it look spent and clapboard. I'd seen stage sets that were more substantial. Anyone could push over the house with a mere touch of their fingertips. Maria said not to worry, it wasn't real; it was just something the black and white television did. In color the house would look familiar again.

"Why are they here?" Ionie said.

"To talk about Jasmine?" I guessed.

"To talk about Jasmine or to talk about how the police came to talk about Jasmine?"

"How am I supposed to know?" I answered.

"Will they be here all day?" Ionie said.

"She knows as much as you do, Ionie," Maria affirmed for me, without my asking. "We could call the office. They could send somebody."

"Yesterday, why didn't you want to call the office?" Ionie muttered. She seemed more disgusted than scared, but I wasn't sure. I suppose she thought she had to be an enigma, with all her authority and her professionalism.

"When has the office ever gotten back to us that fast?" Maria said, the answer implicit in her tone of voice.

The doorbell rang and the telephone started going off. The news crews were trying to flush us out of the house. Answer the call, open the door; there could be a cure waiting: the delivery of a miracle on your doorstep. If Barb had been awake, I might have been willing to answer the door. With her passed out, I worried all the confusion would wake her up and set her off into a fit of hiccupping or crying out, asking whether today was the day and could she see Helen first.

Ionie turned the television to a sports channel, and Maria unplugged the phone near the bed. She shut the bedroom door so we couldn't hear the knocking and pounding on the front door. I hoped Barb wouldn't wake up hungry, because our path to the kitchen was cut off. The vertical window beside the front door would give us away, the one with the CAUTION: OXYGEN IN USE sticker. It was supposed to alert people to how dire the situation had become inside. The cops ignored it yesterday. Today it was everybody else's turn.

"Bells," Barb said.

"Bells," I repeated, like I sometimes did with my daughter, when I wasn't sure what she was talking about, what she meant.

"I hear bells," she said from out of her numb stare up into the ceiling.

"So do we," I said, knowing this wasn't going to be enough to dissuade her from further remarks or potential complaints. "We'll take care of it."

"The doorbell," she said. She had breached the first secret we were keeping from her. She'd take even less time to burrow through the next one.

"You're head nurse," Maria said to Ionie.

"Who is next of kin?" Ionie said to me.

"I'm not allowed to do anything," I said. The hospice, as part of preparing the house for Barb's convalescence, had taped notices in the kitchen and the bedroom listing who was to be notified in case of certain events. In the case of financial questions, there was her conservator, her lawyer, and the accountant in the hospice office. In case of problems with the house, her conservator and the repairman he had authorized. If her condition changed gravely, her friends Dorothy and Marion were to be notified. They came every weekend and spent as much time with Barb as possible. There were other friends listed, who would contact still others. I was somewhere at the bottom of this list.

Ionie shrugged. She set down the rags she used for dusting. She might have sighed, muttered again; I don't know. I was trying to watch my sister, to see if she was catching on. She was sinking back into the bed, where she might start hiccupping, then gagging. When morphine was finished with the pain, it would act on the respiratory system. It seemed like forever for Ionie to get out of the room—so I could try lifting Barb on my own without her commentary; so Ionie could say something to the cameras, get them to go away, scatter them to good riddance—though I knew what was going to happen next. They'd go to the neighbors, seeking testimonials about what a quiet, unassuming girl Barb was and how they couldn't imagine her being involved in anything as sordid as this.

"I'm hungry," Barb said.

"Can you wait a minute?" I asked.

"I'll get it," Maria said, and she left the room, presumably for the kitchen.

"Is someone here?" Barb asked. She was blinking heavily, slowly, like she was trying to focus on the television. Or maybe she was trying to keep her eyesight from waning.

"The television stations are here. They want to talk about Jasmine," I said, just to get it over with.

"I don't want to see them," she said, her eyes shut.

"I figured." I didn't know whether she had fallen back to sleep, whether she was listening, or whether she would wake up and change her mind in a minute. I had never seen her this still—smooth but disturbing.

"Tell them I'm dying," she said.

"I think we're trying that."

"Tell them I'm dying today," she said.

"Maybe not today, but we can lie to them."

"I'm ready now," Barbara said. Her eyes remained shut, but her voice was louder and steady. "Let's go."

"Okay," I said, and I took her hand. It was limp but warm. "Maybe tomorrow," I said. By tomorrow the cameras would be gone. Tonight there'd be klieg lights. I'd seen this before at the galas: the arrival of tents, red carpets, news crews, and their machinery. While we got into our costumes or did our makeup we would watch everything on little televisions—the breathless questions from the reporters about saving this grand tradition in drama, choreography, fine art, or whatever words they had come up with for the occasion. Sometimes "cultural institution" is how they'd refer to us. After the show, we'd be marched out of the theater. Maybe we could be on television, too: public access, Bravo, or another arts channel—maybe PBS. We'd catch the eye of some producer and be made famous in an instant! Those klieg lights had a way not of blinding but of blurring reality. We'd take our walk down the red carpet, but no one would notice. We were just bodies, which brought the ballet to life but only temporarily. The next day, the tents would still be up, but the lights and cameras were gone, and we'd be back in classes—in rehearsals and performances. We'd be anonymous again, the *corps de ballet* and soloists. Even the principal dancers felt this from time to time, though I only know this secondhand.

I WANTED TO PLUG THE TELEPHONE BACK IN after Ionie took on the news people. But as soon as we did, it went nuts again, like an alarm clock. Barb became confused and agitated, which meant hiccupping and demanding to know who was calling and why she couldn't speak to them. Whatever had happened over the last few days, or the last few months, was gone to her. It was as if she was just waking up and discovering that Jasmine had died and that she was in hospice. She said Helen was knocking on the picture window, trying to get in, and that she was the one telephoning incessantly. Maria calmed Barb by reminding her our mother would be the last person in the world needing permission to get in. I promised if I saw our mother, I would let her know. But it was Maria who was able to convince Barb at regular intervals, when her limbs had to be stretched, the sheets and diaper checked, and the drugs administered.

We watched television. We watched commercials for that year's governor's race: I remember them more distinctly than the sitcoms and talk shows. Yesterday it had been all news and all Jasmine. Now we got occasional updates from the scene: the scene of the house, the scene of the murder (somewhere in the Hollywood Hills), and the scene of police headquarters. I prayed for the return of regularly scheduled programming. The teen dramas would come in the evening.

Barb used to watch *Beverly Hills 90210* religiously. First when it came out, then in reruns. She said she was studying what high school was supposed to be like. She maintained she didn't know, because Jasmine had warped so much of her experience. I tried explaining to her that *Beverly Hills 90210* was nothing like high school. It was instead a fantasy, wish fulfillment, and the marketing of fashion and a lifestyle. She wouldn't buy it. She said that because she'd been stuck in that genius annex, she had no idea what the real business of high school was, dating, breaking up, and getting over it. I said something to the effect of wasn't that what happened to you? This she could not accept. She got mad, incensed, and out of control. She could do that—her face switched on red and her voice screwed wide open until she was voiceless. She screamed at me for being ignorant and heartless.

"I said, 'The missus is ill. She is receiving care in hospice,'" Ionie told us when we asked what happened. She insisted it was no big deal; she was accustomed to confirming for people their worst-case scenarios. We watched Ionie take on the questions from several different angles. From seven differ-ent angles, technically, as we switched between all the local

SISTERHOOD OF THE INFAMOUS

stations. We could have seen more if we took the leap onto cable. Ionie was right; she pretty much gave them the same answer no matter the question. Did Barbara talk to the police? Was she able to help them? Was there a family spokesperson they could contact? "The missus is receiving care in hospice," she said, like she expected that would settle the matter. When someone asked for Barbara's condition—serious, stable, good, or critical—Ionie replied, "Do you know what hospice is?" in that way of hers, which I was beginning to understand was how she hid her opinions, most of them negative.

I decided, after watching television most of that day, that when Andy Warhol said—and how could you live in New York without knowing this—in the future everyone would be famous for fifteen minutes, he was leaving out something. First you have to go through Los Angeles. Because in L.A. fame was everywhere. It wasn't as hard and fast as it was in New York; you could touch it and have some rub off on you. All you had to do was know where to go, what to be seen doing, and do it in close enough proximity to a source of fame. In this case, it was Jasmine. The news broke into the shows for interviews with Jasmine's manager, her colleagues, her followers—tearful and gracious for all Jasmine had done for them. "We love you, Jasmine!" a woman in her thirties, maybe older, proclaimed into a microphone. I knew how this sounded and what it might remind people of, but on that day there was no comparison between Jasmine and Judy Garland.

When the news came on—the actual news, not the live updates, teasers, and scrolls at the bottom of the screen, but the full package with all the special effects, the music, and the graphics—the knocking on the door started up fresh. We thought we could ignore it for a while; Maria and Ionie were changing shifts, handing off the schedule and notes to the night nurses, June and Yolanda. I had Maria and Ionie go through a back door, across the side yard and down an embankment to the street; so they could show June and Yolanda how to get inside, without having to deal with the cameras. That night nurses slipped in, presumably unnoticed, but the knocking at the door turned to pounding. I wondered if the door and doorframe would hold.

Yolanda suggested we time the knocks and poundings like we would the contractions in a pregnancy. When the knocks came without intervals, our minds were made up. Yolanda and June said we had to surrender, and I had to be the peace offering. The sacrifice is more like it. But I agreed. I was, after all, the sister of a person of interest. We learned that Barb was a person of interest from watching the news that afternoon. No one had told us of course. The newscasters said they couldn't be sure what that meant: was Barb a witness? A suspect? An accessory to murder? What secrets could she possibly be harboring in the recesses of her morphine-addled consciousness? After Barb was diagnosed with cancer, she had no secrets. Maybe she never did since she lived in public, such as her public was. I was part of that public; so I had to be held accountable, I suppose. I prepared to answer the door so that I could answer the questions about Jasmine, my sister's brush with fame that didn't pan out, the broken heart that couldn't be healed, and the whole lousy business of being a nobody in glittering Hollywood.

"Where's your mother?" asked the man at the door. He had his fist raised, like it was still in the midst of pounding. Behind him I could see a few well-dressed men pacing.

"Is your mother at home?" he asked, and he tried to peer into the house, like he knew the layout, how far it was into the living room, or the kitchen, where he could find her, washing dishes at the sink. In a way, he did know, because this was Mr. Silvers, the famous contractor in the neighborhood. He built all the houses before the families moved in, and that was enough to make him famous around here.

"I want to talk to your mother," he insisted.

"My mother is dead," I replied, and I waited for Mr. Silvers to react—with his face or his body—but he was stiff, stubborn against this news, like he could will that it never happened. Barb and I used to play ding-dong-ditch at his house, because he had a fancy doorbell; it was loud and long, so that his deaf granddaughter could hear it. We didn't take advantage of it when the deaf granddaughter was around. But when she wasn't, we'd punch it every chance we'd get, and then run, because the bell gave us time. It gave us the best chance of escaping on the block, the kind of temptation that guaranteed never getting caught. We couldn't resist it.

"We would have invited you to the funeral, except she didn't want one," I said.

"I'm so sorry," Mr. Silvers said. "I didn't know. No one told me."

"Well, I'm telling you now," I said.

"Jeez, I'm so sorry," he said again. Mr. Silvers was already old when he built all these houses and had only gotten older. His shoulders were curved, his pants loose on his frame, like his skeleton had been withdrawing. There were age spots on his bald head. "You know, your mother's family and I—your grandparents—go way back. Before your mother got married."

"I'll try to do better by you once Barbara dies," and I pointed to the "CAUTION: OXYGEN IN USE" sticker in front of him. "Though I don't know if she'll be having a funeral either."

"Christ, what's happened to you girls?"

"We grew up."

Mr. Silvers stood on the steps of the house that he built half a century ago, and he did not crumble. He stuck his chest out and rolled his shoulders, like he had forgotten why he had returned to this scene. I could guess: the noise; the traffic; and the inconvenience Barbara's life and death caused him, the neighbors, and possibly the reputation of the neighborhood. Mr. Silvers was always worried about the value of his real estate investments; it's why he called us vandals and delinquents as we ran away from his doorstep and why he held Neighborhood Watch meetings about it.

"You know I could have said something a lot sooner, like when your mother started letting this house rot like she was some kind of hillbilly, but I didn't."

"That was generous," I agreed.

"I thought your sister was supposed to be the smart one," he said, peering in, like he could see all the way to the back bedroom.

"She still is."

"Oh, I didn't mean it like that," Mr. Silvers said, and he might have buckled; I thought I saw him exhale, his chest falling. Maybe if I waited long enough, he might slowly melt on the steps. He'd faint and I'd have to call an ambulance. Maybe the news crews would be interested in that. They could put it at the beginning of the next newscast. "But we—people—we're just trying to live our lives here. There's a lot of retired people living here now, and—"

"I didn't invite these people here."

"But all this commotion," he said. "It's so," he stumbled in his voice and used the moment to turn around and look at the news crews and their equipment. When he turned to face me again, his lips quivered to form the words: "tawdry. Like a festival before an execution."

"Is it," I said.

"Look," he said. He stuffed his hands into his pockets and shuffled his feet on the wooden steps. I knew what was coming, because it always came in this neighborhood. The original sin: the foundational offense. "I know it's been hard for your family since your dad left—"

"No," I said. "You don't."

"Your mother would not appreciate this attitude," Mr. Silvers said.

"You didn't know my mother," I reminded him, and with that, I shut the door unceremoniously. I knew it was a temporary solution, but I could think only so many minutes ahead. I knew Mr. Silvers might be back, that others might follow him, and that for me and the nurses, we'd spend more time playing games getting in and out of the house and staying away from the cameras. The news crews weren't going to go away, but they might fan out into the rest of the neighborhood where the famous heart surgeon lived and the famous architect; everyone was famous in this neighborhood for something—working at the big hospital, surviving the Holocaust, or playing the best tennis at the country club. I guess Barb and I were supposed to be famous, too—she with her math skills and I with the ballet, but we all know how some of that worked out.

CHAPTER 7

HOLLYWOOD IS CHEMICAL. Not "a" chemical or "the" chemical: both are reductive. People assume that Hollywood is something you might isolate or distill. I'm talking about the power and action of Hollywood—the insidious formula and everyone's got to have a taste. Foul and fetid: no one cares. They'll line up for a piece, a rub against, or perhaps a touch. That's why all these people are here now lined up outside the sick room. Hollywood is inside. They've got it cornered. Now's their chance to get some. Up close.

You don't need to bottle the air here to know it's got Hollywood. You can't measure its parts per billion to figure out which level is toxic. You only know you can get it by seeing me live, seeing me die. Otherwise, you'll have to count on Hollywood infesting, insinuating itself into someone else you know, so that you're assured of enjoying the slightest of encounters. But even then, with Hollywood on your hands or mouth, within your nostrils, it's never enough. You must be consumed by it—have your heart and mind monopolized by Hollywood—if you hope to get the true experience. In this way it is much like a cancer, with its appetite and industriousness. But it is not a cancer per se, because it does not die. Or more specifically put, it is not suicidal. It does not require a host to carry out its destructive purpose, though we might all be hosts, which would explain its joyous efficiency in carrying out its program.

Hollywood outlives both addicts and the casually intoxicated. It is as close to the eternal as we are able to imagine, with our small, linear minds and dependence on outside stimuli to confirm for us our most recent beliefs, particularly in Los Angeles, and potentially its satellites—anywhere the local talent congeals and rises to the level of a "scene." There and in various nightclubs, theater departments, organizations, and disparate lonely hearts, in anyone seeking an unattainable sense of importance, chemical finds its refuge, its self-replenishment, and its stores for the future.

How else might you explain the people ready to witness my death-drama unfold, up close and personal? My bad breath, the sweat in my pits—I don't know how long it's been since I've had a legitimate bath. Those sponge numbers can't get to the root of the filth, every wrinkle in my crotch and ass. And this smell around me, the talcum that gives women ovarian cancer, and yet everyone's still using it; that's what they're going to get. Is Hollywood so worth it? They are in the kitchen, in my bedroom, and outside on the patio; there are even people outside on the driveway in full view of the cameras. Perhaps they are my sister's friends. Perhaps they were my mother's. But they must believe they will be touched by something. Otherwise why would they come? It's certainly not for a blessing; that comes only in conversation.

I sense them at my side, at my feet, inches away from me, crowding the room, watching my bouts of unconsciousness. They think cancer is like measles or mononucleosis, not in terms of rational immunity, but something like the odds of getting it, their placement in the cohort. If they know, or have interacted with someone so plainly afflicted, how could the cancer gods, their demi-sprites and demons, be so cruel as to inflict them as well? They confuse correlation with causation, believing they can place themselves outside the odds. Like people who fly only after the worst air crashes. It can't happen twice, can it? Not to me, with all the precautions I've taken.

Or perhaps I possess an antidote. To know me is to be cured. Or to know of me. Not to touch me or truly care. There are other reasons why these people have come, reasons that may have nothing to do with Hollywood. They have come here to prove something. Not to me. But to their children and spouses, to themselves: that their decisions have been better or more righteous. They have been more careful with their diets and their television and movie viewing habits. They wear sunscreen, have given up whatever drugs they used if they used them, and seriously curtailed their consumption of alcohol to socially acceptable limits. They have not let the disease into their lives; their lifestyles have made them impervious to tragedy and accidents. It is their DNA that is good and triumphant. Only the most resilient get promoted into the genome, not the prettiest or the smartest, but those who do what they did, whatever it was they did. They might not even know exactly what it was, but they did it. Now they win.

Or they have come because they lack something that I have. They want to be associated with this affinity. They are not so bold as to think it will be transmitted through the air, the water, or their contact with any number of surfaces in my home—the plates or glassware, the television remote, or my blankets—or from the blades of grass outside in the yard, direct inheritors of the greenery we trampled each time we played tag and I was It. Of course I was always It, they said, because my legs were so short I couldn't run as fast and catch anyone. When I was It, the game lasted longer for everyone. But the point is these people have come not to boost just themselves. Nothing as garish as personal gain or comfort. They're after something bigger. They're after a piece of history now. Because I'm the famous person. I am the focus. I am the fulcrum of this world, this house, and all the people in it; all the people coming to it, seeing it, thinking about it. The cameras, the news people, the speculation, the police, and hospice security controlling the crowds. Hospices do handle security, don't they? They will either have to now or learn how to do it. Because I've got what everybody wants. I am the celebrity now.

Yes. I confess it. I have always wanted to be a celebrity. Maybe I started out wanting to be famous for a reason. My singing and songwriting talent, my performances, or even my mathematical acuity. I would have taken that kind of fame. Why not? It has its privileges. But I also needed more: the bigger and the brighter, if not the blinding; the red, hot ball in the sky kind; and one that is necessary for all living creatures, divides night from day, and determines what time of the day it is. What time is it? Time to pay attention, it says, to this person because of her brilliance, which is natural born, God given, 100 percent certified, and algorithmically proven. I wanted people to see, hear, and feel me in every possible direction. I wanted to be the prize at the bottom of every cereal bowl, to flood eyeballs and eardrums, and to rest on the tip of everyone's tongue. I would be accessible, memorable, notable for my rawness and honesty, praised for my candor, and respected for my lack of persona. I'd be unafraid of my vulnerability; inviting, brave, and open with people I didn't know; and generous with those

I did. Everybody's best friend, the one anybody could count on. Philanthropist. Actress, if necessary. Model citizen.

Jasmine said she would make me famous. That was the narcotic she fed me. I didn't ask her for it. I knew about her parents, I knew she was popular, and I knew she was talented; but I did not go into the relationship expecting to come out of it with anything material. I did not go into the relationship expecting to come out of it, period. I did not go into the relationship expecting anything more than whatever it is people get out of their relationships, because I don't know what they get. Maybe it is a lesbian thing—this expectation that your own kind will treat you better than your opposite. But my sister says no, pain is a product of all kinds of combinations of people who lock themselves into all kinds of possibilities and obligations. But two women are not controlled by the slavish imperatives of testosterone or the directives of competition, status, and acquisition, I argued. She said no, people are animals: hungry, compulsive, confused, and exhausted. I wondered if she understood she was describing herself and all the men she had slept with. I had only one lover, after all. And I am proud of it.

I did go into the relationship expecting to come out different. I expected a transformation down to a level my genes could no longer interfere with. I would no longer be typecast based on my looks or my affect. I would be more than my height or lack of it and more than my genius for mathematics. I would be less like myself and more like Jasmine: entertaining, charismatic, quick with the witty repartee, and intuitive with musical instruments. I would have an accessible affinity, rather than a terse and obscure predilection for something that nobody understood or appreciated. The world is made of math: I can't tell you how many times people said this to me. My professors and career counselors. My teachers and parents, too, though they had no idea what it meant. But I did not want to describe the world or reinvent it. I only wanted to reinvent myself on a scale that I could handle. Not on such a universal-cataclysmic level, but still compelling and dynamic. The story of my life as I evolved it, without the baggage of the ancestors.

I suppose I am famous now. With all these people promenading through the bedroom, kneeling at my bedside, and asking if I might take something of them with me where I'm headed. Because the famous go to Heaven. They want me to put in a good word, make a recommendation, and confirm for them that God errs on the side of justice. How can I get a message back to them? Could I agree to a signal, some sort of supernatural occurrence it will suddenly be in my power to perform once I shuffle off this mortal coil and am shot through with light and love and the ability to dispense forgiveness? Perhaps I will drop a penny in a fountain or elicit feedback from a microphone at a concert. I'll open the shutters in this room long after I have left it. If I leave them closed, it means that I haven't been able to get my appeals through or that I've gone to Hell. It seems to me the most viable option.

"I can't believe your mother's life is going to end this way," a woman says as she strokes my hair. She must be older, to say something like this, a friend of my mother's. Her hands smell of talc and glue, as though she also is coming apart, her nails cracked beneath the polish, her skin yellowed in patches where the powder has fallen off. I don't see this, but I expect it. All of my mother's friends were made up, teased, and sprayed; they were held in place by rules and methods that failed to apply to my generation. How much easier my life would have been had these regulations still been in force. I'd be repressed, but that has to be better than whatever I was, my punctured heart soaking through my sleeve, a purgative cycle that for me was all month, all year. "Such beautiful hair. No one ever had it better," the woman says. I think her name is Ruth. She played tennis with my mother. She is the one who said my mother was too solicitous of me when I was a child. That was why I never moved out, grew up, or had any kind of independent life. I have to give her credit, just as I do my sister. At least she showed up to see what she has hated, what she has always been able to compare herself, or her own children, against. One of her children is a lawyer, the other a financier. They own their own homes and have given her grandchildren.

The girl from elementary school is here; the one I organized a gang against. Or so that story went, according to my parents, the principal, and the teacher. They put it on my permanent record. I suppose that record really will follow me to the grave. Imagine the satisfaction all those dead adults are getting now from that. They always said I was a runt and a mean, manipulative little kid. My father called me The Bad Seed. But he had no idea. He hadn't seen or read the play. He'd only watched the movie. Was The Bad Seed a lesbian? Or was she just a selfish, homicidal terror? Whatever she was, she couldn't have been as smart as I am, because she went wandering in the middle of a lightning storm. And she couldn't have been as passionate, because—I understand this now, just as I am coming to understand everything—I had to have been in love with that girl I organized the gang against. I was in love with her so she had to be eliminated if I were going to be able to live with myself. Of course I lacked for positive role models back then, and my obsession with a pretty, popular girl who developed early, as we used to say at the time, drove me to shame with a strange exhilaration. If something offends you, I remember hearing someone say in a now-forgotten context, remove it. Her removal is what I sought after that lesson. Her removal was what I sought, assiduously.

She sat at table three, and I was at table six, her back to me at a forty-five-degree angle; I had calculated it. But when she turned, got up, collected papers for the teacher, or came back to her seat, I could see them, bosoms, boobs, tits. She had a chest that gushed out like a wave of fascination—and betrayal to the other girls. But all of us, boys and girls, got swept up in the attention those tits demanded. They rooted through her blouses and T-shirts and they tempted me, in the same way a complex blemish on the face pulls you in. The cross section of a human breast is very much like a map in the same way that the lines on the palm of your hand are or the threads of a feather. In the human breast, every tremulous inch of that feather pleads with passing carcinogens: come drink from me. Drink from me until I'm dead.

The context did not matter for my record. It did not matter that *West Side Story* had been on television the night before. The salient fact was that inconceivably for the location and the income level of these children, two gangs emerged on the playground, one named "Jets" and the other named "Sharks." Their object was not to control the schoolyard, the classroom, or the position of hall or bathroom monitor. Their object was to dominate the other, destroy the other if necessary, or at the least, render it ineffectual. I myself was out only to eliminate that one girl in particular. I could not have cared what happened to the other boys and girls. I was out to eradicate that girl because of how she made me feel, the commotion she produced in me, the hot and cold, and the hate and envy. At some point that day after *West Side Story* had its world television premiere, the teacher sat me down and yelled at me as though he knew me better than I knew myself. "You're your parents' last, best hope in this world," he said. "Do you want to sacrifice that? Or do you want to confirm their worst nightmares?" He said if I did not confess my intentions my parents would be notified and that I risked suspension. At most I could be expelled if not from the school then its gifted program.

"Is that what you want?" he asked. He had a habit of disposing of all personal space between himself and the subject of his interrogations. I could see how ruined and yellow his teeth were on the bottom. On top the teeth were obviously false. "Is that what this is about? You don't want to be scholastically challenged?" Since I had not asked to be in the gifted program, I could not tell if he was threatening me or just making something up, the usual course adults take when they have run out of options. "You'd rather take it easy, be bored, sleepwalk through life," he went on, but I knew then that this would eventually be kicked upstairs to the principal's office, and anything he said or did was academic. His nose was running and his speech was competing with spit. "Stop smirking!" he demanded, but I wasn't smirking. I was closing my eyes and buttoning my lip to stay away from the fluids he couldn't control.

He should be here now, instead of this woman. But of course he's dead. She's the lucky one, walking among us, and she's apologetic—her speech distending into a wail. I can't pick apart the individual words. All I hear is the saccharine, whimsy and regret locked together or perhaps only an imitation of those sentiments. I cannot speak; my own voice is weighted down by morphine or perhaps by the tumors. There are probably so many of them now. They stopped scanning for them once the cancer breeched into my bones. They're like armies of independent thinkers, slogging through my various systems, in search of fresh tissue where they might reestablish themselves anew. But there is no room left, only territory that has already been spoken for. Perhaps the tissue is worn out, atrophied, emptied of nutrients, or perhaps there are only other tumors, the rubble their predecessors deposit in the midst of their renovations. How am I to know: how am I to know anything, with all the contrition on display from the other humans. I'll forgive you anything, girl from elementary school, if you quit asking for forgiveness. I'll absolve you of everything but your point of view—yourself at the center of everything because how else could you perceive anything, when everybody has always put you there, arranged their circumferences and symmetries around you. And your age, your weight, how far you have fallen from the girl you once were. I can't resolve all that because as you see, I have fallen so much farther.

Some of these people must be friends of my sister's. People I have only heard about or met on rare occasions: at her performances, her wedding, the showers my mother held for her. Not exactly my milieu. These are the people who have changed their names, adding vowels to sell themselves as more continental or more feminine. Ellen became Elena. April became Aprile, the one who feigned a pedigree from the theater. Henry became Enrique, though I'm sure he could have worked out something simpler. My mother called my sister's friends "affected," though I have always preferred "fake," a quality that I take pride in not only recognizing but outing. I grew to be expert at it, since I had so much practice in this climate.

My sister's friends are not celebrities. They would never consent to that. They are artists, or perhaps another vowel is needed here to be consistent. Or conversational. Because that's what they speak, "conversational French." They learned it through traveling—through the names of the dance steps—however artistes just pick up a language as though it were a part of their metabolism. How else could they carry on the way they do, lathering themselves up in all those chemicals from the makeup, and it has no effect on their hormones, their lung functions, or their immune systems? Their art must have inoculated them against the ravages of the masses. They spent their careers abusing and bargaining with their bodies, but to see them now, or to sense them at the edge of my bed, as I lie rotting here beneath too many blankets: they seethe with enthusiasm, something like youth, because so many of them have discovered civilian life, day jobs, and second careers. They are in and out of here as if they are patrons in a museum. Something in this exhibit might rub off. So they leave before whatever it is gets into their systems and curdles their inherent limberness.

I could have wound up like this: superficial, yet haunting. Or still capable of leaving an impression. I could have been healthy, resilient, and flexible in my needs and outlook if I hadn't been born with all these smarts. If I had been like my sister, stupid, I could have been so much more easily satisfied with my life, without my fatal need for prestige and the opinions of other people. I wouldn't have had to go to college, for instance, and I wouldn't have had to worry about all that homework. But it was decided before I could say anything about it: I had to go to college. The object of my life was assigned to me—this constant striving for numbers, letters on a report card, then numbers and letters on pieces of paper;

diplomas, fellowships, designations among other hairsplitters, bean counters, and other academics. That word already has enough vowels, though sometimes we wish we could change just one of them for effect.

I certainly was impressive to strangers. To my parents' friends whom I never really knew and to relatives whose exact relationship to me was possibly counterfeit, although how would I know—we saw them only every other year or less than that. Our branch of the family was shipwrecked here in Los Angeles, as if the city were a colonial outpost. We were necessary only as long as we continued to supply the rest of the world with our otherwise unattainable products. My grades, I suppose, made this strange, untoward experiment of living among the beautiful and the damned acceptable to the rest of the family. Perhaps they made the distance and different mores and conventions of Los Angeles damn near kosher to them, proving that you could still get a good education without the right schools and their vaunted reputations. If one daughter had all her brains in her feet, there was not much that could be done about it. But with the other one, only the Nobel Prize was the limit.

My parents, my father in particular, said I had responsibilities because of my gift. Not a responsibility to myself or to the family, but it was my duty to perpetuate and protect the body of knowledge. He or they, my mother included, saw me dedicating my life to a monastic pursuit, the discovery of new bodies or new fields of study, a kind of controlled growth plan that may not pay off immediately, but with dividends that might come after my death, making me if not prominent then necessary. School—elementary school, junior high, high school, college, graduate school, my post doc—these were the vital, inaugural steps that I was destined to take if I were going to meet my obligation. And I had only one obligation—to this amorphous, diffuse, almost god-like structure of facts and knowledge, of reward and attainment, that they themselves had failed at or were too frightened to try on their own, knowing the pursuit would be lonely, dull, and difficult. My sister, meanwhile, was worthless; so it didn't matter what she did. If she could walk and talk and feed herself without embarrassment, that was more than anyone had a right to expect from her. Just be glad of that.

And look at me now, putrefying on this mattress. Every grain of my being is converting into its apotheosis. My bones to liquid, my blood to sludge, and the air I am somehow still driven to take in practically like a solid in my lungs. My organs are bubbling, metastatic hovels for whatever structures still survive within, denuded glands and absent hormones. I am dead, a total system failure. This is what people have come to see, the waking death, a wholly artificial condition. A miracle of modern medicine. Only through chemicals can we extend the suffering; if the body had its own way, the death would be fast and pure, unpolluted. Not like this time-elapsed, stop-action chase where every cell and its contents must have their moments, their suffering accounted for and checked off, before the next can begin.

My body is my celebrity, though I suppose Jasmine should get some of the credit. This is my comeback, my victory lap! Finally, I am recognized as beautiful or beautifully damned. I am to be if not admired then recognized now as one of the gang, a true human person, with sensitivities and perceptions that are uniquely shared among an even narrower division, the female of the species. I'm a girl, a woman! My approaching death finally confirms for all those present that I was too open, too generous with the world, and its forces were so numerous, they just waltzed in and took advantage.

I am the center of attention because I'm dying of cancer. I'm a spectacle. A theater for the rude, compulsive animal that refuses to be domesticated. It cannot stop its inextricable course, even in the face of far more horrific tragedies. Like Jasmine's, for God's sake. God forbid, just imagine if you were murdered, the collapse of millions of life systems simultaneously, a far more catastrophic event. No one to hold your hand as you suffer; no one to wipe your eyes, your nose, your ass. No time to say goodbye, to make arrangements, and to be appreciated—your life celebrated by friends who are mostly acquaintances, but celebrate your life we will. Let's have a party! Everyone gather around. We know about you only what we care to, but we can celebrate that just as easily. Someone put in an order for food and plenty of alcohol.

Now, murder: that's altogether more tragic. Brutal and thankless. Something no one deserves, so horrifying and no way to prepare for it. Jasmine was murdered. I wonder who had the nerve to do that: take another person's life away and leave us to live with the aftershock?

CHAPTER 8

IT WAS OFFICIALLY GHOULISH, the next day, if you can have a ghoulish circus. If it's a thing that exists, without my having to make it up. I'm basing this on the crowds that globbed on to the doorstep; I'm basing this on all the other kinds of circuses I've seen before. As a New Yorker, I've seen plenty. Living in New York, I've had the pleasure to learn about perp walks, paparazzi gauntlets, police riots, and surges of rock fans, helicopter parents, and dog and cat enthusiasts all trying to get into the same place at the same time—crowds and people rejoicing in whatever utter chaos they could possibly create. Been there, damn that accomplishment. But what happened at my childhood home as Barb subsisted on her deathbed was something else. Maybe it was a dirge, a vigil, or some kind of funeral service in slow motion. Maybe it was none of those things, and it was how people die young in Los Angeles.

"Did you know Jasmine like your sister did?" one of the reporters shouted. I had made the mistake of going outside to get the newspapers. Helen subscribed to two of them, and Barb refused to cancel the subscriptions after her death. They went unread, sometimes still folded or rolled up in protective plastic. But we couldn't let them pile up at the end of the driveway. That wouldn't be neighborly, especially when our neighbors were threatening us.

"Is your sister a person of interest in Jasmine's murder?" I didn't know how they figured I was Barb's sister. I hadn't shown my face before, and I doubted the news crews even knew what Barbara looked like. "Isn't it true your sister was stalking Jasmine for years?" Apparently they didn't have the problem I had with that word, and they were more than happy to share it with the masses.

"Five minutes. We're asking for only five minutes," another shouted as I opened the front door to let myself back in. "Can you send someone out later?" Finally, someone said, "It looks worse, not saying anything," like this was supposed to scare me. Like I'd get on issuing a statement right away. Maybe I'd hire a public relations firm because I didn't know how to say that there wasn't enough to do, with the cleaning and bathing and cooking and grocery shopping, and the waiting. I could tell them about that—the work involved with a dying sibling. But that was not what they had come for. They wanted me to say something inappropriate, possibly cruel. They had fanned out in the neighborhood the night before to interview the people who had lived beside Barb all her life. They must have found out how she never moved into her own place; that the family was troubled, by divorce and death; and that I, her closest surviving relative/next of kin, was an idiot.

"It's Day 3 of the investigation into an emotional Hollywood tragedy," one of the reporters was saying on television as I walked into the bedroom. "Tragedies for two families, really," the reporter continued. "Here at the home of Barbara Ross...." It was year six for Barb's illness; the doctors gave her five to ten years to live once the cancer got into her bones. At the time, it seemed like they had given her a lot of time. I imagined my daughter as a teenager, able to form solid memories of her aunt.

The time did not necessarily go by in a flash but now, with so much unfinished business thrown at her, the present was tedious.

"We're also expecting an update from the LAPD sometime this Thursday," the reporter said, and I wondered how could anyone know what day it was without the television constantly reminding us. "We'll bring you that briefing as soon as it happens," the reporter promised, and with his pledge, I switched to another channel.

"We're not sure if Barbara Ross is a person of interest, a witness, or someone, maybe the last person, Jasmine talked to before she went on her run—"

"What run?" Maria asked.

"You don't know?" Ionie said, like she'd been studying up on the case. "Don't you know she was running the trails in these hills," Ionie intoned, "when she got attacked?"

"Not these hills," I said, and I pointed at the shuttered windows, so Maria and Ionie would know the threat here was not immediate.

"Aren't all these hills connected?" Ionie said.

"No one's going to get you, Ionie," Maria assured her.

I changed the channel again, like I could find some kind of neutral station. Something without news, dates, or coming attractions—anything that would not remind us what we were really doing: waiting. And anything that would not remind us what we were really waiting for.

"We have reason to believe that Barbara Ross is seriously ill, possibly in hospice." Another newscast. Maria motioned for me to join her at the far corner of the bed, to help with the sheets. Barb had an accident.

"Possibly? Didn't I tell them that yesterday?" Ionie complained.

"You're head nurse," Maria said. "Maybe you've got to tell them again, today."

"The thanks I get," Ionie said. "And what kind of day are you going to have, Miss Barbara?" she said to her patient, who had to sit up now so we could replace the sheets and towels, give her a second sponge bath, and recheck her pain patch and the port in her chest. "She's going to get right out of this bed and talk to all the people. Tell them to go home and mind their own business," Ionie said playfully.

"They think I'm interesting," Barb said, though she was half awake. Her head lolled but she was not blinking. Her eyes were closed, and when she opened them, she did not seem to like what she saw—this room, Maria and Ionie, me, and the television. She shut them instantly and kept them shut.

"Doesn't everybody think so," Ionie said as she held Barb around the waist, like Barb was in her lap. "Lift the feet now," she instructed Maria, while I grabbed what I could of the fitted sheet and stretched it out beneath her. Barb had a look on her face I'd seen before, almost smiling, eyebrows raised, the potential to laugh, or to be surprised.

"Something funny, Barb?" I asked.

"Hilarious," she said.

"What?" I asked.

"Am I interesting in the right way this time?" Barb asked.

"As far as I'm concerned," I said, and I looked at my sister, all of her, the body that was kept under the blankets. She was stringy and stiff. We could see her bones—all of them, delicate and cartoonish. What was left of her muscle appeared loose, untethered. Her arms reminded me of curtain rods, and the fabric when it gets bunched up and tangled. This was the last of her, what was left after six years of cancer treatment. You'd have to say it was a failure, wouldn't you? Or this was all that was left after forty-seven years, after all the other remedies for all the other illnesses, diseases, physical, congenital, or psychological.

Since birth she had been the subject of so much speculation in our family, the great feats she was capable of, and the best way to ensure they were accomplished. My father had great plans, which my mother thought would ruin her childhood. Then her childhood became her adolescence and my father had more plans, though Irv and Helen still disagreed on what they should do and how Barb would do it. Then her adolescence thinned; it disappeared in a snap, with anorexia, therapies, feeding, and the constant watching. We had to put her under surveillance. And then she finished school, she had her degrees and her career researching whatever she was researching, and she was an adult; it seemed like she was an adult. She had money and a car, but she was still living at home, not just single but celibate, and committed to going nowhere and having to do as little as possible with other human beings. There were titles, articles, grants, and even more money, a lot of it, but we hadn't expected things to be so small for her, shrunken and so restricted. This was how it would end, in much the same way—all that speculation, potential, and expectations shriveled into next to nothing.

"Maybe we ought to show the reporters this," I wondered aloud. "Maybe they could really do something with this."

"Are you out of your mind, miss?" Ionie said.

"I didn't mean it like that," I said, though I did want to give the cameras something that would shock the audience at home, shock everyone, and make them rethink their twenty-four-seven coverage of this nothingness. But I wasn't going to say that, either.

"Wasn't it bad enough when you brought the police in here?" Ionie said.

"I didn't have a choice about that," I said.

"So this is the one choice you would make?" Ionie accused.

"I said—"

"Okay, stop it, guys," Maria was almost yelling.

"Am I head nurse?" Ionie asserted.

"So start acting like it," Maria said. "Call the office, call her lawyer, or call anyone. Get them to fix this—this situation."

"Will it get me away from her, this calling?" Ionie said, meaning me, of course. Maybe I should have, but I did not, let myself imagine all of what Ionie thought about me, what Maria must have also thought, given this and whatever Barb had told them. My husband, who did not list my sister among his favorite people, had said I should concentrate on how Barb had finally relented, granting me permission to visit; that she had said I could stay for as long as I wanted. She had decided to tolerate me at what had to be the end. If I could tough it out, not start a scene, take whatever abuse Barb or anyone else lobbed onto me. I wasn't good at that, naturally. I had to get better.

"Don't worry about her," Maria said, her head nodding in the direction of Ionie's scramble for the kitchen.

"Because I've got enough to worry about, right?" It didn't come out the way I wanted it to, but there was nothing I could do to take it back or to take back everything I had ever said or done that led up to this day. "You know what my mother would say about you," I said to Maria. "She'd say you have nerves of iron and steel."

"Iron and steel," Barbara said, and I thought I saw her lips curl, her dimples push through, a kind of unconscious smile trying to overtake her face.

"I've worked with Ionie a lot," Maria said, sitting down at the edge of the bed. "She needs to get over herself, sometimes."

"Iron and steel," Barbara repeated.

"She'd say that about people who could put up with anything," I explained, because I was relieved to have found something to talk about, to have found a way to tick off more time, to delay or stall or postpone whatever was coming next, because it was going to be awful. We were running out of options, or Barbara was. Maybe we all were. "She also used to say that she didn't raise us to be tough enough for this world."

"Your sister is strong," Maria said. "Very strong."

"I don't think that's what my mother was talking about."

"Your sister is a fighter," Maria said, and she took hold of one of Barb's feet through the blanket, like I'd seen Ionie do. But Maria didn't pull on the foot to get Barb's attention. She patted it, like she was including Barb in the conversation.

"She got it from running, you know," I said, because what else could I say: thank you? Or, I know? I could have listed everything Barb had to fight through because she was always up against something—dumb kids, bigger kids, though she never had any problems with boys like the rest of us did. No teasing, no threats of violence. Boys she knew how to handle. She did what they did: science, skateboarding, and athletics. Girls are what got her into trouble. The rude, the cruel, and the snotty: she was attracted to them, or was it that they were attracted to her? Always the most catastrophic in symbiotic relationships. She knew how to find them, or they found her. Then there was the band, always breaking up and getting back together. It was like she found the worst people to grow up with. "If you're not part of the solution, you're a part of the problem," she used to say. I couldn't figure out what the problem was—being gay before the world was ready for it? But there were lots of gay kids in school, even more at the ballet studio. And not just the men.

I'm not saying it wasn't hard. I have no idea how hard it was. I wanted to be a ballerina. I fit into all the prescribed slots of sex, gender, and profession. I fit in without question. Barb was a tough girl, a tomboy, the genius kid. She fell for the pretty and imperious types and wanted to be one of them; she got close by falling for Jasmine in high school. The sun rose and set on Jasmine's word, and when they stopped talking, the world stopped spinning for Barbara. That always seemed to be the end of her life to me.

"She didn't tell me she was a runner," Maria said.

"Oh yes. Among many other things," I said. I understood that I was supposed to head off the oncoming lull in the conversation, the awkward silences that would be filled by the television, the noise from shows and commercials. But I had never known how to talk about my sister to the people who knew her. "What did she tell you?" I asked.

"That she was going to burn in Hell for being a lesbian," Maria said.

"Oh my God. I'm so sorry—"

Maria waved me off. "People say a lot of weird stuff when they think they're dying," she said, although I was not sure if this was true. My parents certainly didn't say anything weird—they were passed out and comatose, as they waited for their ends. They both had strokes, how lucky was that, everything quick and efficient, if not neat. They hadn't seen or spoken to each other in years and yet the same thing pulled them under, like they knew only one way of suffering and that was together. They had suffered each other so much that they couldn't conceive of suffering in their separate ways.

"Your sister isn't ready to go yet," Maria said, like she was trying to reassure me. Like there was more time for us to reconcile any outstanding grievances and for us to be sisters.

"You could have fooled me," was all I could think to say in response.

I DON'T KNOW WHO IONIE CALLED, but there were so many people I hadn't seen in years—people Barbara hadn't seen either—who braved the gauntlet of news cameras to grace our front steps. They had heard Barbara's name on the television, probably, and had to see if it was the same Barbara they remembered from high school or from kindergarten. Or they had seen the house on television and had to know first-hand if it was the same house where they played baseball, climbed the ivy, and tried to make the patio into a skate park. Of course it was. The living room had the same furniture though the patio was larger, because Irv got tired of taking care of the lawn and poured cement over half of it. That was in 1976-ish, I think, the bicentennial. Irv disappeared just before the Fourth of July, like he finally had something to celebrate on the occasion.

"This yard isn't half as big as I remember," one visitor said. He was one of the boys she used to play with, a neighbor or elementary school chum who thought Barb was cool because she wouldn't wear dresses and wasn't afraid of dodgeball. "We could really have made use of a patio this size," was another variation I got; the real estate that was our childhood home that our mother maintained and that Barbara had inherited always seemed to be a subject of great excitement for visitors, like they were astounded it still existed. Soon it would be liberated. One woman, who I had seen only in a housecoat while I was growing up, arrived at the house fully reinvented. She brandished her real estate license with her swift walk and her knowing inspection of the premises. She wanted to know what my plans were. I told her my plans were to get back home to my husband and daughter. The woman shook her head and probably muttered something about how I was as dense as everyone had always said. She didn't know I wasn't inheriting the house. Barb had made certain of that in her will, which she once brandished before me, so I couldn't get greedy.

Those who had been astounded by the size of their memories, or the yard, were disappointed when I told them that they were right; they must have thought they were having profound moments of reckoning. The near-death state of the neighborhood tomboy, apparently, wasn't enough to inspire the same kind of reflection. They bowed their heads, ducked out of the bedroom, and said they were sorry, like Mr. Silvers was the day before. Others said they wished they had known earlier. They would have come by; they would have brought food from their wives, or flowers, or cards. None of that stuff would have changed anything or, I think, made the outcome easier on anyone. But I was so surprised to see these people—so shocked and amazed that after so many years they yearned for Barbara, that I could not say anything. Or I could not say the right thing. Or I could not have said what probably should have been said if I even knew what that was.

"I wasn't expecting to meet you this soon," one of her former coworkers said. He was from the insurance company where Barbara worked between college and graduate school, writing computer code for actuary programs. She calculated risk factors for people buying life and health insurance and became fond of telling her friends and myself what was most likely to kill us: cancer from sleeping under electric blankets, cancer from living near oil wells, or cancer from eating canned tuna fish. Cancer, cancer, cancer. It was the inescapable conclusion to all modern living. She saw it in food, in clothing, in shampoo and makeup, in shoe leather and in kitty litter. You could not go anywhere or do anything without encountering it. We may have been prone to other diseases or were heading toward early deaths from other causes, but cancer was like her personal demon. The irony went unspoken.

"When did you expect to meet me?" I asked.

I remember he was overdressed for the summer heat in a coat and tie, like he had been expecting to find a memorial service once he got to the house. "I thought maybe after—"

"After what?"

"I—I—that wasn't how I meant it," he said, and he took a handkerchief from his jacket pocket and blotted it around his forehead. I might have felt sorry for him, but he managed to get himself swallowed up by the crowd before I could have told him.

I wondered why they came—I mean, I knew why they came. But why did they keep coming? We told a lot of people to come back on another day—Barbara was exhausted and could handle only so much. Or Maria and Ionie could handle only so much in the presence of gawkers, curiosity-seekers and a few who thought they knew more about hospice care than the hospice nurses did. "Why don't you call my supervisor, and you can discuss it?" Ionie offered to my mother's friend who wondered why the bedroom was so dark and whether light would improve Barbara's mood. Why wasn't Barb on a morphine drip? It would have been so much easier than administering it orally. "You have a degree in medicine? You set it up," Ionie said, which sent the woman skittering out of the bedroom. Ionie kept up with her dusting and straightening as the people marched in. They marched out, I think, because they were afraid of Ionie, her composure and determination, and her efficiency around the dying.

"Could you show your mother at least tried to teach you some manners?" Ionie demanded once as she got ready to check Barb's diaper, in front of a group of men who said they knew Barb from graduate school. They looked at me like Ionie wasn't speaking to them or like she was speaking a foreign language.

"Give the patient some privacy," Maria instructed and herded them out onto the patio. "Don't bring them back," she whispered to me as I tried to help her; the men kept looking back toward Barb, like they had been pushed away from an auto accident after they had fought their way through traffic to see, like they were being denied some kind of explanation.

They came for all their own reasons: to say goodbye, to say that they had said goodbye, to prove to themselves and to one another that they truly cared about my sister. Perhaps they were even trying to prove it to me. I didn't know why this had suddenly become so necessary, although it was; I mean, I was there, even though some of it was embarrassing. These were the people Barb had bragged to, I figured, or maybe they were here when Barb called me a cunt in front of her tough punk friends. These were the people Barb entertained with the story about how when I brought my first boyfriend from New York home to Los Angeles, Barb told him he might as well break it off with me since she had all the money and I had nothing. I assumed they remembered all this stuff because I remembered it; I had assumed it was ugly enough to keep people away. But it wasn't, because come they did, even as the television and newspapers rattled on about Barb's fraught connection to the murder, like the television stations were saying, of an American sweetheart. Jasmine.

Helen's friends came, those who stuck with her until the end, women she knew from college, her book clubs, and volunteering in the thrift shop, who knew Barb and I only as adults, though surely Helen must have told them how difficult her daughters' relationship had been. Barb's sworn enemies from grade school came, too, and they brought people with them—their spouses and their parents: their parents were young couples who knew both my parents when Barb and I were babies, and everyone thought everything was turning out pretty well for us—I mean the entire neighborhood—and their children and Barb and I would grow up together and maybe some of the boys would marry some of the girls, how cute it would be; and even though they were only in their twenties and we kids were toddlers, they could see how the whole story would go, all neatly tied with pink and blue ribbons. That the story didn't go that way and that lives had diverged—run off the rails and landed in the gutter for those who hadn't bothered to come say goodbye to Barbara—didn't seem to matter much. Because no one had it as bad as Barbara. In her they saw pity and a chance for a kind of reprieve.

They came for days, up until the very end, which we all knew, when they started coming, was days away. They came as Mr. Silvers got a group of neighbors to sign a petition saying no one else could come. They came until there were so many that Dorothy and Marion had to be called, and they proclaimed that no more could come. Dorothy and Marion: Barb's best friends in this interim. They had to make that call, because I could no longer distinguish in my unconscious sister whether she was approaching death's door or was right up against it, furiously knocking. Dorothy and Marion appeared as their work-home-life-Barbara-balance was upended. They stated their case to the nurses and left. But people kept coming, even when we ran out of morphine, and there was no one with the proper credentials from the DEA to pick it up at the pharmacy or the hospice. The hospice had to deliver it to us, and the van got stuck in the neighborhood traffic.

The people kept coming after the police arrested a local homeless man for Jasmine's murder. The police had witnesses to place him on the trails where Jasmine jogged; they had his skin under her fingernails and her blood on an item of clothing they would not specify to the news cameras. But they admitted they had no motive for the murder. They dared to call it random. The television and newspapers refused this verdict. Through their anchor people and reporters, they insisted there had to be more to the story. Half of murder victims know their killer, I remember hearing during the coverage; there could be only so many accidents in this world—or in the world of icons and superstars, people nobody really knew and yet they were embedded into the national consciousness. Someone doesn't get to be as big as Jasmine solely by knowing the right people. There has to be merit and talent involved, and that kind of gift that brings a light onto all of her audiences can't be snuffed out like that. It can't be that arbitrary.

The cops knew all of this of course. They can tell you how two halves make a whole, and half of murder victims don't know their killer. Violence is indiscriminate, strangers are malevolent, and the homeless are desperate. The murder could have been a robbery. How was it, I asked them, that all these people spontaneously appeared on our doorstep, after Jasmine died? How did everyone seem to know who the person of interest was and where she lived? Even if Jasmine could have been killed by someone who surprised her during her run and thought they could hold her up for money with a knife or a rock? They weren't discussing the method on television, yet. That, I knew, would also come. Detective-Sergeant Simpson and the officer-with-the-strangely-exotic-name-to-me drew blank looks like they were stupid beyond redemption, which is something I know about. They weren't fooling anyone.

"People die every day," Simpson said.

"Not like this," I said back.

CHAPTER 9

FAME IS A GAME OF NUMBERS. And of choices. Choices are what make it a game of numbers, ultimately. Like binary code. If you're going to be famous, you've got to make a choice, to do this one thing. To do it over and over again until you're better at it than 99 percent of the planet. I'm actually reversing the equation here and not being wholly accurate, but this is for you to understand, not for me to make it comprehensible in your language. And that is also my choice. I should have been good at it—the numbers and the choices. I wound up writing code in the end for a living. So I know about how you choose a one or a zero but never both in the same way, and how this choice must be asserted again and again, until you have something that produces a result, a result that produces an action. I know every moment is a decision and that I could have decided better, harder, more sincerely, or with more gusto; and then I could have been famous. I'm fairly sure of it. Maybe not 100 percent but close enough. I should have been good at trying to be famous, but I wasn't. Because fame is finite in its various contexts, and various contexts will only support so much fame. Or such is the case in Los Angeles.

In a population of 7.4 million (the population of Los Angeles and its surrounding suburbs when I graduated from high school), or in a population of 6.9 billion (the current world population), how many people can be famous? The answer is 0.000086 percent; a venture capitalist figured it out for obvious reasons. How many people will have the money and influence, or just the influence, to be worthy of the attentions of said venture capitalist? To be harassed, hustled, extolled, denigrated, so that said venture capitalist might become one of those people himself? He was not actually investigating the chances any random person might become famous, but his own odds. Because everyone wants to be famous, or they lie about it when they say they don't want to be. The supply is limited but the demand is something else.

When Andy Warhol talked about the future, he wasn't talking about numbers or sequences. He was talking about time. And time is a relative concept. What seems like fifteen minutes to me may be two minutes to the on-air television personality, such as those now congregating at my front door. But only if my life can provide enough material for such a daunting limit. Because I don't have much to say myself, and those who might testify on my behalf won't talk to the cameras. So the cameras have only the closed front door to film and the people who come and go through the door as they shield their eyes from the attention. You can show only so much of this before the audience will change the channel in search of more exciting footage. Or more titillating footage because fame is about titillation—the idea that you too could be famous. All you need do is walk through the right door, smile, and be wholly consumed—or dedicated.

I wonder which is my problem: that I walked through the wrong doors, that I did not smile, or that I didn't offer up enough of a sacrifice? We watch so much television in this room that I'm beginning to think the television networks are supplying me with a security camera. I can see my own front door virtually on any channel. Wall-to-wall coverage, they call it, but the only things I can see are the exterior walls of my house if you don't count the front steps, which the cameras occasionally pan out from. There are rare shots of cars driving up and down the street—for the record, shots of the throng holding its position, and coverage of the media circus so that the media can continue the circus. It's a kind of self-evident justification, a decision that yes, this is important. My front door is important now. Let's everyone look at it. See what you can intuit from its color, its length and height, and the decorative doorknobs my parents had installed when they built the house. And of course, let's judge the people who walk through that door in and out. What can we learn from them?

They come only out of a sense of duty, and once that duty is discharged, they are free from further responsibility. Never again must they return to this spectacle. Their action of appearing here now on television and, by implication, in my bedroom speaks of their decision. I will associate myself with this woman one more time, and only one more time. If they touch me at all, they touch my hand; they say that I look good and say how strong I am; they would mutter platitudes about courage and fortitude if they knew any. But they don't; so the visit becomes awkward.

My sister has to translate for them: the meaning of the look of my eyes or the movement of my head. She translates for me as well, raising her voice as she repeats what anyone says, as though I am in such a fog that only the most familiar voice can reach me. But I hear everything. I hear "good luck," "stay strong," "goodbye friend," and all the other platitudes twice, as my sister is intent on repeating them all if I miss them. When people leave my bedside, I look up at the television to either see them leave or confirm that they have closed the front door properly. I wonder why I am not on television myself, given what everybody has said about my appearance and my bravery. This is the peak of my fame, in the time I have left, fighting the unctuous cancer demon. I can only do this, however, behind closed doors, not for a live audience.

Who is on television the most, of course, is Jasmine. She always had that ability to eclipse me; she eclipsed everyone. She is on television more often than my front door is or so it seems to me. It's very possible that she is the only television I am capable of understanding now, aside from the pictures of my house. The world gets so small when you are dying. Only the minimum is comprehensible or can be bothered to be comprehended. Concert footage, interviews, replays of speeches, red carpet moments, when she won her first Grammy award, or was invited on stage during the Oscars: these are always shown in the same succession. Jasmine in concert at Wembley Stadium. Jasmine interviewed on *60 Minutes*. Jasmine wearing that hooded, sequined dress when The Regent won for Best Original Song and said he couldn't have written the tune without her, and he begged her to join him in adulation. Jasmine took The Regent's arm once she was up there and ducked her head behind his shoulder, as if to dodge all the attention. Her dress was red, and she looked like an elf on fire, an aura rising to buffet her figure.

We didn't have a color television in this house until after my father left. Color television was unnecessary and expensive, he said. Our father told us to imagine the colors on the screen, rather than just accept the dull pictures television gave us. My sister really fell for this. When we'd watch *The Wizard of Oz* or *Cinderella* every year, she claimed to feel the colors and sense their qualities, like range and thickness. The color of the ruby slippers was hard and ripe. Cinderella's ball gown was silver with a dusting of gold on the skirt. If you concentrated, you could see the gold dust catch the light and strobe through the camera. It happened when Leslie Ann Warren first turns to discover the prince just behind her at the ball.

I did not believe this, not for a second. The television was black and white, sometimes brown when a tube was about to blow, and sometimes white when the weather interfered with our antenna. I neither felt nor saw any color until it would be made plainly available to me, without any guesswork. Because I knew, and still know today, that there was an objective, documented, easily decided by a jury color out there, being broadcasted from Television City, the top of Mount Wilson, or network headquarters in New York City, and nothing my sister said or felt would change that color. The color of Cinderella's dress or the ruby slippers was a verifiable fact, unchangeable and unchanging from broadcast to broadcast. If need be, we could have called someone, standards and practices, programming, or even advertising, and asked them what color they were pouring though the wires. Was it black, purple, orange, or yellow? Could they provide us with a color still for future reference? How might we go about reading the colors correctly so as not to delude ourselves further? Seeing is believing, and believing is all about excluding the other possibilities, narrowing your options, finding the right horse in its silks and uniform, and betting your whole load on it, with a certain abandonment and confidence.

By the time we got a color television in this house, they weren't showing *The Wizard of Oz* and *Cinderella* every year.

My sister was gone most of the time, practicing and performing. She thought she'd slip into one of those ripe and resplendent costumes and rocket to the top. She thought she was going to be on television—public television—and on the stage in London or Paris. And she was, but not the way she had imagined. She got up on that stage, into those public television settings and studios, and traveled throughout Europe. Except that she was mostly at the back of the scenery, behind the better dancers, and her costumes were neither sumptuous nor bejeweled, but weird, ill-fitting approximations of what had baited her as a child. She got ripped off, but I doubt she would admit it.

I never saw my sister on television. I do believe that the shot of my front door has gotten more time on camera than my sister ever did. When I saw Jasmine in that gleaming red dress at the Oscars, I was a departmental scholar in mathematics. There were only two departmental scholars each year, both graduate students. But I was the third that year and still an undergraduate. The faculty said I had a free pass to graduate school, any graduate school. I was on my way to a Fields Medal. If I could devise a practical application for my equations, I might land a Nobel, possibly in economics. But what was all that, these slashes and marks on random pieces of paper, compared to Jasmine and her TV appearance?

I was shocked by Jasmine appearing in that red dress. She looked as though she had stepped out of a color negative, the green and brownish-red contrast, a kind of terminal condition, the sun unable to set, the world on hold. The thing about it was that it was all an act: Jasmine pretending to be jittery and modest when she was called to the stage by The Regent. That's what he called himself, The Regent, because there already was the King of Pop (Michael Jackson) and Prince (as in Prince Rogers Nelson and The Artist Formerly Known As Prince); so the most logical, next step in this strained succession was "Regent." The honorific of "the" was self-assigned as most power grabs are in the rock 'n' roll kingdom. Jasmine must have helped The Regent's ascent, though, because when she was on that stage with him, she shined like the Virgin of Guadalupe. After that first night, The Regent invited her into his realm, and Jasmine came to embody pure, unadulterated fame, as in no longer requiring some alphabetic or numerical rank to explain the source and rigor of her celebrity. Just look at her or listen to her play. Everything she touched turned to riches, and I was lost somewhere in the math department, trying to derive practicalities from abstract, sequential learning.

There were any number of people who promised over the years that I'd be famous. Jasmine, for one. The girls in the band I had. The producers and photographers, sound engineers, my adviser at college, the chairman of the math department, and the people running the epidemiological study for whom I did the statistics on the prevalence of cancer among people living under or near high tension power lines—the technical term is non-ionizing electromagnetic fields. The principal investigators in this study (the tenured professors who didn't need to publish another study but were compelled to do it) were convinced they had come upon a Nobel prize-winning connection for a series of cancers in California's Central Valley.

It was never clear what it was about these fields that caused childhood leukemia or inspired the growth of brain tumors. It was never clear what was similar about these cancers, since one is a disease of a system and the other affects an organ. Leukemia is entrepreneurial, original, and a pioneer in pulling down a body and making it untenable as a body. Its work is far cleverer, more ambitious in design, than simple brain cancer; although, to be fair, brain cancer can be original. It is not always the product of metastasis; the lazy route cancers take when they are dissatisfied with what they have destroyed. I tried to point some of this out to the principals, though not exactly in these words; I said dissimilar cancers might not have the same causes. But they were undeterred. They ploughed on under the belief that they might not find a magic bullet, but there was a possibility of finding a tragic bullet—a single, isolatable factor responsible for a spate of erratic cell growth in the blood and tissue of innocent bystanders.

I did my work: I added, divided, compiled, collated, and indexed the numbers that were handed to me. The numbers came from the records of people who lived on farms within two, three, four, eight, and sixteen miles of the power lines; cancer clusters can be remarkably porous, depending on the will of the researchers. These researchers willed that numbers from the health records of farmworkers who picked the vege-tables growing beneath the power lines would be added, and they were if you could call what was turned in for them health records. The records were more like notes school nurses took on farmworkers' children if and when they were enrolled in school. Since the records were spotty, the researchers began to add in statistics taken from farmhands who lived on the farms beneath the power lines, because the owners of the corporate acreage would never deign to live where it smelled like cows all the time, or manure, or the perfect distillation of those ingredients: ammonia.

Does constant exposure to ammonia cause cancer? Who knows? Who cares? As long as it is not combined with chlorine, the question isn't relevant—or it wasn't for our purposes. I kept pouring in numbers from the histories of families in the study area; statistics that stood in for socioeconomic conditions, the temperature of and pesticides applied to the vegetables as the farmworkers picked them and the farmhands oversaw their storage—another factor, although I was told not to make too much of it. Not if I wanted to be famous, like the tenured professors and their graduate students; not if I wanted to be known for accomplishing something that truly affected people's lives, made them better, and made them worth living until the end. Not if I wanted to be held responsible for an advance in the annals of humanity itself, forever preserved in the pages of a medical journal, and after that, perhaps for an eternity on microfilm.

I could have massaged the data, or I could have looked away as others massaged the data; it happens, more often than people care to admit. But I didn't. Or perhaps I should say there was no data to massage. I was always told to look for patterns, repetition in the numbers, strange consistencies or inconsistencies, but there was nothing. Only a morass of unquantifiable aspects; in other words, nonsense. Nothing to tie a few instances of erratic cell growth in disparate populations to the emission of what might as well have been nonsense. Nothing to tie a few instances of erratic cell growth in disparate populations to what powered their microwaves and their radios—which are also sources of the same kind of radiation that we were studying. We published what we had and then retreated into the anonymity that had always been waiting to engulf us. Because shouldn't something as horrendous as cancer; something with such power and mystery; something that seemingly changes every molecule in the chain of events that governs our breathing, our beating hearts, even our minds and our five senses; shouldn't it have a simple, easily digestible, believable explanation? Shouldn't it have a source, a catalyst, a particular or peculiar anteced-ent that guarantees the disease makes sense? Because cancer cannot be as simple as randomness, which is essentially what we discovered. We did not give the people what they wanted, and so we were not to be made famous.

So, in sum, as in an abstract, we could say that my hopes for fame spread and multiplied; they burrowed into me like a sickness. And now I have cancer. This is a huge leap, I understand, but still. The coincidence is damning. I am a compendium of failure. Only the cancer has succeeded in its task. It is what I will be famous for.

I wonder, does this mean I have overcome my need to be famous? That I have liberated myself from the defining, driving need of my life? Wouldn't that be the height of cruelty, of cosmic jokes and mordant tragedies, to be released from my need for people in these final moments? Now that I am dying, I have been emancipated from the compulsion to name, to collect, and to display the people who will remember me after my death. I see now that it doesn't matter if it ever did; I might as well have been dead all those years I was trying. I was trying to confirm my humanity by looking in the face of other humans, but how absurd was that? Because humans see only what they want to see. They do not take the time to plot out the subtle measurements. What I wanted to see validated in myself by comparing it to theirs: now I see how irrelevant it all was, because I was never like them. I was locked into my own path, set out for me by my genes, my environment, and my parents. I have always been faced with two choices:

celebrity status or annihilation, and my body has picked the most convenient option. Gone, forgotten, extraneous, but in so being and in so becoming, I am emancipated.

Now I'm ready. I'm ready to see them now. I'm ready to see them break through the television screen and appear at my doorstep. Perhaps they will be denied entry by whoever is gatekeeping—the nurses and my sister. My sister hated them, the girls I started the band with. My bandmates. Or should I say, the members of my band. It was my band: I started it. I can say that now, without reservations, because of my newly emancipated status. I owe allegiance to none of them. I named the band; I paid for most of the sound system and got my father to take us to the gigs in his pickup truck. I did all the heavy lifting. The drudgework nobody else wanted to do: for this I was treated like dirt, an interloper, an outsider, and a fame whore, because I was serious. I was serious about the band, because I thought we had something. I thought we could be famous.

California Youth Authority. I came up with it, because the best name was taken already. They wanted names like "Juvie Hall" or "Juvenile Delinquents," but nobody was calling the prison for adolescents "Juvie" by that time or even "Juvenile Hall." The California Youth Authority is where you went when you were real trouble. All the other names out there were weak iterations of the real thing, like The Runaways and The Minors. People thought The Runaways was a better name because they had looks, talent, and a label. But California Youth Authority, or CYA, would be the cleverest name. I promised the girls in the band that when I unveiled it to them. CYA would be shocking. You couldn't look away from it. We were the CYA: outsiders, castaways, rejects from school and any other setting we had been inserted into—music classes, gymnastics, glass blowing, and ceramics for gifted children at the community college. We'd been through them all, suspended from some, and dropped out of others due to boredom. Bound for the California Youth Authority prisons scattered throughout the state, obviously, since we couldn't make a go of any other extracurriculars.

Me, Nicky, Jack, and Bev (Beverly)—the drummer. I stood out, because I was the only one with a name sheared of its diminutive. I stood out because I was stunted, as tall as a first grader. I was BR, my initials, because I wasn't going to be owned by my stupid birth name. We became a band when we started writing our names in the bathrooms at school, the bathrooms at the Baskin-Robbins, the bathrooms at the Santa Monica Pier—disgusting, but necessary. That's where the action was, or what we called the action back then: cigarettes, Quaaludes, boys-on-girls, and girls-on-girls. I'd kissed boys in elementary school and felt nothing. We met an aspiring surfer named Frankie Stevens on the pier, a little guy. Just my size: runty and short boned, as though his growth was impeded, like mine. His hands were fat and tiny, like mittens. He wanted to surf but couldn't handle the size and weight of the board. He had a black eye from trying. He was playing pinball in the arcade next to the carousel; Jack and Nicky found him. They brought him to me while I was playing air hockey. I was the king of air hockey at the pier; I could see the disks coming at me before the players hit them. I was good at anticipation, people said. Following through. Guarding my goal. I knew when I could abandon it to really sink one on the opposing player. In the slot, down the pocket, back out the bottom, and back to me again. I was a champion.

This dwarf, they said. We found him for you. I'm busy, I said. But I felt sorry for Frankie Stevens. The bottoms of his feet were black like raw asphalt. He had that black eye and gunk in his fingernails, probably from sleeping on the beach, or wherever he slept. His clothes smelled like smoke. I fronted him a few games and then he said he needed to get into the girl's room, you could buy soap and toothpaste along with the feminine hygiene products, so I took him in there with me. Then he pushed me inside a stall and grabbed my arms, forcing me to sit in his lap.

I laughed, because it felt too stupid to scream. Who was going to hear me in the first place, and what would they do when they saw us? They'd think we were a couple of kids, making out. I thought I could push him off the toilet but he had a blistering grip on my wrists. Whenever I tried to move my arms, he pulled so hard I thought he was going to break them, break me. His mouth went looking for mine—he was trying to kiss me—but I wouldn't let him, especially when he said Jack and Nicky told him I wanted it and I needed it. I was feeling as though I was back in the brace when I was a kid, the brace that was supposed to straighten out my pigeon-toes, something I didn't remember myself except for people telling me about it. This was how it must have been, trapped and struggling in my crib, but it was for my own good. I couldn't describe what was happening because I was too young and inarticulate to comprehend the how and why of this treatment, or to get out of it. Frankie Stevens pushed my head down into his crotch and though I couldn't see his dick I could see the whole scene from above, and I knew I'd have to wait for someone, anyone, to interpret this experience for me to get a handle on it.

Frankie Stevens smelled like cleanser—ammonia—when it turns rancid. He said, "Be quiet," and was pressing on my neck. I couldn't tell if he was raping me or giving me a swirly. He let go of one arm, probably so he could jack himself, and I pulled myself up to get off of him. He forced his tongue down my mouth, and I wanted to gag. Then he got up so fast, I fell in the stall. When he opened the door, it smacked me in the face square, gifting me with a dent in my forehead that is still there, that is here now, that is such the notable feature of my visage that it would probably be included in police reports, should one ever needed to be filed relating to my person. I will die with this ridge dividing my forehead, as if a legend to where the left brain and right brain begin and end. On this ridge the crap this city coughs up, soot and clay, sand and soils, mixed with the requisite filth on my skin, and I became an acne case after that night. For the rest of my life, to be accurate, even this life I am allegedly now still living.

I felt smeared, gritty, and swollen. I felt inflated—the palms of my hands, my kneecaps, and my feet—as though I had no more sense of myself or my skeleton. Whatever foundation or scaffolding I had was submerged under my puffed-out tissues. My face swelled up on the left from getting hit by the stall door. By the time I got back to school, my cheek had ballooned into my eye, which was threatening to turn red from an infection. Around my jaw the skin was turning green, as though that part of my face had gone stagnant. I looked like a victim. Or maybe I looked like I had radiation poisoning. For weeks afterward, Jack and Nicky kept asking me if I was pregnant, if I was going to give birth to a homunculus. That's how they're made—a dwarf and a pixie getting it on. Somehow Jack and Nicky knew about such things. I didn't.

We didn't have allies, pronouns, or a flag. We didn't have clubs or support systems, or rights and privileges thereto pertaining, or a parade to celebrate ourselves. All we had were stereotypes: the lesbian as hideous, lesbian until graduation, and lesbian because no man would have her; we had bull dykes and butches, but there was no variety beyond that. No soft or stone butches. And no afternoon talk shows, and no celesbians. We had rumors. Maybe Agnes Moorehead on *Bewitched* was a lesbian. Maybe she wasn't. That meant no role models, no spokeswomen, none of the infrastructure straight people find so charming and now go out of their way to mention they watch, or donate money to, or otherwise associate themselves with. What we had was Jack and Nicky's lesbian test, starring Frankie Stevens. If you haven't figured out how it went, I passed. Barely.

Jack and Nicky looked like lesbians. Nicky wore a chain on her belt loop. It was connected to a watch in her pocket. My father said Jack was a real beauty, but I thought she was kind of freakish. Her mother was a model and Jack was also tall, but she grew too fast, so that her face always looked like it was trying to fill in the vast space of her head. But no one saw that but me. She had a wardrobe of her father's and brother's clothes: her father's vests, her brother's aviator's jacket with the military stripes safety-pinned on. It was very punk, and we all coveted her look. But I just couldn't get it. My father gave me his T-shirts to wear, and I looked like I was drowning in them. I had to borrow my friends' blue jeans. My mother was still buying me Wranglers from Sears, but there was no way I was going to wear them. I wasn't in elementary school anymore, though I wasn't a woman or becoming one. I was somewhere out there, attracted to Jack and Nicky, their command and confidence.

Ten percent of the population is gay. This I learned in college. I don't remember how this came up; if it was something I plucked out of the ether or if I was told directly by another lesbian admonishing me for my lack of lesbian-signifiers in my manner or dress. Or perhaps I got this from some problem I was working on. Maybe I was in graduate school by then. Of course, lesbians have a higher risk for breast cancer than the rest of the population. But why? Is it genetic, somatic, a common factor in their environments, the result of stress, discrimination, low self-esteem, the miasma of doubt and pity that follows each lesbian as she makes her way through her family, her education, her careers, even her lovers? Breast cancer is what happens when your life is terminally unsatisfying. The current explanation is that lesbians do not seek medical care in the same numbers as other women. They are more apt to ignore the signs of any cancer. If and when they arrive at the gates of the medical establishment, their fear and trepidation have made all of the necessary decisions for them. By the time I went to the doctor with the lump I had found, two more lumps had commenced construction beside the original tumor in a manner that prevented me from readily identifying them.

But it's the fact that matters or, in my case, the facts: three tumors, three facts, and not the conditions that produced the facts. This is what I hope to illustrate for you. When I was in junior high and high school, people said we were "experimenting," though what were we trying to prove? Plus, we lacked this new "value-free" vocabulary that's meant to be supportive, encourage natural tendencies, whatever they might be, in children nowadays. My tendency was not against boys, per se. Girls were more interesting. Boys were slugs. They collected records and bragged about collecting records, and they gave speeches about the records they collected. But they weren't joining bands or making records. They weren't even trying to. So I picked women.

I kissed Jack and Nicky and a few others, and I did feel less vacant, less of a dead thud against my face and lips than I had with Frankie Stevens, but probably because I loved those girls—Jack and Nicky. I worshipped them. They were real musicians, with lessons, practices, and recitals. They read music and counted off in their heads, while I was self-taught and could barely keep up. They said that was the point of punk, DIY, but I felt left out as they played their instruments as if they were born to them—the bass guitar and the piano. I was always dragging on the bottom, or I was too studied. They were also born to Hollywood. Their parents, aunts and uncles, grown cousins and their spouses, their neighbors, friends of the family, godparents, and babysitters were all in on it. Hollywood, that is. They had all kinds of connections. Jack's father was "in television," though what he did in television was never clear. I made idols of these people—extras and advance men, editors and personal assistants—all remote and unapproachable, and if I did approach them, I thought I might be blinded by their authority and experience, because they had once touched someone, spoken to someone, or witnessed a bit of history that was Hollywood legend. More likely it was some apocryphal B.S., but they knew I wouldn't know the difference.

I would have done anything for them, Jack and Nicky, and I did whatever they asked. The things I did for them made me hate those girls. But I loved them. I loved and hated them. I loved them and broke up with them. I asked to come back and they asked for me back. I loved them as if they were addictive, illicit, rare, and far above my rank and standing on the playground. I loved them like diet pills and cigarettes, imported vinyl, and swigs of Southern Comfort or Jack Daniels. I sacrificed my tongue to Southern Comfort, sweet to the point of truculence. I scorched my tonsils on Jack Daniels. But I didn't throw up. I could hold my liquor; I could keep it in my stomach. Its effects galloped everywhere, from my arms and fingertips to my crotch, where it was magnetic. The liquor fell through me as if it were iron filings and hit critical mass between my legs. With Jack's laugh and Nicky's arms around my shoulders everything took to those membranes like a riot of attention and kinetics. I was what they used to call "sailing."

We drank out of sight of the liquor store where we got someone to buy us the stuff. Sometimes we'd stand in line at the Whisky on Sunset Boulevard as if we had tickets, but we didn't. We couldn't stand in line at the Roxy because that was the new club back then. A-listers of rock 'n' roll were patronizing the establishment. You couldn't see them—Alice Cooper, John Lennon, a guy from The Monkees—because they had some kind of VIP entrance. At the Whisky everybody had to go through the front. The Whisky was for the raw and the grotesque; the audience stoked on drugs and alcohol, descending into anarchy because the sound wasn't right or the show wasn't long enough. How it looked on the inside and what went on there, we didn't know, because we could never get inside. We had only the descriptions that emerged through photographs, articles in the newspaper, and what our parents told us when they begged us to stay away from it. But the Whisky was punk. We couldn't get close enough. We stood in line and hoped someone would notice us. Give us backstage passes, get us on the permanent guest list. There was no permanent guest list at the Whisky, but we didn't know that. We did come to recognize the people who worked there. They were older, bordering on ancient for us, their hair wild with starch and dye, sometimes screaming with shocking colors, sometimes a naturalistic black, applied so uniformly it could not have been nature that made it so dull and perfect. The hair dye was one way we knew they were older. The other was the tattoos. They wore leather or second-hand suits, the pant legs shining like mirrors on the thighs. They were obviously failures at stardom. They looked at us and maybe they sighed; then they told us to get lost.

We were failures too, at looks and influence. Or I was the failure. That's how it worked out eventually. But that is another story that I believe would kill me to fully acknowledge, a story that would change my breathing, my body temperature, and what is left of my pulse and heart rate. Such a change in my condition would require additional dosages of morphine, possibly force the hospice to notify the DEA. I could tell that story, or all the stories, of all the times I kept Jack, Nicky, and Bev from getting into the Whisky because the bouncer didn't like the way I looked—the blithe openness of my expression. I could tell the stories about how I kept Jack and Nicky from making it, from getting their own contract or their own agent, but I won't because I'm not supposed to upset myself. I'm supposed to not be upset—according to my sister and the nurses, the guests, and the news on the television—by thoughts or the fact of Jasmine. I am trying to maintain.

In the beginning, when we didn't get in, we could blame it on having no money, no fake IDs, no names that mattered in the industry. No juice, Jack liked to say. Though she was supposed to be the juice at first, wasn't she, with all her connections through the realm of television? The harsh ugly truth of it, the bottom line, the thing for which we had no excuse was that we were a bunch of 14-year-olds who had no idea what we were doing, and we looked like it too. Our faces had that soft resilience and possibility of youth. We could not disguise it. We tried makeup, but it would not adhere to our lips and eyelids. We drank and smoked but the coughing and hangover melted off our skin and muscles. If we could affect pain or toughness for a moment, it refused to remain permanent. We were either too impressionable or unprepared for how much life would throw at us. Or at least my face was that way and stayed that way. Jack and Nicky learned how to do surly and petulant in high school, but I just couldn't. I could never fake it to anyone's satisfaction. I was always so much myself, wide-eyed and open to harassment.

Jack might have looked older because of that stretch-intraction expression glued to her face, owning to her gruesome dimensions: 5'8", nine, ten—she couldn't stop growing. Nicky might have passed for 18 in her junior year, with that glass coldness in her eyes, a kind of "come hither" look she was born to, though she was not interested in men. I would never reach 5 measly feet; so in junior and senior high school I wasn't passing for anything post-elementary school age. I was a terminal brat, the arrested baby sister, blatantly juvenile, tagalong nightmare, and a weight around Jack's jaw and Nicky's ankles. Because of me we had to retreat to the alley between Larrabee and San Vicente, where it was relatively dark, in Sunset Strip terms, because of the apartments on the other side as their inhabitants desperately tried to maintain their privacy. When my father found out we were spending our nights there, he laughed, and then said it figured: some guy famous for being a criminal once had a store on that block. It was as good a training ground for delinquents as any other. I didn't know what he was talking about; we weren't delinquents. We were playing hide-and-seek and freeze tag in the alley because every other place demanded money; it was like they charged rent for the space between your feet, for walking through the aisles, for their look-don't-touch. We played games—any game with an It because I was always It and had to earn my way out of it—and sometimes we'd pretend to play "chicken" with a car that occasionally came through, but the alley was mostly our office, where we channeled our despair and embarrassment into songs or song lyrics. We thought someday there'd be a marker, alerting tourists to the birthplace of CYA's "Teacher's Got a Rap Sheet" or "Mom's Habit."

The office was where I wrote the words for the title track for our long-awaited record, "Jail Break:" "CYA! CYA! /How'd you like to check in today?/It stands for Cover Your Ass/ You'd better work fast/'Cause I'm running away/From the CYA! CYA!" We wrote the music at school during recess and lunch. We wrote at school until we found Bev, our drummer, because Bev's parents let us play in their house and didn't bug us. But before Bev it was as if the music didn't matter as much as the words did: words to be screamed, shouted, shoved down the head of the microphone, jammed past its diaphragm. "Statutory rape! Statutory rape!/Whatever happened/To your mystery date?/Screw that bitch!/She's jailbait! /If you don't haul ass/You'll be too late/Statutory rape! Statutory rape!" Then we started hanging out at Bev's because her parents didn't care about their neighbors and the noise, and we had to rehearse the words with the music.

Bev loved my songs. Jack and Nicky said they were simple, but punk was about being simple; so they let me have my way.

Jack couldn't stand Bev, saying she was a sellout. Bev was too mellow, smoking all that dope with her parents. Punk was not about mellow. It was about protest, channeling rage. Bev had no rage, Jack said, and Bev begged for things, like clothes and additions to her drum kit and joints. We saw this happen. Bev was shameless. Bev was also straight and wouldn't drink with us, but she loved my songs. She played everything the same. Hi-hat on the eighth note, the snare on the 2nd and 4th, the bass drum on the first and 3rd. For different songs I'd speed it up or slow it down. The angry songs we did the fastest: "Lesbian Turmoil" and "Mom's Habit." Jack said we couldn't play rage with so much consistency. We needed to be erratic and unpredictable. She wanted Bev to hit the bass drum on the 16th note, but Bev couldn't deliver. Bev quit the band eventually.

We all quit the band at one time or another. We were all kicked out at least once. I got kicked out the most, because I complained. Everything would be fine until some outsiders got involved: people we met on the Strip, who came to hang out with us at the office, people who said they knew people who knew people who knew even more people still. Photographers and A&R people from nonexistent labels, men who said they owned studios and would help us get a demo tape, until the time came to actually make it. There was a chain of people from the Strip down to the Santa Monica Pier, our former headquarters, and they were lined up along the bus routes, waiting for us in the gas stations, coffee shops, and movie theaters to give us some tips, snag us backstage passes, or introduce us to someone who mattered or someone who knew someone who used to matter and might one day matter again.

Bev quit the band because she got a boyfriend, I thought. She said it wasn't worth sacrificing her relationship to come to the office, to rehearse and write songs, because we couldn't get any dates. We were just three unclaimed lesbians, she said. She would have rather been making out in a car up on Mulholland or in a movie theater than spend another minute trying to hit that 16th note, especially when I couldn't keep up on the guitar with Jack's bass or Nicky's singing. Bev made her decision, Jack said. There was no going back on it. She was out of the band and out of our lives. When we graduated from junior high, Jack, Nicky and I went to the same high school, and Bev went to the rival school. Then she was definitely, permanently out. She was out because she lived in a different high school district. She was out because she went to high school; she should have dropped out. She was out because she wasn't a lesbian and because Jack and Nicky wanted her gone, exiled, and banished from their existence. It wasn't entirely about music. She just wasn't good enough.

This is how I met Jasmine. Because Jasmine was someone who was supposed to make things happen. Not like the junk Homo sapiens we met on the Strip. Not like the losers we found at the bus stops, or the wasters who started tagging after us whenever we tried to get into some club and failed. One of them, a photographer, wanted to do a layout with us. We call this "grooming" now, this arrangement of girls in towels, girls in showers, girls naked under blankets or raincoats and posed like paper figures, but this photographer said she'd take our pictures and then she'd show them to people at Capitol, or people at Slash, or people she probably never knew and never had a hope of knowing. But Jack liked her, this Santorini—she called herself by her last name and called me, Jack, and Nicky by our last names. This was her greatest feminist statement, next to her leather, acne, and terminally greasy hair. She was a feminist, she told us, and wouldn't sell us out as objects. Sometimes she got us into clubs—not the Whisky, but clubs downtown, clubs on Hollywood Boulevard, clubs that weren't quite at the center of the action, but they were clubs, and clubs had music, bands, and sometimes liquor that could be sneaked over to us, and sometimes the clubs had nothing and no one who wanted to meet us.

But Jack liked Santorini. Jack said Santorini was down-to-earth and a very together woman. Santorini had taken pictures of Blondie, the Ramones, and the whole New York scene and had shown Jack the negatives. That's how Jack knew the pictures were Santorini's, though how Santorini could have gotten to New York and back was mystifying. Whenever we asked if she could take us off the Strip and take us to her place, she didn't seem to live anywhere. Jack looked at those negatives on a light board in a closet-like photography shop where Santorini supposedly took her film. Jack described how she had to bend over, her butt sticking out in the plank-covered walkway from the shop's entrance to its darkroom. Each time she heard a step on the planks she had to right herself so someone could get by. I wondered who was being naïve then but said nothing. There was a mattress in the dark room, Jack said. Perfectly normal for a fellow struggling artist-photographer, she said.

And Santorini liked Nicky. She wanted to photograph Nicky and didn't want us in the picture. She wanted Nicky to model for her, and she'd get her an agent. Lots of rockers have a modeling portfolio, something always ready for commercial directors, Santorini said. It wasn't selling out. It was being prepared, like in the Girl Scouts. Santorini was going to photograph Nicky and maybe Jack for a few shots, and I said fine. I was quitting! We were a band. A band was a pact. A contract. A family, but one of our own choosing. No more liars and broken promises. Declaring ourselves a band was our first act of rebellion and of asserting our independence. From our families, from our other friends, and from the adults who would prey on us, just like this Santorini was doing. She was dividing and then she'd conquer. If I wasn't going to be included, what was the point of having a band or of being in one? We were in a band because we had statements to make about our lives, about honesty, and real friendship. Real friends don't hold each other back, Jack and Nicky said, so fine, go ahead and quit. They didn't need me. I could be replaced, easily. My guitar playing sucked and my songs were clichéd rip-offs of better material. So yeah, fine, and don't come back.

Then I met Jasmine at school in the Mentally Gifted Minor program. So Jack and Nicky asked me to come back. We didn't have a drummer anymore, with Bev being at the rival high school. But I could still introduce Jack and Nicky to Jasmine, couldn't I? It was all I could do, chasing after Jack and Nicky, trying to keep them out of the hair of all the frauds and poseurs we were running into on the Strip. Grift was the Strip's primary employer, somewhere beyond the music business. Everyone worked for somebody, and everybody was working on a deal. Commercial artists wanted to draw our album covers, provided they could sketch Nicky solo. Sound and light people invited Jack to their tech rehearsals because only she understood the lingo. One woman in a sailor-like cap, except it was leather, said she was a scout and took us to a party on Harratt Street behind the Playboy building. She was always looking for talent and she blew cigarette smoke in my face when she said, every year the talent got younger. The talent in those days was all kids. Management was all adults, though they had to have been kids at some point, probably during the last youth movement or the one prior to that, whatever it was. There was this one talent scout who wanted to make Jack and Nicky into a duo, and I was kicked out again. The band didn't matter. My father said, what did I expect? Nicky's father was Italian, and her mother was Japanese: she was a mixed-race beauty. It's hard to compete with that, he said. My father had to know everyone's pedigree as though we were all dogs being put out to show. He said Nicky had the look of a mermaid on her face, as though she had been washed ashore in Santa Monica from Shangri-La.

But I knew Jasmine. A grifter our own age, though I didn't know she was a grifter at the time. Or I might have known and purposefully ignored it. Jasmine never came to class in our special gifted program. Since we were so far ahead in intelligence, we didn't have to come to class. Or sit at desks, do homework, call the teachers "mister" or "missus," or collect report cards for our parents to sign. We were empowered to make our own decisions about our education, unless we screwed up. Then the adults would take over and we'd be back where we started, with teachers and administrators acting as proxies for our parents. But I was in class every day, and I did my homework promptly with a double-check and triple-check when it was necessary, because I was not going to give my father any daylight. By this time, I knew how he worked, boring down on weaknesses and guilty moments. He had said the only way he'd allow me to enroll in the program was if I didn't take advantage of its primary selling points. I had to resist temptation and delay indulgence. So I deferred. I postponed. I waited for my moment. It had to come, considering how many other moments I was giving up.

Jack and Nicky were going out every night, including Sundays. Without me they were getting in everywhere, at Madame Wong's, the Rock Corporation, even the Whisky. They saw the Buzzcocks and The Motels. They said they talked to Martha Davis. They spent the night at the squat where The Go-Go's lived, when Belinda Carlisle was between her cheerleading phases and her hair was as spikey as a toilet brush. Jack and Nicky talked business with real musicians while I clawed my way up into the top 12.5 percent of the California student body, so I could get into my father's college. The one and only university in existence as far as my father was concerned. I didn't then, and still don't, see what was so shock-and-awe inspiring about the place. He had gone there, after all, and he could barely keep it together: our house, his job, taking care of our mother, and raising my sister and me. But the university is an idea, he used to say, as if it were the last, pure idea untouched by the expediencies of the 20th century. The university did not care about my purpose at age 16 or 18 but would allow me to discover it naturally. The university was unconcerned with all the spurious trivialities I tortured myself over. People would treat me with respect and reverence, he said, once I exhibited my intelligence. I'd find my own kind there: the brainy, the boring, the socially inept, and the isolated. He didn't say that exactly, but I could tell it was what he meant.

To get into that college I had to do the work everyone else thought was lame, stupid, and conforming to what the Man wanted, whoever the Man was: my father, the principal, or the president. I wasn't the only college-bound student in the school, and there were some, a handful, who got into the Ivy

League or something similarly exotic for us public school kids to aspire to. But the great lot of minds in the gifted program were agnostics when it came to school. They thought we were being fed a dead end: science, math, and history were meant to distract us from our real futures as musicians and artists. Whatever class work I was doing wouldn't prepare me for the street and the real world, discovering my true self and my passions. I was dragging myself down with mindless repetition, corporate brainwashing, and the drills the establishment had cooked up to keep children gainfully occupied and out of the workplace. I was giving in, surrendering, and rolling over like an old dumb dog that couldn't learn resistance.

But I had something that Jack and Nicky didn't have, because they weren't in the program. They didn't meet the qualifications. They had to attend the traditional high school in the permanent buildings. I was in the bungalows, and that meant access—to Jasmine. It meant proximity. I was in and they were out. They could do nothing but watch me march off to the bungalows and gain admittance. Much like my sister would see me go off, and there was no way she could join me, because all her brains were in her feet, my father said, which meant there wasn't much room for brains in her at all.

Jack and Nicky were unmoored and disoriented that I was on the inside. More than two can play at this game: who's got the keys to the castle and who's the most celebrity adjacent. It's just like musical chairs, this game—not for me this time, but for them, the gorgeous pair. They had to walk, or maintain an awkward, butt-first posture so they were always ready when the music stopped—and Jasmine might show up. They always had to keep in mind where their chairs were, or the right places to eat lunch. They had to keep an eye on where they had been, so they knew how to get out. They couldn't forget who was in charge and what I was capable of; they had to stay wise to the people around me, the other gifted kids, and be prepared for their arbitrary boredom—their potential for social violence.

I had classes with Jasmine; so now I controlled the real estate. I was the master of geography. I guarded the passage to Jasmine. Now I was the drug—a narcotic. I was the object of stupefying worry and yearning. Now they couldn't afford to offend me with their demands and what they thought were pranks. In the office I was the one who could send either one of those girls to get gum and cigarettes without any money and demand they come back with merchandise. They could come back from shoplifting to find me gone. Because I'd gotten a better offer, a ticket to some concert for which there was only one ticket left. I could have been a free agent, gone off with the highest bidder. Or I could have Jasmine all to myself. Instead of their brat, baby sister, a mass of undifferentiated need and want, I could become Jasmine's burden, no matter what it did to Jasmine's gait or how uncomfortable it made Jack and Nicky.

But I am not that kind of person. And I was going to prove it. I would show everyone. For one thing, I was not nearly as selfish as Jack and Nicky. If I had some kind of opportunity, I did not hoard it. I shared it with my bandmates. Because that's what being in a band is all about. When I got paired up with Jasmine on an algebra/geometry assignment, I didn't say anything about myself. I asked her if she knew Jack or Nicky. I emphasized their Hollywood connections and their prodigious musical talent. I told Jasmine she had to meet these girls. They were the real thing when it came to punk, DIY feminist politics. Jasmine should come over to my place and see them. They were in my band, though we didn't really have a leader.

We weren't into labels or positions; we were real punk, not some kind of vehicle for me, though I wrote a lot of the songs. We wrote songs only about what we cared about—inequality, abuse, identity, and what's wrong in the world that doesn't give teenagers a choice in anything. Jasmine listened. She smiled. She murmured affirmations, like "yes," "yeah, I know," "cool," or "bitchin'," but she barely said anything at all. We didn't have school bells ringing all day like a regular high school, but the teacher might start announcing the next homework assignment or say, "that's it," and Jasmine was up and out of that room as quickly as any victim of Pavlovian conditioning. I could not find an angle to make her stay.

Jack and Nicky wanted Jasmine to come to a rehearsal and hear us play. Her parents were musicians, they said. I knew that. Who didn't? Who didn't know that her mother was a percussionist, one of the only women on the studio scene in Los Angeles? Who didn't know that her father sang backing vocals and was a guitarist for the Beach Boys with Glen Campbell, that he played for Stevie Wonder, and that he wrote songs with the Eagles? Everyone knew, of course, or everyone who knew Jasmine knew, because of how Jasmine was, with her clothes, her hair, and the girls she selected to hang out with her—the girls who were named deliberately, so their name meant something. Not like me, Jack, or Nicky, but girls named Carole with the all-telling "e," for the actress Carole Lombard; girls named after characters in books and poems, or girls named after animals (deer, lynx, and leopards). As long as they were girls whose names came with an explanation, that said something about how they were being raised to be iconoclasts by their most unusual parents, then and only then could they be in Jasmine's inner circle. Jasmine was named for the night-blooming trees that grew in the hills and that her father planted for her mother as a wedding present.

We knew that Jasmine's parents were musicians because of the concerts she went to and the T-shirts she wore to school the next day. We knew Jasmine's parents were breathlessly adjacent to fame, because of all of Jasmine's uncles and aunts, godmothers and godfathers, and the presents they gave her—albums and sentimentally significant rings and necklaces. Jasmine wore a gold chain with a star at its center against her throat; Holly Near had given it to her or maybe Laura Nyro or maybe someone else, Maria Muldaur. It was impossible to keep up. Jasmine did not walk or run but glided on campus, propelled along by the girls who followed her—Bambi, Guinevere, Althea, Montserrat—with their paisley scarves and velvet hats. If Jasmine and her entourage were coming to one of our rehearsals, I knew we had to be ready. So I waited until my parents were out of town and began making arrangements.

I couldn't get rid of my sister, but she was rarely home. She was in charge but too busy dancing to care what I was doing. I was taking apart my parents' bedroom. I separated the mattress from the box spring and put both against the street-facing walls for insulation. The pillows, I put in the picture windows and held them in place by closing the wooden shutters on them. The oriental rugs in our living and dining rooms I used to float our instruments and amplifiers. I cleared the chest of drawers, moved it into my room and kept the door shut on that crime scene—that's what my father called my room when he wasn't calling it anarchy. The chairs from the dining room I put in semi-circular rows. We had only eight dining chairs, so it was a most exclusive venue I had put together for Jasmine, and then I invited her over.

Jack and Nicky would be there, of course, and our new drummer, an older girl, maybe she was twenty; she called herself Howard. Jack and Nicky had found her somewhere—the classifieds, through Santorini, maybe through Bev—I didn't care. Jasmine was coming over. I expected her to say no, so I asked in a rush, telling her my parents were out of town on the other side of the world in Israel, or maybe by that time Europe. She could bring her people; we'd make it into a party. I gasped when she said yes. Jack and Nicky couldn't quite believe it, until they convinced themselves this was not something I would lie about.

Jasmine was coming to hear us play and Jack and Nicky were convinced she'd get us into a real studio; so we could make a demo. Jasmine could get the demo to her contacts, through her parents, and then we'd get some gigs. Not out in the Valley or at The Masque where everybody could play, but at a real club, maybe as an opening act. Maybe Jasmine could get the demo to some programmers she had to have known, through her parents (maybe Rodney on the Rock) and make the demo our first hit single. Jack and Nicky also wanted to be famous, though they probably wouldn't have admitted it. They wanted to be famous, but they just wore it better, making it less obvious, though it was right there on their mouths. They figured out how to put on lipstick the right way, so that it didn't smear off and didn't make them look like clowns or drunks. And they knew how to use makeup so that it was not merely painted on. It complied with their vision of themselves. Not like when we were junior high punks and the lipstick we tried went from our lips to the corners of our mouths like we were kids with grape juice moustaches. Purple lipstick: Jack and Nicky knowingly called it "smashed fig." There was a private significance to figs for Jack and Nicky, but they wouldn't tell me what it was. I had to find out for myself.

Jasmine came to see us in this same bedroom. The room I'm dying in now. I have lived my entire life in this room. Conception, stardom, and death. These things should not all occur in the same room. There should be more than a beginning, middle, and end to a life. There should be padding, space, breathing room, a chance to forget the embarrassing parts, and embellish the better ones. You need to create a life out of a life, but I didn't do that. I have only this time, this event, this room where Jasmine showed up with her entourage—she traveled with a group of girls who were always with her, their faces hidden underneath big hats and long scarves so I never really knew who they were—and the people poured out of the bedroom into the hall, out of the sliding glass door and onto the patio, and we held our rehearsal. It wasn't even a real gig. We played what we thought would be our hits, "Jail Break," "Teacher's Got a Rap Sheet," and a new one, "I Hate Homework." "So you're going to college/But I piss on your Golden Book of Knowledge/Shove it down your throat/Everything you know is rote." I howled out the words on that one, because I had the most credibility on this subject.

Jasmine said we had a sound and that she was glad she'd come to see us. We tried to get her to say more—to get her to make a promise. Take us to your connections, show us your inside track, and give us a chance; please, please, please, we're desperate. I was desperate. When you're dying, you can't be desperate. You might inadvertently speed up the process, miss that birthday or anniversary you're holding on for, one last milestone, one more achievement—one more chance to say that you exerted your will, this time over your dying biological systems, and you succeeded. So I am not desperate now. I am too drugged, too slow and buffeted, to exert anything or avoid what is coming. But when Jasmine was here, in this bedroom, we were four high school girls who had always gotten what we needed but not what we wanted. What we wanted most of all was an improbable, near-magical, potentially diabolical chance at being big—bigger than our parents, our teachers, and the high school seniors, bigger than anyone who had ever been bigger than us. We wanted revenge for being small, invisible, and irrelevant. And we wanted, we needed, we demanded that Jasmine give it to us.

Things started to happen pretty fast after that. We hadn't broken through, but we had a place in line. We had a number in the queue. We did not know what the number was, but we were heroes when we got back to school after that weekend. Somehow, we had been promoted, elevated, or touched by the hand of the powers that were. I felt as though I had penetrated the nucleus of how everything is run. I was observing the mechanics of the universe. I observed the orbit of Jasmine widening to grant me admittance before it closed up again.

Jack and Nicky tried to play it cool, as though it was all inevitable. Deserved even. Someone other than Santorini wanted photos, to build us a portfolio. I was breathless. Much the same way I am now, though the sensation is far less pleasant now than it was that week. Then I was deliberately running out the clock. Until I could get to school in the mornings. Until I could get out of school in the afternoons. Until I could get to Jack's or Nicky's. Until I could finally get to Jasmine's to meet her parents, see their studio, and find out how we would sound when we played in it. Until I could distract Jasmine away from the crowds that seemed to choke her and have her talk to me about my songs and my musicianship. I was going to have to use more of the minor chords if I wanted to write a real hit, something with a hook that would slither into people's ears and then reach down to their throats. You want to compel your melody and words onto their tongues and lips. I was also in need of a look, a stage persona, and switch it on and off when I needed if I was going to be able to live through this. I was going to have to quit being such a baby about school and homework because I had to undergo an entirely new course of study. I had to learn how to really listen to music—hear how it was made and hear the contact between mouth, hands, and feet on the instruments—the banter of fingers on the keyboard, the guitar pick bright and steady as it thrashes against the guitar strings, the drumstick balanced among the fingers as it summons the cymbals, or the foot pommeling the pedal on the drums. I had to be able to use all my senses, and my commitment had to be total: I had to choose between myself and my parents, music or college, what I wanted and what people wanted for me, the friends I have now, or the friends I might get.

Jasmine walked through the front door of this house and changed my life for a couple of months. Maybe for several months. For the space of a school year, which is nine months. But a little less than that if I'm going to be accurate, because it was all over by the time I graduated from high school. Done. Finished. Everything was irreparably completed. The band's run, the band itself, my relationship with Jasmine, and my shot at being famous. My life almost changed and then it changed back. My life has been like that shot of my front door—the camera trained on it in case someone walks up to it, out of it, or through it. But cameras are like mouths that feed off shadows, obstructions to the light, or silhouettes that manage to have more than one dimension, and there are no figures, no shadows, or silhouettes darkening my door. No one has ever walked through it as Jasmine did. No one is coming to see me. My life has been a backdrop for my parents' lives and my sister's. I was a yardstick for their parenting skills or the lack of them—their devotion and selflessness, though the needle ran in the other direction for some of the skills. Fill in the blanks; the answer should be obvious. All I did was provide perspective to the people who made it—Jack and Nicky and all the Jacks and Nickys out there, the people who rarely look back because they don't need to look back. They don't need to take stock of where they've been because they're never going back. Jack and Nicky are never going to visit me and neither is Jasmine, and that is almost a relief. Because I do not have to wait, I do not have to take my turn, I do not have to be polite or patient, I do not have to do any of the things you do to hide your desperation, because I am not desperate. I am simply decided. I have been decided for some time.

CHAPTER 10

SOMETIMES, IT SEEMED LIKE A PARTY, with all the people coming in and out. I guess that's what funerals are, or wakes; reunions on unhappy occasions, though in our case, we still had the body alive and in front of us. We talked over Barbara's body, across the big bed, while Barbara slept. Technically, Maria reminded us every so often, Barbara was not sleeping. She could hear everything we were saying. And she could understand all of it, too, like when we laughed or when we had nothing but pity to add to the conversation. Morphine was responsible for part of her silence, and exhaustion and boredom were responsible for the rest.

I told myself I was going to learn about my sister from the visitors. I thought I'd finally be given the missing pieces: the facts that explained how she came to be who she was. I wanted to know why she stopped living after the whole punk and Jasmine escapade. Or anything I didn't already know: hobbies she picked up; acts of kindness she performed; friends she'd made who had nothing to do with all her grievances, the record business, and Jasmine; and friends untainted by the whole kindergarten-through-12th grade experience. Outside of work, Barbara had made a few lasting friendships; we called these people who were high on the notification list. But they were unavailable during the week or inconsolable about

Barb's condition. So we wound up treading over the same old experiences with familiar characters, the same years, places, and guilty parties.

"Are they coming?" Barb would ask every now and then. I knew who she was talking about, those girls from her band. But I would try to act stupid, like I had no idea who they were.

"Why didn't they come?" she'd ask constantly, like whenever she pulled herself out of unconsciousness, and she must have thought the day had ended or was starting again. So her obsessions had to start up again with her.

I said to Barbara, "I don't know why they're not here. Maybe they don't know what's going on."

"What's going on?" Barb said.

"A lot," I said. I was trying to keep things simple. "I already told you."

"If they were coming, you'd tell me?" Barb asked, because she knew no one really liked them. Our parents didn't like them, and the friends Barb made after high school couldn't have liked them, since Barb must have told them all of the trials and humiliation they put her through. Always baiting her, cutting her out. Jacqueline and Nicole: they were a pair if not a couple. Barbara was the third wheel. Jacqueline and Nicole went by their nicknames, Jack and Nicky, because they made them sound tough, maybe butch, or dangerous. Barbara wanted a nickname like theirs too, but she obviously had nothing to work with. Sometimes they called her "Bra Bra" just to be casually cruel.

"If they come, you'll wake me up?" Barb asked.

"Of course," I said, because I had asked people—people from junior high and high school who passed through those days—where I could find them. Everyone remembered them, but no one knew where they were. They'd gone off with Jasmine to become rock stars. They were famous, I think, for a while; I wasn't exactly paying attention. Then they came back, or they stopped being famous, or they went into hiding. Wherever the formerly famous go once they've been brought down by time and more upwardly famous people.

"At least your father isn't here," a friend of Helen's said. Her name was Lillian, and she had gone to college with Helen. She knew Irv when he was still marriage material, fully employed and sober. "Can you imagine, he'd be out there with the reporters, telling them I don't know what for," Lillian said. "Then he'd be back here, hassling the nurses, acting like he was the doctor."

"That's not the Irv I knew," said Alice, another one of Helen's gang. My mother and her friends thought calling themselves a "gang" was edgy, like they spent their days marauding through department stores and tea rooms on Wilshire Boulevard.

"Nevertheless," I said, because I could not tell whether Alice was defending our father or lamenting how far he had fallen. He supposedly had so much promise, though no one could say what that promise was for. "That was the Irv who raised you girls," Lillian said. "I was there. I saw it."

"You know, it's a shame your mother's life has to end like this," Alice went on, and what she meant by that could have been anything—as in Helen's life had been completely contained and packaged in this house, and once Barbara was no longer living in it, all would be lost. Or Alice might have meant that Helen had poured all her life into Barbara, her mind and emotions into the maintenance and sustenance of her younger daughter, and what did Barb do with it? But Alice couldn't have been thinking like that; she must have understood that cancer is neither someone's fault nor secret wish. Or Alice could have meant that I was extraneous, as unnecessary to the story of Helen's life as Irv was. I had always been merely passing through, in and out, and I had no kind of impact. My husband reminded me, before I came to California to be with Barbara, that all this was not about me, and it wasn't. But how could I not feel that way when I was going to be the only one left to live with the damage.

"Let's leave Barbara alone," I said to Alice, "and maybe make it last a little longer." As she obediently shuffled off, Alice promised to visit in the next few days; so she couldn't have understood the turn our conversation had taken, unless she was as dull as Helen indiscreetly said she was. I tried to take some comfort in that.

"I can't believe I'm not going to have my little Barbara anymore," said Leslie, who had grown up around the corner from our house. She had a sister my age, and the four of us were in Brownies and Girl Scouts together until we got to that age when Brownies and Girl Scouts became humiliating. "That's what I used to call her, my little Barbara," Leslie said. "What am I going to do? She was the littlest..." Leslie went on. I was tempted to say Leslie had done well enough without seeing her little Barbara for decades. But I was pacing myself. I was nursing my outrage.

"You think she's still the littlest?" Leslie asked, but I shook my head ambivalently. "You think she remembers how I used to call her that, that I missed her?" Although together we dropped the adult-sanctioned after-school activities, it was Leslie and her sister who made the final break. The high school we were destined to attend was notorious for the usual reasons—violence, lax academics, a prison atmosphere, and an undisciplined approach to learning—and Leslie and her sister transferred to another high school with more cachet than ours, somewhere in the San Fernando Valley or west of Beverly Hills. So long as it was not seedy old Hollywood.

"I'm sorry I didn't come by earlier, I've got so much going on," Leslie said. "So much work, so many properties…." I wondered whether it was hellish to be so weighed down with tangible success, but it must come with some intangibles I could not dare to imagine, like stress. "Is there anything I can do? I know a doctor—"

"Nothing that should have been done a long time ago," I said. I don't think Leslie understood what I meant, because she offered to pay for a masseuse, someone who could perform miracles through foot rubs. I was intrigued but also dubious, not just about miracles but also about Leslie's ability to follow through on her promise. It might take her weeks to deliver and no one was sure how much time Barb had left.

Leslie promised to come back and possibly bring her sister, and then she dissolved in the distance, like so many other kids in the neighborhood. Everyone was seeking higher ground when we were growing up, but technically, we were living in a canyon. I couldn't decide whether it made the social climbing natural or more desperate.

"Your sister was a good friend," a woman named Adele said. Her face and name were familiar, but I couldn't place her. She said she was in junior high school with Barb, that they worked on the yearbook in ninth grade together. While they were laying out the faculty pictures, they changed the name of a teacher from Smith or Richards to "Asshole," because this was the creepy teacher who was always hanging around the girls at recess, at lunch, and after school or in class when he could pull them out of math and English. Asshole was his nickname and he might not have been a teacher; he might have been a counselor or an administrator, and everyone called him Asshole, although I don't remember. He had a harem, a stable, or a fan club—nowadays we'd call it a cult—and all his girls used his nickname with the strictest affection, though I can't consider how much fear there was and wonder at the attentions of an older man. In the meantime, though, changing the man's name to Asshole went unnoticed by the editors. When the yearbooks were delivered, the Asshole was still there beside the other teachers' names. Barb was hysterical, thinking she'd be suspended from school, possibly expelled.

The entire yearbook staff was summoned to the principal's office. Or maybe the principal was summoned to the yearbook classroom. Adele said, as she told the story, that she was losing her grasp on the details, but she was sure about what Barbara said to her and a few other girls. "'You guys have nothing at stake, like I have,' or something like that," Adele said. "She was saying, 'you guys aren't like me. I'm going places. I'm going to college. I can't have this on my record. It'll ruin everything. It doesn't matter what happens to you.'"

"What?" I practically shrieked, because here was a missing piece I thought I wanted. But it didn't fit. It conflicted. Barb would never think of herself as better than someone, anyone, except her big sister, or maybe Irv. We were the equivalent of financial hazardous material sites to her. I was just a plain idiot. Irv was venal, selfish, and potentially narcissistic. These were criticisms that she could explain if she needed to, criticisms that could be proven like her mathematical theorems. But she'd never do this to her friends—the friends she once had; the friends who returned as she was dying. To them she was desperately fair, egalitarian, and this her allies believed was the source of her problems. Jacqueline and Nicole certainly didn't subscribe to this principle; they were stuck up on top of their cruelty. That was the rap against them, the rap Helen and I heard over and over again; sometimes it was the rap against Jasmine. How could someone Barbara had picked—someone she had picked for love—turn out to be so much her opposite, conceited and belittling? Some of what I thought made her so sour over the years was how she must have turned this over in her mind without ever reaching an adequate conclusion.

"You've got to be kidding," I said, thinking back to the yearbook story.

"Nope," Adele said.

"What did you say back to her?" I asked. "I mean, what did you do? Did you do anything? I—"

"We might have laughed, I don't know," Adele said as she shook her head. "That's just who she was. She was under so much pressure."

"To do what?"

"Be on the Honor Roll, magna cum laude, win a Nobel Prize, I don't know," Adele said. "Whatever she was supposed to do."

"That was a lot," I agreed, because wasn't this the crux of everything, when it was decided that Barb had to be able to demonstrate her genius if the world was to continue spinning, and that all my brains were in my feet? Not that I'm complaining; I loved dancing. I thought it was understood that while I was dancing, my career wouldn't last forever and eventually I'd be forced into some kind of conventional scenario: a husband, a child, maybe even college. I wasn't getting off easy, even though Barb told me that I was. Why did she have to be the smart one, the one with aspirations and responsibilities? And why did her aspirations have to be so acceptable? We talked a lot about this, the summer before she started college and started starving herself. The anorexic summer, or ano-rectic, as Helen used to say. She could never bring herself to pronounce the word properly. I thought that was about denial, but I wondered how responsible Helen felt about it all, since as a parent she must have had a say into what her daughters were supposed to do—if she even looked at us in that way.

"Your sister could be so nice, but she also could be a real whack job," Adele concluded. I know I was wrong to take some comfort in that, some confirmation that something was definitely off in Barb; people would so rarely say it. But her statement also carried a kind of sting. Not a direct sting, but something a little far off, maybe scattered the way pain can be under anesthesia. Like with liniment or a numbing agent, camphor or eucalyptus and mint oils. If there were a way for me to avoid pain while I was dancing, I would find it. Tape on my toes, wraps around my knees and ankles. I did not power through injuries or flaws; I inoculated myself against them through any means possible. Usually they were artificial. But the time for that was over, I knew. There was nothing I could do to avoid the inevitable with Barbara, and she was going to have to do all the hard work, again, while I just watched.

CHAPTER 11

ROT BEGINS FROM THE OUTSIDE. In most cases, I will concede. Gangrene, for instance, doesn't occur spontaneously. Neither does jaundice in newborns, since there is some external event—bruising in birth, incompatibility with the mother's blood type—that precludes the official damage. You might say that its beginnings are certainly self-generated when it comes to jaundice in old people and alcoholics. Yet didn't some of them have to imbibe a great deal of irritants to reverse the work of their bloodstream? And for the others, the innocents who find their blood suddenly wanting: couldn't they have lived too long, gone slow motion overboard on too much of the world's blights and venoms? I didn't think I'd ever die this way. I always thought I'd starve or drink myself to death, stimulus or the lack of it from the outside. Others, I recognize, aren't so lucky and blame it on their hardware. I suppose the real answer on rot depends on where you draw the line. I'm drawing it at the skin.

I'm drawing it at the mucous membranes of the eyes, mouth, nose, and ears. The digestive system and genitalia are internal and certainly not the cause for any of my issues, at least none of the issues I'm talking about here. It was what was exposed on me that invited the rot in. In other words, it was not a conscious decision. Rot was ubiquitous. It still is. An artist, for another example, may pick up rot from the audience. This is not a complaint against the free market. This is about human nature and how it can be corrupted. When you are dying, most everything boils down to human nature, particularly the intractable aspects of it. I am the same person I was in high school, everyone tells me. That's been my problem; I demanded too much of people and I still do, even though I should know at this stage that no one is perfect. Certainly I'm not. Look at me, septic and practically disintegrating. But shouldn't people be nicer?

Think about the artist again. Any artist, not necessarily myself, and not Jasmine. An artist, based upon the reaction of her audience, may wish to retrench or expand her repertoire. Or a previously unseen, never before digested artist may arrive and deign to present something altogether different. But the audience insists on the same routine, a kind of reclamation. Not a recycling of familiar elements per se, but the audience clamors for product that is a reflection of itself, a recognition of its own clever tastes and remembrances. If people cannot see themselves in your art, then they will have a hard time seeing your vision. So don't make anything that is too tart or recalls too much of the ancient. You can remind the audience of its age or give them something that will be recalled as the advent of a new era, yet not so far out as the avant-garde or the difficult.

This is where the rot comes in. Success is the result of careful navigation among these thickets—the old, the new, and the repetition that reinvents not just the artist but the audience as it perceives itself. The longevity of any performer depends not on resilience but on how judiciously she attends to manipulating these elements while avoiding the rot inherent in this process. Too much of the same and rot becomes exponential, doubling, tripling, and overwrought with its own awareness. It consumes the performer, though the audience might be happy, even satiated. I know I said this was not about Jasmine, but this is the situation she mastered: the juggling of style, substance, image, and content. By the time of her death, she had poured herself through every cultural trend and every legacy. She was a punk, then a hedonist-bohemian, a woman with big hair and massive lipstick, then a savvy businessperson who knew when to call and when to bluff. She continued to thrive as a mentor, a music business sage, or stateswoman.

Jasmine did not rot. Instead she "grew up," she "matured," or she "aged." She indulged in all the stages in life that I never got around to; she went from rejecting "Jasmine" to embracing it, creating a moment of national reckoning in the process. When we first met, she was "Jasmine" at school, but on stage she was the leader of The Tainted and referred to herself as "The Taint." But as she burrowed through all the musical trends, from punk to pop to jazz, she became known for her covers of standards and orchestrating her own lush arrangements. She was "Jazz I Am" for a while and eventually became Jasmine again in a moment of homecoming, a recognition of who she truly was. She happened to come out that day as well, and her risk-taking and honesty was hailed as a cultural statement, a new day for gay rights and reconciling the gay-straight divide. I was just a lesbian from the beginning; so my sexuality, and everything about it, meant nothing.

Hence the rot: I never "came out." I never sat my mother and sister down at the kitchen table and explained to them myself and my desires. My desires just *were* and always *had been*. There had been no phases or questioning, no softening to sweetness, to bitter and rancid. My sister says everybody's on a spectrum and all that matters is that you find someone, but I was never that enlightened. I am a homosexual, and I like a certain type: patently gorgeous, maternal, and authoritative. I have been this way for so long that I have soured into a poison against myself. I am a study in overgrowth and fecund imaginings. If I had thicker skin, perhaps; if I had not been so open to the world, porous to its trends and afflictions; if my intelligence was not so sponge-like and I had to do more than be exposed to some material in order to master it, inculcate it completely into my being, then perhaps my life would have been different. Because once Jasmine rejected me; once I was informed of what I was, the damnable, controlling, hounding, stubborn, inhuman perfectionist, then nothing ever again happened for me; nothing in love and nothing in music. If I am going to do anything, I have to live the life that I know, what I was able to process. And I just keep reliving it, the life I had for a few weeks, a few months, and I try to figure what went wrong and who, besides myself, I might blame for it.

My sister has seemed to manage to survive a similar collapse: not in love, but in her career. It has to be the case that she survived, because if she hadn't survived, why would she ever come back to this city, which stands in such fierce judgment of its failures. Outcasts and exiles, or the people who couldn't make it, even though they came close: people who were shown a way in. You should come back to Los Angeles only if you've figured a way through—been there, done that, it was beneath me, I've still got my soul. If you can't affect this attitude, then you should never leave, because you will not be permitted back. Because you have to have something to show for your time in the wilderness. Autographs, film clips,

photographs of yourself mingling or interceding with the rich
and fabulous. Or everyone knows that you've failed, because
they always expected you to fail, and in these beliefs, they must
be confirmed. Someone must suffer when the system does not
fulfill expectations. Someone must, or how else will we know
it's working when we have invested so much in it?

My sister is talking to me. How appropriate when we are
discussing rot. The least that can be said of her is that for once
in her life, she has excellent timing. She hasn't said a word to
me in days, it seems, and yet she is suddenly overcome with
urgent matters she must divulge. She is sorry, or she says she
is. She was never a good actress: I looked it up, what the critics
said about her, and they said she was a lousy impersonator of
genuine emotions. She did not know how to listen or wait for
the other dancers' actions. She just danced her steps as though
she were up there alone, and her execution was often small and
rushed. I don't know what all of that meant. I mean, she had
music; she had to dance to it. I don't see how she could have
moved any faster than the music demanded, but there you have
it. Then again, she never seemed to be able to demonstrate any
patience. The cops are coming, she's saying, and she's going to
call people, because she can't wait any longer. She's not supposed to call people without my permission, but the cops are
coming, and she can't stop them once they get here.

My father used to call this a "song and dance"—whenever we got excited about something and couldn't sit still
long enough to explain it to him to his courtly satisfaction.
My sister is alternately moving away from the bed and then
rushing back to it to squeeze me on the arm or run her hand
over my forehead. This is what is coming through the static
of my exhaustion-saturated consciousness. That my sister is

able to move around at all, I want to tell her, is proof that she hasn't rotted away, as I am in the process of doing, but I can't tell her that. Even if I had the wherewithal to speak at this moment, I could not say that—without her recitation of every orthopedic insult her body has withstood in the name of her art (an art that is dying, I'd like to add)—because it's irrelevant. The same stories, told through the same dance steps, the same costumes, the same sets, and none of it addresses what's going on outside in the world. It's a cult that she was in, that she's still in, something entirely self-contained. But the rot got her anyway, didn't it? She always thought she was better than I was because she was selfless, dedicated, and unconcerned with what people thought and stuck with it until time and her body made it impossible. She can barely walk, she likes to say. I'm dying, but she can barely walk. You decide which is the greater tragedy. Let the cops come. What are they going to do, arrest me?

I suppose the cops could arrest me and haul me off to a hospital ward. They could put me on a heart-lung machine, or a ventilator, once my kidneys failed and my liver stopped working. They could bypass the death of my life functions and keep my organs from rotting until they were ready to make a decision—let me go, keep me alive for trial, and then dispose of me with all the other killers, though imagine the confusion that would inspire. Pull the plug or kill me while the plug was still in? Just as long as I don't rot, stink up the gas chamber and the prison. Sometimes I think of Jasmine rotting. She must be coming apart after the stiffness and bloating. Her hair will fall out, her skin will retract, and the structure of her face—what made her so beautiful, desirable, and attractive—will collapse. She will no longer stand out but be, like the rest of us, another petrified skeleton. Soon I will experience everything that she has or will, and there is nothing anyone can do to stop it. Death: the great leveler. It's the timing of death that makes it a source of so much frustration.

I died when Jasmine took off for Chicago to play with The Regent. People said I should have followed her. Jack and Nicky were going. They were no longer part of her entourage like I was. They'd been promoted. They were backing musicians. Song writing partners. Muses, inspirations. But CYA was my band in the beginning. I had started it, kept those girls on a schedule, and gotten us to the point where somebody started to notice, and I wanted more. I wanted to go all the way. But I had to go to college. I owed it to my parents, and I owed it to my intellect. Someone with my smarts comes around perhaps once a century. Use it or lose it, my father threatened.

My sister didn't have to go to college because she owed nothing to anybody. All her brains were in her feet, my father said. If she had any brains at all. Gray matter, white matter, and the fat required to power either: when they were handing out the equipment, she didn't get the memo. There was nothing to be done to change that, so let her dance. Let her dance her head off. My father had a million explanations why she couldn't go to college, while it was my responsibility to attend, achieve, use the gifts that had been given to me, become somebody, and make a contribution to society. I stayed behind and followed this safe route, the one dug up for me. No rotting away for me, just math. Numbers, probabilities, and binary thinking.

I stayed behind and everybody went off to Chicago, the new home of the rock 'n' roll vanguard. Or so it seemed in all the newspaper reviews and photographs. You'd think that Los Angeles and everything that had happened here—including

CYA, just starting to get the big gigs—were entirely inconsequential. Perhaps the L.A. scene had never existed. As if I—we—had never played before 350 people at Madame Wong's before it burned down or opened for Jasmine and her band at the Whisky. We got through a half-hour set even though there were probably more than 500 people there, 500 seething, spitting, untethered men waiting and anticipating our nerves, our gaffs, and feedback—however we could blow it and we would, because we were kids. We were green. Untrained, unarranged, possibly talented but definitely, defiantly raw. We were not like Jasmine. We were amateurs.

We opened with one of Jack's songs, "Genocide Diary," and we dove into it as hot and feverous as we could get. You can never open slow at the Whisky. If you do, you risk all kinds of abuse. But the audience threw bottles at us anyway. They spit at us, and they would have jumped on the stage and torn our instruments away from our hands if we showed any sign of weakness: if we cried or complained, if we asked for a time out, or if we flinched at the flying glass and asked the bouncers to stand up there in front of us, as though we were some celebrity act and had to be protected. But no, we did none of those things. We were CYA. We were invincible. We were heinous.

Next was "Savage Lesbian" without any introduction or banter, just straight into the power chords, and we barricaded the place with them. We meant for ears to bleed with those opening power chords, for the rafters to crack. The chaotic wash of that song flipped back and forth, but I finally had my look right that night, and nothing was going to stop me. I was wearing one of my father's vests and ties and a white T-shirt; Jasmine dressed me. And boots instead of tennis shoes for safety. "Savage Lesbian" was another Jack song, but I could play that one barbarically. My arms, hands, and ears would hurt for days afterward, but I didn't care, because on that stage, I was elevated. I was the tallest I ever had been in my life. I don't know whether the other stages we'd played measured higher, but at the Whisky I was looking down on all those people—a few more women now, into "Savage Lesbian," and they had to look up to watch me play, see how my hands handled the frets and strumming. They had to crane their necks if they wanted a legit shot of what I was doing. I was so tall on that stage that no one could correctly guess my height. No more stomping on my feet or pushing me around as if I were some kind of overstuffed trash can.

After "Savage Lesbian" we went into "Get the Door," one of mine, and it was all 1-2-3-4, E-F-E-E, "1-2-3-4, Someone's at the fuckin' door/5-6-7-8, Drug dealer's running late." I could see some of the guys in the audience running toward the back of the room as if it would give them more space for momentum for whatever they were planning. Rushing the stage, an ambush, who knows what they wanted? We were wearing boots instead of our regular tennis shoes and when we paced or swayed, we were crunching glass under our feet. I couldn't hear it, but I could feel it from the way my feet seemed to want to slip out from under me, as if I were on a treadmill, and I would survive only by keeping up the pace.

"You want to see some spit?" Jack yelled at the crowd after we'd done a few more songs—we had to do a lot of songs, because each one was probably only two minutes at most, and we had 30 minutes to fill. We'd just done a new one, "Private School Rules," which we'd never done before, and some people were booing. Those who weren't booing were spitting, little globules of petroleum jelly, it seemed. When the saliva landed on the stage, we could see it, distinct little ecosystems with greasy atoms and their rancid electrons. They made picking up the glass impossible. There was no place not to catch some disease. "I know you really want to see some real spit," Jack yelled again, and people hooted and shouted back "yeah!" and wiggled their tongues at us like we were working girls, and then they shouted some more. "We'll show you some real spit," Jack declared, and then she lunged toward my ear and yelled, "Get down on that floor, and lick up all the spit down there."

This was my moment of truth. And I knew what I was going to do, because I wasn't like all these leeches—these poseurs who were coming in and out of our lives, promising us record deals, studio time, and introductions to this band or that DJ or photo sessions that never materialized, because they were fame whores or they were worthless sponges who would do anything to get next to us because we were girls or because we knew Jasmine. I wasn't going to be like Jack and Nicky and the new drummer, Howard, who didn't show up for rehearsal or said she'd rather go off with the poseurs and spongers because they really could do something for us, when all they really could do is get her some kind of contact high. I wasn't going to be like the way Jasmine turned out to be; I was committed.

So I kicked away some glass with my foot and got down on my knees and put my nose to all the stage's sneaker grime, the brackish strange discolorations where people had spit out gum and let it harden, and the guck people collected in their mouths and the bottom of their feet and then upchucked it or smeared it on that stage. The stage was glossy with this stuff, the spit and glass dust and the residue of aborted blowjobs and circle jerks. It was all there, practically bubbling at my nose, and I opened my mouth, shut my eyes, and then I licked it. I licked it a few times in one spot that may have been slightly less disgusting, and I licked to the left and to the right; so it seemed as if I were lapping up a whole bunch, even cleaning the stage. People hollered. They shouted out their disapproval and their amazement. They shouted out my name. I licked it and then I got up and wagged my tongue at them and then gave everyone the finger. It was my night for the taking, and I collared it. It was all mine after that point. I was entering the rock 'n' roll monarchy. The underground division, but still, a different class. Higher than the audience.

Howard had taken off her shirt, down to her bra, and was panting. Nicky had her back turned toward the audience as she pretended to adjust levels on her amp and speakers. Jack applauded until I stopped taking my bows and then she revved us up for the pile-driving notes of the next song, "Jail Break" by yours truly. And then it was quiet, or more than quiet—obedient—and people jumped and threw their fists in the air or stared at us in awe and holy admiration. We drove that song home as though it could scatter the glass at our feet and blow the roof off. "We are California Youth Authority! Cover Your Asses bastards!" we shouted in unison and the crowd hooted, and then Jasmine jumped on stage because she was going to play a number with us, and we had arrived. We were the hottest, wettest lesbians on the Sunset Strip. We played a shredded version of the Bee Gee's "More Than A Woman" with Jasmine singing. Punk could make pretty much anything sound better, and we could have torn into the entire "Saturday Night Fever" soundtrack, but the sound guy was waving and blinking lights at us. Jasmine mouthed to us, "That's it." So we took a few more bows with Jasmine announcing our names, and then we were finished.

The body is a font of hungers and hazards, I learned that night, and I tasted all of them. I've always hated it when I can taste myself—my own salt. I don't think you should be able to taste yourself. You should be seamless and neutral, with a chameleon tongue, and blend into the dominant sweat or pattern. On that stage I could be satisfied only by the taste of outrageousness, of spectacle, and of famousness, and it was gross but filling, in the moment, entirely necessary. But in the green room lit with black lights, where people were ghosts and rioted as if to prove they still existed, I should have been cold, phosphorescent. Instead my mouth was all grit and particles, a rough transition between breathing and swallowing, as though I'd contracted something. The flu, an oral disease, something venereal with sin. I wanted a drink of water. We were being showered with foam: beer or champagne. They tasted the same to me, like sand, smog, or what you might crunch on if you were caught in the inversion layer. The residue of the Whisky was on my tongue, its friction on the back of my teeth. Jack grabbed me and tried to pour something down my throat. I wanted to spit up and vomit out the night so far; so I could get a better look at what had happened and who I had a chance of becoming.

I wanted to see myself on that stage, playing and licking up the remains of a million other shows so that I'd know what happened was real, not a cliché, and that this was it—the authentic experience that no one could take away from me. Jack, Nicky, and Howard were screaming. Jack had her arm around my neck and was jumping. If she had any awareness, she might have known she was choking me, and I had to jump with her or she'd wind up socking me in the jaw. People were shaking beer cans and spewing the carbonation as though it were fireworks. "Wash this girl's mouth out!" Nicky was saying. She was talking about me. One of the bouncers was shouting, "Under 21! Under 21!" to no avail. It must have been the first time he found his voice and body useless.

Jack told me I stank like the girls' shower at school; so I kissed her on the mouth and then she stank too. She hugged me as if she were about to fall. The only thing that got me out of Jack's grip was Nicky, who picked me up by the waist and tried to parade me around the room, but it was too crowded with adults. They seemed to be pouring in like insects, colonies that had previously been trapped in walls. Jack and Nicky were meeting people, and I drank beer and coughed. I coughed as though I had the dry heaves, as though I still needed to work in reverse to know what I was experiencing. My nostrils had been singed with cigarette smoke, my eyes watered, and I didn't know where Jasmine was, though she couldn't have gotten far.

After the screaming, the shouting, the jumping, and falling, Jack and Nicky announced they were going back out, into the audience, because Jasmine's show was starting. The Tainted were the main attraction, the headlining event, and we were just the opener; no one was supposed to remember us. As soon as Jasmine started playing, we would be nobodies again. Or I would be. But Jasmine took me by the hand, suddenly, and led me into the wings, stage right. She yelled something into my ear, but I couldn't hear with the surge of people around me; her voice was a blur, her words rushing by so much faster than she usually spoke. She was a different person, infested with the smoke and panic of the club. She even squeezed my arm, as if drawing encouragement from my example. She walked onto the stage and was playing her guitar before I realized Jack and Nicky were in the pit, but I was there, alone, Jasmine's chosen for the night, her muse and confidant, her protégé, or her lover.

My back and neck were drenched, and I tried not to smell myself, hot and metallic, something ferrous and volatile. I could never just drift. I was combustible, ready to catch fire. I tried tapping my feet, nodding my head, but it wasn't enough. I wanted to be devoured. By Jasmine and the music, the glances Jasmine threw my way, and the awe of the audience whenever I could be spotted standing in the wings, my importance so obvious. No one else could get this close to Jasmine. Not even the other band members. They were there only to support her. She played and sang, and I was split in half, quarters, proportions of prime numbers. My voice was separated from my throat, my skin from oils and acne, and blood from what coursed through my head, heart, and lungs. Blood pooled like sparks, embers in my crotch. I let everything go, but not because people were watching. I let go because I belonged finally. Finally. I had found my place. At the nexus of everyone's needs and wants, their aspirations and envy. I was the girl in the band, the girl beside Jasmine, the girl at the glaring aura, in the light after the debris settled. I was that girl.

Once she ran through her set and encore, Jasmine had the bouncers pull Jack and Nicky from the pit. Our drummer was AWOL, but Jasmine had us on stage for one more song, a cover of Nazareth's "Love Hurts," at 99 rpms. Jasmine was wet, her blouse transparent. Jack sang. Jasmine was breathless. I sang too, the words that I knew, and I was seriously shredding my instrument. I wanted my fingers to bleed, and my lips to blister into the microphone. We walked off that stage as though we were killers, mercenary geniuses after a serious plundering. We were not gods, but demi-creatures on our way there to the top of the pagans.

And that was just the beginning of the night. But my sister wants to talk to me now. How could I ever make her understand how I felt that night, how that night felt around me, the beginning of my life, finally, after all that fighting and practicing and bargaining and fighting. It was actually happening. How could anyone who wasn't there understand it, especially if they hadn't heard us play. We were loose. We were natural. We screamed like that was all our throats were made for—the pump and the rush of notes and syllables. My sister would never understand this. She wasn't a creator. She was a receiver and unoriginal, copying over the same steps and the same expressions as every dancer before her had done for years and centuries. You might say that my sister and her ballets brought to life pieces of history, incidents and actions that film and recordings could not capture. But that's the point, almost. To watch my sister dance was to watch a Civil War reenactment or something at one of those Renaissance festivals, everything preordained and perfectly decided. There was no history to make, only to imitate. When I played, I was establishing ramparts and plateaus; I was writing the textbooks. If you came to one of my shows, or to any rock 'n' roll show back in those days, you'd be present at the creation. You'd smell the blood and taste the oxygen it took to make the performance. My sister and her ballets were like memorial services—funerals in comparison.

Nevertheless, she still believes she has something important that can't wait and must be communicated. She wants me to confide. She crowds her face right in front of mine and says I can tell her, but what can I say? She never did get it, and now it's too late. Wherever we go or wherever we've been, she always needs to sit down and take a load off her feet. Her back hurts, her hips ache, and the bottoms of her feet are on fire: she is exhausted. Is it motherhood that does this, or is she still feeling the effects of dancing? I got nothing from that night at the Whisky. If you saw me, you might think it hadn't left a trace. No one remembers I was there at the moment of conception. The meeting of minds, disparate parts, individual cells that foretell an explosion: I was there, and I rocketed straight into the minds of the audience. But who cares now. My only scar is from the mastectomy, and no one wants to see that. They only want to see the tits on a lesbian when they're not damaged.

I hear doubt in her voice, though this is nothing new. My sister lives in doubt and feeds off it; it's how she has made her way in a life, acting as dumb as she is, precisely, so she can get people to do the more difficult work for her. She still doesn't know how to balance her own checkbook. She's saying something about my bank account and large cash withdrawals the police want to know about. I'd tell her that's none of her business, and I wonder whether she's trying to steal my money. I always thought it would come down to this, my sister always broke and tedious when it comes to numbers. How much less she has compared to how much more I'm pulling in. I wrote her out of my will when I was first diagnosed; so she'd know where we stand. She said it didn't upset her, but now she is riled.

I know it's doubt in her voice because this is just how she sounds when she's in over her head. Desperate to convince you she's anything but desperate, but you can hear the rheumatism between her breaths, shaky and uncertain. That's how she rots, the great artiste. You present her with a truth she can't deny, and yet she tries, she struggles, and she folds, and you can hear it in her voice. I heard her do this whenever she brought a boyfriend around, even that piano player she married. I sat those men down and treated them to an unexpurgated education on life with my sister: the hysteria and stupidity they would be saddled with. I had given them fair warning. My sister would try to protest and convince them otherwise, but the doubt in her voice often persuaded them that I was correct.

Except for the man who married her, the musician. I've got to say, he must have guts. I had a conversation with him once about his playing the piano for the ballet company during classes and rehearsals. I asked him how could he consider himself a real artist when he's merely riffing and repeating those riffs, the dribs of other compositions, for people who weren't really listening to him. Before he could answer, my sister was between us with that voice on the verge of hyperventilating. I wonder whether he understood what I did, and the implications of her sorry defense of him: that this would be the so-called foundation of their relationship.

True, they are still married. I don't know how or why because they fight. Or as my father tried explaining to me, they have "disagreements." He told me this as he was pontificating on the difference between science and art; so I would finally comprehend that there is an art to good science, like medicine; that he never meant to imply there was such a stark separation between the two that I couldn't do both. Marriage was also an art, he said. I suppose the statement served as a discourse on what had gone wrong between him and our mother, because he was no artist. The fights he had with our mother, he said, were like a failure of art—a failure of the imagination. Neither he nor our mother could see clear to the other's side of the conversation; so they fought, trying to enforce their views upon each other. He did not tell me what their views were, but he said my sister and her husband, who called himself a musician because he squeezed out a living by playing keyboards, had the ability he and our mother lacked. He could tell by the way they talked to my niece and how they dealt with each other. I'm glad he figured out the secret of marriage after he left our mother as if he were a criminal, and the crime was our household.

So this is what my sister will be passing on to my niece. History, art, and most of all, doubt. I can tell by the way she talks to her family. Once, when she and her husband were visiting us, they had a "disagreement" over when my niece should be put to bed. He saw no problem with letting the girl stay up, allowing her to fall asleep on the couch as we sat around talking. But my sister said no, emphatically, as in hell no, over my dead body, because my niece would wake up cranky and inconsolable. She told him, none too convincingly, he'd have to "deal" with the consequences the next day, because she couldn't. She ran out of the living room, and I chased after her. I wanted to know what she was going to do about this schism. "Nothing," she said. "There's nothing to be done." I told her this wasn't good enough and that she had to take a stand or he'd be walking all over her for the rest of my niece's life, and I didn't want my niece to see her mother rendered powerless. "Well, I could divorce him," my sister said. "Would you like that?"

With my niece, she is worse than robotic, as though she's afraid to go beyond the most basic instructions: "Go to bed."

"Finish your dinner." "Clean your room." But I should give her credit. At least she did not say the same things our parents said to us. None of the "You don't do for me, I don't do for you." Or the "Is this how you want to be remembered after you die?" Or "What am I supposed to say, when the neighbors find out? After you've dragged all of us into the mud with you?" At least my sister is not on automatic pilot. I have to give her that.

But another time when she and my niece were visiting—without the husband, because he had to work, as he called it: a new ballet to rehearse and he was the favored rehearsal pianist—my niece hit her after the bath, probably out of some kind of frustration. My sister said, "Okay, time's up, you're finished," or something like that, and informed my niece she'd be going straight to bed, no songs, no stories, nothing. My niece began to cry. Apparently, these lines had been used on her before to maximum effect. But my sister was resolute. There was no going back after that swat. My sister turned off the light in the bedroom, and my niece emitted a piercing, pitiful cry. She shut the bedroom door, and my niece was howling. "You can't do this," I told her. "You're going to screw up that kid for life. Withholding affection. That's cruel, devastating." She said to me, "You have no idea what you're talking about," as though, if she said anything more, a sclerotic rash would have crawled out of her mouth and onto her face. I wanted to laugh in her face to show her how certain I was, but she was gone, back to her own room. She thinks she knows everything, but she knows she doesn't. She knows it.

She is asking me to concentrate and to give her something. Words? A sentence? What should it be composed of: a confession, an admission that might lead to a confession, an acknowledgment that might provide someone with leverage to get an apology on my deathbed? None of this is my problem—the bank account or anything the police want—so I don't understand why it's my sister's. Then again, that's how she operates, taking someone else's problems and making them her own. Because she glories in all the suffering. When she told me I had no idea what I was talking about, she also said it was none of my business how she and her husband raised my niece, whatever their "parenting styles" were. She told me to have a child of my own first, and then maybe we could talk about it. I said that was ridiculous. I'm human, and I know how to treat my fellow human beings, I said, and then it was her turn to laugh. Like you treat everyone around you, she asked. Look around. Who's here? Who have you been treating so humanely all this time? That weak and whiny strain in her voice had deserted her by then, and she was yelling as though she meant to permanently clear her throat of whatever rot and fear had previously accumulated there. Because she was my sister and she knew too much about me then, just as she probably knows too much about me now. She may not have known how we killed it that night at the Whisky. She may have lacked the ability to comprehend just how much of a landmark my performance at the Whisky had been. But she was to know everything that happened after that night at the Whisky: my precipitous decline into humiliation and now this—rot and death.

CHAPTER 12

"WE'VE GOT SOMETHING TO SHOW YOU," Detective-Sergeant Simpson said, once I got him and W-Y-R-E-C-K-A in the kitchen. I had managed to keep them out of the bedroom this time, no thanks to all the proactive mourners floating through the house. One of them had let the cops in, but I was able to intercept them in the hallway; I heard their march, heavy and perilous.

"What?" I asked, taking a seat the table. Simpson sat down beside me, a little too close, but W-Y-R-E-C-K-A's positioning was more disturbing—right behind me. They thought they had me cornered. Maybe they did.

"We think you could enlighten us to what's going on here," he said, and W-Y-R-E-C-K-A plopped a stack of papers down in front of me—computer printouts, they looked like.

"Can you leave it? We're a little busy right now but later—"

"Can't do that," Simpson said solemnly. "This is evidence."

"Okay," I agreed, because agreement seemed to be the best option.

"Can't break the chain of custody," the cop said.

"What?" I asked, though I had an idea of what he was talking about if not the exact meaning.

"Do you know what evidence is?"

"Yeah," I said, which was kind of true. I mean, I knew what evidence was, but I couldn't imagine how it could be a stack of papers in this case. In Jasmine's case, that is, because it was still Jasmine's case, strictly speaking. Jasmine's case had nothing to do with Barbara; we had already established that, by virtue of Barbara's death march. Unless the stack of papers tied her to Jasmine's case, in which case, I wasn't saying anything.

"Do I need a lawyer?" I asked.

"Whoa, Nelly!" Detective-Sergeant Simpson declared, and he cracked a smile across his lips, which were chapped, and his teeth were short and yellow. "We've got a way to go before we get to that," he said, trying to sound good-natured. But he still had evidence, and I still had a sister dying of breast cancer and a house full of people trying to pay their respects in advance. Once she was gone, they wouldn't be able to remember what they respected her for.

"So I'm going to need a lawyer," I said. "Eventually."

"Who said anything about needing a lawyer?" Simpson said, as sweetly as those stout teeth and that awful mouth would permit and as if he had made too big of a deal over nothing—this evidence. Like he and his partner had rehearsed all this, blocked it all out. They were a stagey pair. They were using all the dramatics to their best advantage. Dramatics was something I knew about, of course, although people said I was no good at them. I anticipated too much. I concentrated more on my part than on reacting naturally to what happened on stage—to what my partner did. I was always acting in a vacuum, like mine was the only character that mattered.

"Okay," I said. "Sorry."

W-Y-R-E-C-K-A began unfolding the printouts, like he was stretching out one of my daughter's toys, the Jacob's Ladder. He was wearing surgical gloves, I noticed; maybe he thought breast cancer was catching or he didn't want to get his fingerprints on the documents. "Do you know what these are?" Simpson said.

"No," I said, and thought, good answer, because I didn't know anything.

"These are your sister's bank transactions, ma'am," W-Y-R-E-C-K-A said.

"Every check, every deposit, and every withdrawal for the past year," Simpson went on. W-Y-R-E-C-K-A traced his finger along the columns as Simpson spoke. "So here's a check for fifty bucks, the day the bank received it; the day they paid it out; here's a deposit for $325, probably her disability check."

"Okay," I said slowly, because I really wasn't looking at the numbers. They always seemed to cramp up on me and dissolve into a language way beyond my comprehension. I was like a dyslexic at math, even with the gloved hand pointing them out for my benefit. It was the hand that I was really following, like it was showing me where to sign a document or steering me to buy a particular product. "Okay," I said each time it pointed. "Okay," I said, because I could not stop myself.

"Don't you want to take a closer look—for yourself?" Simpson tried to sound gentle, encouraging, like he was not so much tempting me into doing something as he was inviting me, giving me permission.

"I can barely balance my own checkbook," I said. "I wouldn't know what they said even if I read them."

"We thought you'd say that," Simpson said, looking at his partner. "People say you're good at acting stupid so everyone will keep thinking your sister's the smart one."

"Huh," I said, and I tried to make it sound like there was something in my throat instead of something stuck in my head.

"It's no act," I said, "and if you knew anything about me, you'd know I'm no actress."

"Okay," Simpson said. "You got me." He leaned into me, in a way that was both fatherly and threatening. His face so close to mine, it reminded me of something my mother used to talk about, when she would take me to the ballet when I was still a kid. She always refused tickets up front, because she did not want to see the dancers' strain and sweat in their performance. She thought the dancers strained and sweated because that's what I did when I danced. I was an amateur. Professional dancers don't gird or grimace on stage like that. They hide that sweat and strain, but what they do—what you can see easily, no matter where you sit—is run out of breath. You can see how hard their hearts are beating at the end of a sequence, the pounding that seems to translate to their clavicles, suddenly visible, just as suddenly hidden. That's why they are professionals, or soloists and principals; they have set their bodies and minds in perfect service of the stories they're telling. When Simpson leaned into my face, I wondered what he could read there, what I might see in his own, and what my mother tried to shield me from when I already had seen it time and again in the mirror, or on the stage.

"Your sister had a lot of money," Simpson said.

"You'd have a lot of money, too, if you lived at home all your life," I said.

"Jealous?"

"Maybe," I said. "Maybe not. I wanted to move out, move away—"

I stopped because I knew he wasn't listening. He was looking up at his partner, and his partner was boring his eyes into the back of my head, trying to pick out some stray confession boiling around in there. "Your mother," Simpson said, and he shook his head, like he was thinking of how she should rest in peace although he never met her. Or maybe he was telling himself not to take the next step, or not make the comment he had planned. "She left you a bundle, didn't she?" W-Y-R-E-C-K-A flipped the papers back and showed a deposit for a half-million dollars, Barb's share of the money.

"Yeah, okay," I said. I had no idea where this was going. "She did. Okay."

"But you and your sister. You argued about this?"

"No, not really," I responded, because it was true in the way everything was true at this stage. I didn't argue with Barb about money. She argued with me about money—money I didn't have, money I didn't carry with me at any particular time in any particular place; money she thought I should have had but didn't because I was harried with the baby or was running between appointments or for whatever reason. But she really let me have it. Once we were at the Jersey Shore for a weekend, I had run out of the beach house without enough money to buy a bottle of water, I asked her for change, and she got furious. How selfish I was, to leave the house without enough money to take care of myself. What did I expect, that she, Helen, or my husband would just take care of all my needs? How could a mother be so irresponsible? Who was I, the center of the universe that I didn't have to worry about leaving the house without money? This was the selfishness that enraged her on this particular situation, but there were many more like that—like each time I was unable to buy my daughter a particular toy, a T-shirt, or stuffed animal she wanted or meet any one of her demands for immediate gratification. It was selfish of me to expect her rich aunt to pay if it was my daughter who needed something because I failed to anticipate those needs and how to meet them.

"Everybody argues about money," Simpson said.

"My mother would say that only people who don't have money argue over it," I said.

That got him out of my face really quickly. He sat up like his spine had been snapped to attention. "Okay," Simpson conceded. He nodded, like he was telling himself he had pushed it too far. For a moment, I might have been winning.

"Don't you want to know what your sister did with her money?" Simpson asked.

"Not really," I said, because I knew. This was what she was doing. She was spending it on her death.

"Here, take a look," he said, and W-Y-R-E-C-K-A's latex hand reappeared to guide me through the columns. There was a song Barb and I used to sing; it was the jingle for a car dealership, a commercial that played with the cartoons we watched. The commercial had a little white dot that went along with the tune, pointing out the words; they were really directions to the car dealership, and we'd sing the words that had no meaning to us. We had no idea where all those freeways and streets were, and yet we knew them. We understood that they were a part of our world, and yet they were far away—too far for us to worry about them much. We sang the jingle at the dinner table once, and Helen was mortified. She wanted to restrict our TV time, saying our brains were rotting. But Irv laughed; he sang with us. Whenever I asked Barb if she remembered something from our childhood, she'd always say there were no good times in our childhood. It was all bad from the beginning up to the present moment.

"There's this withdrawal for five thousand," Simpson said. "And another, in December." The pages flipped. "And another, in February. And another—the last in April. Cash withdraw-als. You know what this looks like?"

"Like she was spending her money?"

"Like she was paying someone off."

"Okay," I said, because it seemed, at first, like it was possi-ble. But then I thought there had to be other options. She was setting up a new account somewhere maybe. She was always doing that, moving her money around, like she was playing a game of Three-Card Monte; so nobody could find all of her money. She was like that, always worried someone was after her money, though who could it have been seriously. Maybe she was buying blocks of concert tickets; she had started doing that, taking her friends to see shows with the best seats, because why not, given her prognosis. Or maybe she was buying something she always wanted that she couldn't justify splurging on when she was healthy, and now what difference would it make, although she could have bought it outright, like all the other things she bought—guitars, electric pianos, a drum set for my daughter, to which I had said, "no way." Not in a New York apartment. Barb said I was being selfish again.

I began looking at the numbers on the computer printouts, columns labeled with dates and times, pluses and minuses; I couldn't help getting confused between the amounts, −123.23, −500.00, +420.00, −15.59, and the times they were recorded, 0930, 1215, 1645, 0100. I couldn't figure out what Barb was spending her money on since she never had any expenses, but she must have had some after Helen died, and she had to fend for herself. Barb always talked about numbers, and how they made patterns; it was seeing those patterns that made people think she was so smart, she explained, but there was really nothing to it. It was about recognizing repetition and the purpose for it. This I could get; there's repetition in music and in choreography. It's a language; it conveys an emotion, the meaning of a gesture, and a quality of the character or the setting. But then Barb used to say something else: patterns are something our minds make. They do not necessarily exist. We make patterns to master the data, but the data changes. Data is not aware of the pattern; it has no investment in it. This was why, she said, all the studies she did—counting cancers and their causes, determining whether there were clusters or coincidences, what was a cause, and what merely correlated—always had provisos or exceptions.

"You want some advice?" Simpson asked.

I tried squinting at the numbers, like it would make me look like I was really concentrating, looking for something, anything.

"Your sister's gotta get a lawyer," Simpson said.

"She already has a lawyer."

"She needs a criminal lawyer," Simpson said.

"Wait," I said. W-Y-R-E-C-K-A swept the papers back in order and picked them up. I was staring at an empty table.

"We're not going anywhere," Simpson said. "You know who she's paying off?"

"No. I mean, I don't know—I don't know what you're talking about. I mean, what are you saying? That my sister was being blackmailed? There's nothing to blackmail her over. She's dying. I mean, she could die tomorrow," I said, and I suddenly felt hot and out of breath, like I was blushing after having embarrassed myself, because I had said too much. I had said something I hadn't been sure of, but then realized this was what I had to face. "My sister hasn't done anything—she's dying. She's been dying for six years. She's a computer person. She used to go to work and then she came home. Maybe she went to a few concerts. But that's it. Now she's dying, okay? Maybe tomorrow. Maybe by the end of the week. She's in hospice, that means she's dying, right? I told you earlier. You saw." I looked behind me and found W-Y-R-E-C-K-A there, the papers folded under one arm, the other arm around his chest; so he'd be menacing, like he was impenetrable. This bit of staging was just the point; so I had nowhere to go, no one to appeal to. It was clever and maddening.

"We're trying to do you a favor," Simpson said. His arms were crossed and rested on the bulk that was his stomach and he frowned, like he was apologizing. "What we're giving you is a head's up. Because the next time you see us, we'll be asking for a list of associates and business interests."

"My sister doesn't have 'associates,'" I said. I was pretty certain about that.

"Everybody's got associates—especially people with money," Simpson said. Score one for him, he must have thought. He was grinning. "Okay, it's back to work for us. Come on, son," he said as he stood, and there was suspense in that second, as he sucked in his gut or made it look like he was, as he maneuvered past me.

"We'll be in touch, ma'am," W-Y-R-E-C-K-A said.

They left me staring at the blank space where the papers had been. I could have at least followed them to the door and watched through the window as they went outside. I could have seen if they were mobbed by the reporters and cameras; I could have been prepared for whatever was going to hit the TV screen that night. I didn't even have to get up, though; I could have leaned over, peeked through the shutters in the kitchen, and seen the same thing. Instead I sat there at the table where I used to eat with my parents and sing TV jingles with my sister, and I thought again about what Barbara had said: there were no good times in her childhood, no happy memories of Irv or even of Helen. This always bothered me, not because I had so many but because after everything—the fights, the divorce, even Barb's anorexia—there were good times. My husband came here. Helen bought my daughter a highchair, and we used to feed her; Helen taught her how to make lemonade and bread at this table. I saw it. But Barb sat here, day after day, eating whatever my mother could fix or maybe take-out or delivery, with that void in her heart, whatever it was that Jasmine had so thoroughly taken from her. Nothing could fill it or take its place, and the rest of her life fell through it until the cancer came and settled things.

CHAPTER 13

WHEN MY FATHER TAUGHT ME HOW TO DIGRESS, he imparted another lesson: how to disappear. This was not a result of direct instruction; I don't believe he intended it as a corollary or his sick sense of extra credit. But his tactics left an impression. So when someone asked me to explain some topic, a proof or theorem about which I did not have a complete grasp, I was able to delay and divert until the problem resolved itself into the ether. If you asked me to solve a polynomial on a computer, for instance, I could discourse on the history of said equations, their invention by Descartes, although he was only perfecting and streamlining what the Greeks and the Muslims had long before given us. If you asked me, what is Hilbert's thirteenth problem, or his fifteenth or sixteenth, I could tell you that the thirteenth was a problem of math analysis, something beyond calculus; and that the fifteenth and sixteenth problems were for the algebraists. I'd tell you that there were originally twenty-three of Hilbert's problems altogether, or maybe twenty-four, depending on which manuscript you were looking at, although maybe there were really only twenty-three, since one of the problems was really about physics.

If you asked me why anyone would want to know about my bank account when it's been the same account I've had since childhood, I'd tell you there's a lot of history in that account. It could be made into a kind of sociological case study. My grandparents opened that account for me when I was just a few days old. It was to be my college account, because in my life, there were no other options. College or bust, and if I went bust, I wouldn't need any of the money. It would just sit there, collecting interest but losing value to recessions or inflation; I wasn't an economics major. But I recognize a metaphor when it's shoved up against me. My intelligence could keep pace with the achievement race my parents enrolled me in with all of my contemporaries only if I exercised my intelligence to a degree that impressed the elders. If you asked me what would have satisfied them, I probably would have talked about medical school, or a doctorate in some obtuse and highly specialized research topic that would foreclose further conversation and judgment.

I thought I emptied that account long ago because my father didn't make, and couldn't have made, any provisions for my future. My father did not believe in savings accounts, investments, or pensions: all of the things other kids' dads believed in, because savings accounts, investments, and pensions implied that work was a necessary part of life. My father believed in work, though not necessarily for himself, because for himself he believed only in scheming. If you could score big, and get it all at once, then a savings account, an investment, even a pension was not necessary. You walked away without looking back or perhaps you turned on a spigot, and the money just flowed based on some previous and magical action you had taken. He was always going back, trying to figure what he could muscle out of some past arrangement: what he was owed and how long he could stretch it out. A highway weigh station, a tire dealership, a business selling campers and recreational vehicles: he started all of these things but did not see them through. Yet he could not let go of the possibility that they could still pay off if he approached them differently somehow in his mind or in the historical record.

For me, however, there was only one road: college. Only college could hook you up with a decent living. Or a better living than any he could put together for himself, though he went to college too, but his education was another story. I wouldn't regret college, he promised, because look at all the money I'd be able to make. The world runs on money, he said, but not the way you think it does. Spending money was just as important as earning money, which is not something that everybody understands, but he did. If I wanted to spend money like some people earned it, I was going to have to go to college, because he didn't want me doing what he did. Which may have been nothing or dealing with fly-by-night operations run by people who were here one day and gone the next, and back on the third day but with new names and empty pockets. What I wanted, he said, was money that I could predict, just like the answers to some problems would be predictable if you could solve them up to a certain point. For me, he wanted money to be inevitable.

That account at the old Home Savings & Loan, down at the corner, was the only inevitable money I ever had. The only money given to me without asking, the only money that came without strings, strange terms of exchange; the only money that was logically collected and spent for a purpose. Because I was a mathematician, remember. I understood the basic principle of money while no one else did. Money is a special problem, a unique type of paradox. It's a tangible, practical problem because it doesn't necessarily require the abstract thinking and theoretical calculation that is the hallmark of a difficult mathematical problem. Money is accumulative, its amount dependent on the simplest of functions. Yet money is not limitless, infinite, or inexhaustible. There is only so much, or it becomes worthless.

Money was not some inscrutable, single-celled animal that spontaneously reproduces, like my father thought it was. He thought that if he could isolate this single-celled animal, discover it where no one else thought to look, he would strike it rich. He'd sit back and let the money do the rest. Jack and Nicky did not necessarily believe that money was the result of clean, asexual reproduction. But they did believe in some kind of perpetual quality of money: it would always be there for them, and they might do no more than reach out and touch it to claim it. I wanted to save money for studio time. I thought if the three of us all saved money, we could get what we needed three times faster. They would save their money, then use it to buy concert tickets for a big show—Aerosmith or Queen— and go without me. I couldn't go because I was saving my money for studio time. They squandered their money on sellout bands, KISS or Steve Miller, whatever everybody else at school was seeing. They threw their money away and then asked me how much I had in my studio fund. And I told them, because I was honest. I wasn't going to be like them.

I never spent the studio money though I did open quite a few accounts. I was always afraid I'd go over the FDIC limit. If the bank failed, I'd lose everything. I postponed my gratification and saved everything I ever earned. My sister said this was easy, considering that I never paid any rent or utilities. She said she could be just as wealthy as I was if someone covered all her expenses during her adult life. No one had to be a mathematician to figure that one out. When I told her I was sick and was making out a will, she said she hoped I'd leave all my money to her daughter, my niece. But what would it teach that child? And how long would that money last with my sister in charge of it?

If anyone wants to know about my bank accounts, this is what I would tell them: the money's there because there was no other place else for it to go, although I've thought of places. I've fantasized and imagined. So yes, I have many bank accounts. My conservator is taking care of them. He knows which ones to empty first for expenses, which go to charity, which one account, and only one account, will go to my niece, provided my sister can keep her hands off it. The conservator knows everything. Why would anyone else want to know about my bank accounts now that I'm being forced to use them, only because I'm about to die, to dissolve and dissipate into a kind of permanent digression, a tangent?

People will remember me only through association: when they hear one of Jasmine's records or some other music, probably female and probably acoustic; or when they smell something I liked to eat, when I liked to eat; or when they see someone jogging down the street as I did. I will recede in people's minds. I will no longer be a first thought if I ever was one, like a real priority or an only consideration. Or I could be deliberately purged, out of sight, out of mind, and not of further importance, which is how I've registered to so many people for so long. And if I perish or persist in any memory, how will it be any different from now? Or ten years ago? Or even further back than that? To ask about my bank account, my accounts, is to leave open the more pressing question: why delve into this minutia when I am in this process of becoming residue and erasure, ablated like bad heart muscle, surgically resected so no one need adjust to my disappearance. I may never have existed, to some people, to most people, or to myself.

I might say that I am disappearing, though that would not be accurate. It's more of a matter of my anatomy disappearing, vacating the premises before my consciousness is ready to release it. For my organs, this is their moment to give up and stop fighting. Whether this is the direct result of the disease or an attendant case of exhaustion, I don't know. I only know what is happening molecularly. My liver is refusing to separate toxins from what little I eat and from the medicine I imbibe. My blood is becoming either sludge or water and is unable to perform its duties of exchange and nourishment. My heart and lungs sag from a lack of stimulants, primarily oxygen. My brain is starving from all of the distractions.

I've done this before. Not the death part, but the disappearing: my mind battling my systems and metabolism. So I am familiar with all of the signs. One sign actually, and that is fatigue: the need for sleep consuming hours, days, and a weekend. But sleep is only an avenue for passing the time. I am being absorbed into sleep—not into the ether or some other cosmic location: Heaven, Hell, and Purgatory. My father always loved Purgatory. It fascinated him, as if it were a hoax someone had run and gotten away with. Where else could you get people waiting for something promised, with the bunco artists never having to deliver on it and without facing any consequences?

I slept a lot the summer before college when I was anorexic. Actually, once you are anorexic, you are always anorexic; it's like alcoholism or malaria, a disease that can be theoretically acute, but ultimately reveals itself as chronic. In this vein it is much like an obsession, as psychological a disorder as it is physical, and it is through various types of accommodations—indeed, diversions—that a patient is able to live with it. You make your peace with it, in other words. You try, and sometimes you succeed.

If I told you I became anorexic after Jasmine and I were finished; if I told you that anorexia was the diversion from Jasmine, from the band and Jack and Nicky, because Jack, Nicky, and I weren't really anything more than a novelty act, an homage to much better, more aggressive teenage girl musicians, and it was novel to see us sell ourselves beyond all the possibilities of our experience; if I told you that college was a diversion from anorexia, and then my graduate work after that was a diversion too; if I told you that everything I have done with my life, or in my life, because I have not done anything "with" it—if you listened to my father, his retinue of complaints, the chorus of other aggrieved parents he organized who said yes to him in his every interrogation of the subject—if I told you that everything, all the jobs I've held and code I've written, articles I coauthored and money—money I earned and donated, all the 5Ks, 10Ks, and relay races I ran to raise money for all the right causes, stopping teenage suicide and the shelters for teenage runaways, that the concerts and movies I went to, and cruises where you got to meet celebrities and Disney characters, and the times I let my niece bury me in the sand at the beach as if I were already dead, that if the sum total of days, distractions, paychecks, and resume padding were just a big distraction away from the real issue, Jasmine and the whole Jack and Nicky saga over whose band it was, after I came up with the name and wrote the best songs and hosted the most important rehearsal in my house; if I told you all this, would you still be asking me these nonsensical questions about my bank account or accounts? Wouldn't my recitation of every detour or circumnavigation I devised around this bottomless, unremitting hurt that has been mincing away at me for decades; wouldn't this unburdening of myself, this disclosure or declaration, persuade you to stop bothering me about some petty financial machinations?

It's worked for my sister. She seems to have given up on the questions, though she remains determined to sit it out and see me through until the end—much as she did when I had anorexia, although by the time it was over, it was more her disease than mine. It was more her disease than mine because she knew more about it, and therefore more readily identified it and understood its implications, its consequences, and how it would always linger. There would be no real recovery. She knew all this because her body was perfect; it always had been, and always would be. So she was the one who knew what anorexia was: nothing more than a shortcut, a dead end, and an easy and deadly way out. She also knew that these things had to be done with patience, deliberation, and no willy-nilly get-thin-quick fads and schemes. Her body is the only thing she has ever done better than I have. I used to think the thing was her career, her artistic career, but she never got beyond a certain point with that company. She could get only so far, just like me.

To say I didn't take into account how I had committed myself to the disease before I picked it up wouldn't really be fair. You cannot plan out your bout of anorexia. Neither can you summon it or affirmatively decide that you'll make use of it once it's around. Anorexia doesn't work that way or in any way that other diseases do, or so you find out once you have it. Anorexia is more like a haunting, a visitation you cannot put an end to. You can't simply ask anorexia to leave or ask for your body to suddenly be rinsed of it. It lives on after it has taken what it wanted from you because it has always been there in your basic intelligence. It "preexisted" in a sense. Something in your environment, your tissues, and your mind, separate from the brain that controls your hunger and heart rate, has always been waiting for the disease's entrance. It must be this way because how else would the rest of you—your skin, stomach, hair, fingernails, joints, and uterus—know how to demonstrate so forcefully the blossoming of its symptoms.

Only my sister understood this. She was the one who noticed the signs, the ones I hadn't anticipated. She did not necessarily see the weight loss; of course I was losing weight. I'd always been chubby, short, and squat where my sister was lean. We had descended from a long line of short people; my father and others never ceased to remind us. But my sister seemed to stretch out all the conceivable permutations of our inheritance. Or it might have been just how she carried herself. I tried to carry myself that way but failed without the benefit of ballet lessons. I tried holding in my stomach. I thought of stretching, traction, isometrics, and calisthenics, but they bored me. So I took up running, weighing myself, and measuring out food in precise, tidy increments. In the mirror I appeared as I always had, but it was my sister who saw the transformation of my body as though she were experiencing it vicariously, and I was experiencing nothing.

She saw the scrapes and bruises I'd collect on my legs from running settle into jaundice and scabs and then into a weird festering stasis. She saw the fine hair that gradually over- took my flesh. It was like something spun out of a deferred childhood, cotton candy or a cashmere blanket. What jarred her most of all was something she didn't necessarily see but smelled: me. She said she smelled something from one of her dance studios. Sometimes it was like laundry detergent, fresh and overpowering; sometimes it was like ammonia, irritating to her nostrils. Sometimes, she said, it was like all of the cleansers in the world that couldn't hide the scent of something rotting. In the washing machine she stashed all the boxes of Tide, Ajax, Brillo, dishwashing liquid, and Spic and Span our mother ever hoarded. She shut the lid but still said she could taste it, something between boiled spaghetti and ammonia. Her nausea and curiosity were relentless.

Once my sister caught on to my plans—though I never planned it out; I never practiced or professed it as a lifelong ambition; nor did I ever outline my intent, publicly state it, or invite others to advise me on how best to proceed—she set out to ingratiate herself to my illness. She asked what she had done and what had our mother done to deserve such treatment. I might have answered that they had nothing to do with it. No one did. No one was involved. Jasmine may have been and Jack and Nicky, but they must have left for Chicago by the time my sister noticed I was receding. I was withdrawing. From my skin, my clothes, the dimensions everyone knew me by, the surface area that people had come to expect. According to Jasmine, or maybe it was Jack and Nicky who said it, I was a disposable person. Unnecessary, easily replaced. Someone of my type came by every minute, one of them said. I was so common; they probably wouldn't have to hold auditions to replace me. I was a waste of space. A waste of skin. If that was the case, I had better make myself less of a burden on others and the world. I had to redistribute my characteristics. I would be lighter, portable, more efficient. It would not win me back into the hearts of Jasmine, Jack, Nicky, et al., I knew, but I would have the satisfaction of having accepted this constructive criticism and not run away from it.

My sister obviously didn't take it this way. She took it personally on behalf of the family. Why was I torturing our mother like this in slow motion? This I did not understand, as I was so busy that summer. I had no time to stretch things out and make them last forever. I had my room to clean up before I went to college, and I had my laundry to do and groceries to buy and then label and place on a specific shelf in the refrigerator so my mother and sister would not toy with them. I had an appetite that summer, but only for hard foods: carrots, cucumbers, and iceberg lettuce under certain conditions. Apples at their peak but not a split second afterward. I threw out a lot of food that summer; my sister said it was criminal. She said that because she lived exclusively on leftovers; so she wouldn't have to spend any money. I was seriously limiting her food intake; that's what she complained about.

My mother lived on everything I hated: the soft, smashed foods, mushrooms, zucchini, and eggplant. She made casseroles of ratatouille, tomato, and chicken breasts. Everything was in a sauce or steamed, like she had become a senior citizen. Everything was tenderized, denuded of all satisfaction. My jaws, meanwhile, were becoming muscular as I sought out the real essence of snap, crackle, and pop. I felt as though I was consuming real food, bones and viscera. Let my sister and mother stay hungry with their gentle habits. I knew what I was, a cannibal. I was simply training with vegetables.

There were cartons of Knudsen yogurt all over the house. By the television, on the side tables in the living room, and by the bathroom sink. This is what my sister ate, and no one thought anything of it. Knudsen, she said, because she had been so homesick for it when she was in New York. A red carton for strawberry, green for lime, yellow for lemon: I had to pick them out like Christmas decorations and make sure they kept to their own private ledge. I didn't want them mingling with my corn on the cob, my one indulgence. No butter, no salt. I would have taken them raw except that when my sister caught me trying, she called me a savage. "You're obsessed!" she declared. I told her I was just trying to be organized. Perhaps I was practicing for college when I'd have roommates. "You're obsessed!" my sister said, and I told her I had neither the time nor the inclination to discuss these accusations.

I watched my sister follow our mother into the bathroom, as if it were a soundproofed chamber. From there I could hear the muffled ranting of two voices as if they were competing. They must have thought I could not make out what they were saying, but the tone and persistence of their arguments told me they were arguing about me and my newfound, exacting habits. My sister also began looking for our father that summer. She was getting and making telephone calls whenever she was home. She left her notes on the next number she should try, where people had last seen our father, all over the house. In the kitchen I found them and in the dining room at our mother's desk. That was all she did at home, get on that phone and call people who might have known our father, or now wouldn't admit that they ever did. She made lists and crossed out the names and numbers that had failed her; she wrote out what people had told her about our father—which business he was trying out now and the names and aliases of recent girlfriends. She tried lawyers, the Better Business Bureau, hotlines, and answering services. Whenever she struck out on finding him, which was all the time, she would watch me and ask if I were jealous of her. Why else would I want to imitate her figure?

"You could not live my life for one day," she told me that summer. "You'd get the heating bill and find out your roommates were ditching you, and your mind would just explode," she said. "You'd find out you weren't getting some part and you'd be destroyed," she said. "You wouldn't be able to go to the movies or concerts, buy your records and your T-shirts. You'd have to save up everything you've got for rent and pray you'd have enough for food afterwards," she said. "Do you think you can just walk in somewhere and have everybody know you're an artist, just like that?" she asked. "Do you think it's supposed to be easy, like going from kindergarten to first grade? Do you think it's just a little uphill jog to get to the top? Do you know how many people are out there, waiting to drag you down at your heels?" To which I would not have given her an answer, because if I knew the answer, it would have made me look pretentious. Of course I did not want to live her life. She was not only ugly, but stupid. I didn't know why she thought she could succeed in anything, let alone show business, celebrity, Broadway chorus lines, which was as far as I thought she could get. It was more than I aspired to following the Jasmine catastrophe, but I still could not live her life because of what she expected.

She expected disappointment, impoverishment, sacrifice, all without a payoff. The payoff isn't the point, she said. Think about the payoff and you'll drive yourself crazy. So she was going to check all the boxes and hit all the marks of being an "artist" because she didn't have the talent to actually create art. She was average, a follower, and a robot in a tradition that was dying. Whenever she tried to pass herself off as a martyr for her art, which is what she did all that summer, to prove that my suffering was irrelevant, I told myself that in a few years, she would quit. She'd get tired of having nothing and being nobody, although this had always been the case for her; perhaps her life now was no different. Nevertheless, she couldn't dance forever; she often talked about this. Ultimately, this would all be a slight episode in her life, an aberration. She'd tell her kids about it, maybe, something crazy she tried before becoming a wife and mother. What had happened to me, however, hit at my purpose: my needs and desires. I was trying to alter the course of my life by playing music. I was escaping whatever traps teachers and my parents and every adult I had ever met expected to snare me in and put to work for their own benefit ever since everyone found out I was a genius. Jasmine, Nicky, and Jack: together they were my one chance to get out from under the sentence of my intelligence. Now I was doomed to it, its demands and schedules, the debt I owed to the greater good to use it in the most soul-crushingly conventional sense.

"Do you think it's easy, being ugly like this?" my sister asked me. "I started dancing because I was so sick of people telling me how ugly I was. I wanted to do something beautiful." I wanted to tell my sister that I knew all about beauty: the tyranny it was and the sense of control it offered. I wanted to tell her she could never be beautiful, but I might still have a chance. But I knew if I said that, she would have run to our mother and said something dumb like, "She just said I am ugly," as though we were still kids teasing each other and having our parents mediate. We had to have someone referee our discussions because she wouldn't have understood what I meant about how beauty was about not having to care, no matter what situation you were in. If you were beautiful, you could command it. You commanded it because you met the standard. I didn't care about being beautiful. Anyone with enough brains can catch onto the cruelty of that situation, the inherent unfairness and practical eugenics. That's why I became a punk; so I could dispense with these arbitrary forms of hierarchy and punishment.

But I'll admit it. At least I admit my hypocrisies. I own up to my fugitive thoughts and feelings. I am not merely honest, but candid to a fault, while the rest of the world, everyone I know, is fooling themselves about themselves, their secret hates, and their untapped jealousies. They're fooling themselves because they know what hypocrisy is, a type of padding everyone has to protect themselves against the other hypocrites, but if they admitted it, this fat would poison their organs. I'm not going to lie and say I wish I were beautiful, but I am going to say that I wanted the power of being beautiful; if not the power, the nonchalance and control beauty confers on its holders, so that I wouldn't have to worry about first impressions or people's memories. I could exist without automatic judgment. If my sister was clearly failing at wresting out a chunk of some place where people would remake their tastes and preferences in her favor and if she was searching for what she could never get, why should that prevent me from getting my own piece, especially since I was on a mission. Anxiety was what drove her into art clearly. It was all about ego for her and the fulfillment of a childish, impossible wish. I had statements to make and a message to deliver. I had attitudes to change and a world to educate. I'd enlisted for a very long game, and my arsenal could not be limited.

"Do you think it's easy, being this stupid?" That was another one of my sister's questions. I could have given her a real answer, and told her that yes, it is easy: she was living proof of that concept. But she would have thought I was calling her lazy and run to our mother again—"She just said I'm lazy"—or she'd think I was insulting all the hard work she put into ballet and put into trying to be less ugly and not as dumb as a bag of rocks. But you don't get credit for hard work. Everyone knows that. You don't get credit for your potential, even if it is merely one of average intelligence. I know this because—despite all her knowledge about side effects and symptoms; despite how she had managed to memorize some of what she must have witnessed and recognized as its incarnation in her own household; despite her declarations of sisterly love and concern and her pledge to get me through this if it killed not us, but her and her alone—she had no idea what anorexia was, what it meant, and most of all, what her sophistry and self-deception was doing to me, even as she said she was trying to "cure" me of it.

When I had nothing, anorexia was what I needed; anorexia was a reassertion of my brilliance. I applied everything I had ever learned and intuited since I was old enough to intuit things. Anorexia was about the sum total of what had brought me to the benighted stage of life that summer on the verge of college and academe. Anorexia was the same kind of sleight of hand I first performed to the delight of my teachers. Teachers love sleight of hand, magic, or intellectual ability they can recognize but cannot explain, because identifying the gifted and enlisting them in the great effort of socialization that is school (compulsory education) makes them appear gifted, talented, and perceptive. That is why they go on making these identifications, elevating some rather arbitrarily in certain cases, above all the other children, even though the United States is such an egalitarian nation. Fairness, merit, and exultation of effort and loyalty: from kindergarten onwards, this is what we learn in school, and anorexia is the culmination of all those values put to work in the great social laboratory that is the industrial entertainment complex.

The teachers identified me because I was a girl who could add, and not just add, but tally columns of numbers in my head, without using my fingers or a number line or any of the beaded contraptions children are given to learn the rote procession of so many digits. I was a girl who could do these things but could not read or memorize any text; I was a girl who could not copy sentences off the board but knew all the license plates of the cars in the teacher's parking lot. I was a girl when girls should not have been able to do those things, and that made me a wizard. I could do word problems even when "Dick and Jane" did not make any sense; and more than that, I could subtract numbers, without using my fingers or counting out loud, or even backward in my head. I was reversible. I tackled all directions. I could subtract, and I could divide, and eventually I was able to depict volume and dimensions in equations. I had a knack for illustrating the world as it was, rather than simplifying. I understood that people had motives, teachers especially; I knew how to make them look good with my test scores. I was the perfect student.

Now I am a student of anorexia or, shall I say, a student of one particular mathematical function. Call it lessening, or abating, curtailing, or debasement. Any kid can count out addition, but it's the geniuses who take to subtraction as if it were instinctual, the key to all other executions. Anorexia was confirmation of all this; confirmation of who and what I was, confirmation of myself to myself. I still had it: this facility with reduction. I was reducing the circumference of my waist and stomach; I was subtracting from the width of my muscles. I was contracting the amount of space I occupied; I was returning to the visage of my youth, my original measurements. I was going back to the beginning, casting off years and hormonal changes. I was returning that rebate everyone says you can get on adulthood, but, for more than one summer, I was going to make it permanent.

But how to explain this to my sister? How to explain any abstract concept to her when she did not understand that everything is in flux and that no amount is final? How to explain to her when she depended on thinking that every move took her up when she was running in place or moving laterally? "Do you think it's easy having to be perfect for a job?" she asked, and I found this humorous. I found this to be a riot. My sister was as far from perfect as anyone could possibly be, but she insisted, ever since she claimed to have noticed my weight loss, that she was the sister who had to be perfect, not me, and I should give up trying. "This is my territory," my sister said, as if she were the only person in the family with a body, or a body that required attention. Or perhaps I should say that she thought she was the only person in the family whose body counted for all of her virtues and attributes and that she thought she was judged first and foremost for the condition of her body and that no other person shouldered this burden. "Is this what you want?" she asked me several times, perhaps every night, when she came home from her dance classes to find herself famished and me resolute in my discipline. "Do you want to make your body your only instrument?"

That summer my sister took our mother by the shoulders and screamed, "So prove to me I'm nuts. Prove it to me and be done with it!" She found our father, eventually, and made an appointment for all of us at the pediatrician's. "No one needs to prove to me I'm stupid," she said, when our mother and I told her our father would never show up, but he did. The doctor may have been more concerned about my father's finances, or lack of them, than he was about my weight, but he made an appointment for me any way at the special clinic. He instructed my mother that I was not to miss any appointments. "Yeah, I'm crazy, and I'm stupid," my sister said when we got back from the doctor and each time we got back from an appointment. "I should have been a secretary," my sister said, each time she got us to another appointment, another weigh-in, and another meeting with the nutritionist, the social worker, the internist, and the psychiatrist. "Always knew I'd be good as a secretary, even if everyone thinks I'm too stupid to do anything. I'd make a lot more money if I were a secretary. Plus I'd be able to eat ice cream more often," she said, but then she put her hand to her mouth and remembered that she wasn't supposed to talk about food—not in the least. Those were the instructions from every expert we were forced to meet with.

She also wasn't supposed to talk about weight either, but when I asked her if being on television really did add five pounds to your appearance, she was quick to answer. "Do you really think those five pounds on camera are going to make a difference? That your face is going to look swollen or your ankles are going to be fat or that someone is going to be measuring your waist to see the inches you've added? Do you know what really matters? It matters what mood someone is in—the director's, the ballet master's, the choreographer's, the cameraman's—that's what really matters. Their own little dramas, their baroque little worlds and attitudes; that's what matters. They're so busy looking at themselves, they have no idea what you look like. They can barely see past their own toes; they're not going to know if you're 100 pounds, or 95, or 105. Trust me. Most of them are like me, they can barely count, so how could it matter? Listen, do you want to have kids? Do you want to have a life? Do you want to get married and have hobbies, and a decent apartment, or maybe even a house? Your own house without roommates? And your own car? Don't you want anything that anybody else likes?"

The marrow of my sister's stupidity is her smallness. She thinks small, in averages, of the lowest common denominator, of what appeals to the masses, and of what everyone might agree to. She does not realize the range of numbers and opinions possible in those categories; so she always comes to the same conclusion: material goods. They are her last refuge. Or, to be fair, I should note that she didn't have any of those goods. Perhaps that is why she was so prone to putting everything in those terms: what she lacked versus what everybody else had. Ownership of any one of these items automatically pushed you ahead in success and status. My sister slept on a couch, even in her own apartment. She wore other people's clothes and lived off other people's food, gas, and utilities. She borrowed money without paying it back. Hers was an ad hoc existence; everything was mooched or chiseled. It was beyond her vocabulary, fiscal or otherwise, to conceive of other needs, a more substantive type of permanence. But I had what I wanted with anorexia. I was becoming what I wanted—what everybody else was finally. I was becoming a body.

The problem was that you have to be able to lose your body, to truly understand it. Or your mind has to lose its grip on your body if you want to know what's truly in it. The sequence of hormones that fire or not, the cascade of synapses switching on or off, the production of endorphins: these work without you, no matter how much you try to control them. As I lost that weight and as I lost more and was unable to gain it back in a manner sufficient to liking of the doctors and various therapists, I realized that my mind had so little to do with these processes. My endocrine system was nothing more than a set of dominoes, and I was curious to watch them fall or right themselves, perhaps, straightening themselves up as if they were taking time backward. My body had tried adolescence, had dipped its proverbial toes into adulthood, and found those stages sorely lacking, in love, in justice, and in the kind of logic in which I had been schooled. My mind could tackle math and science, the cold and standoffish abstractions, but that did not matter when it was the body that ruled—the body that determined. I could count calories, intake, outgo, and even the weight of my excrement, but adjusting these amounts—those I could adjust—was ultimately irrelevant. My body would do as it willed, whatever gratified it. All I could do was watch and listen.

And this is what I heard: the hollow tang of my fingertips on my ribs, counting individual bones visible in the mirror. I heard the slush, the conclusion of water, as I gulped it down to fill out my stomach. I heard my lips cracking when I became dehydrated and tasted the blood that filled out the skin there. I heard myself expel air, digestive gases, just before I weighed myself each morning, afternoon, or evening. I was getting rid of the supposed 24 extra ounces each person carries around in gas, although that number has been disputed. What mattered was that my body wanted to be rid of it; my body told me how to bend over, in that touch-your-toes position, to accomplish this. I was released from my intellect in my anorexia, and I became something else entirely, without the concerns that had seemingly blocked me from what I wanted, whether it was success as a musician, a place beside Jasmine, or winning, earning, or holding onto the respect I craved from my peers.

With anorexia, I would no longer be haunted by such lofty goals as decency, fairness, all for one and one for all, what being in a band meant, camaraderie, and decisions that you stick to because you made them together. With anorexia I was going to be like all the other girls, all the women, and all the people I had met since I lobbed onto Jack and Nicky; I would be like all the people who tried to lob onto them, like Jack and Nicky themselves, and anyone who called themselves an artist though they had neither the inspiration nor the talent. I was going to be like those people who made us promises; how they bragged of expertise and access but could not bring themselves to demonstrate their so-called acumen in the music business. I was going to be like all the people who wanted, ached for, and coveted a place among the stars ascendant, and all they had to do was survive—or survive their longing, keep it secret and silent. Because going public would blow their cover and ruin their personas. All their lives had been about longing— for love, for attention, and for moments in the spotlights that they could string together into a kind of permanent daylight, and then they'd be safe from the darkness. They were going to survive by hitching themselves to a Jack or a Nicky but not someone like me—never like me. I was too small physically, too emotional, too green, or too transparent. Like these people all I had to do was survive with anorexia or through it: survive another month, another day, another minute. This would be a bedazzling, mesmerizing performance, with such fire and passion people would be afraid to watch and yet, so grotesque and curious they wouldn't be able to ignore it. If sidling up to Jack and Nicky, rubbing against Jasmine, was like trying to get hold of a rocket, I was the star that was falling, falling—a meteor in its last iteration. Both seem to last forever, and yet it is only the relative nature of time and its distortions that make a star and a meteor appear equal in strength and endurance.

CHAPTER 14

"YOU SHOULD HAVE CALLED ME EARLIER," the conservator said. But I hated calling him. I hated asking him for anything. His name was Greg Onderdonk, and I knew him only through the telephone; we'd spoken a few times while I was still in New York. I asked before I made this trip if I could meet him in Los Angeles, but he said no. He was under Barb's strict instructions to have nothing to do with me, I assumed. It was a safe assumption, considering how she usually felt about me.

"You should have noticed the withdrawals earlier," I said back to him.

"I did," he said, and then I thought I could hear him swallowing or maybe licking his lips, like he had been getting ready to admit something difficult—he was sorry, he'd fallen down on the job—but decided against it. "Listen. I think she was bilked by one of her nurses before hospice," he said. "They take advantage sometimes."

"Then why didn't you do anything about it?" I asked.

"Well," he said, probably in preparation for another thorny truth he was about to gift me with, "it's difficult. Given her state. She'd have to fill out a police report and given her state…."

"But that's why she hired you, isn't it?" I was on the verge of going heroic, and Barb would have hated it. She didn't want me for an advocate—she didn't want me for anything. I under-stood that. But I thought she'd make an exception when it came to her money.

"Yes, but it's not that simple," he insisted. "You—"

"You just tell the cops, okay? They think she's being black-mailed or something."

"I'll get on it," he said, and hung up, like he was showing me how prompt and dedicated he was. I was not reassured.

"Hey," I said, by way of greeting him a second time when I called back. I gave him the numbers for the Simpson and w-y-r-e-c-k-a's song and dance act. "Do you have any idea what's been going on around here?" I asked, and I knew I was being indignant, but how could he have not seen any of the Eyewit-ness-we're-watching-when-you're-not-so-you-don't-have-to, action-360-degrees-of-coverage-for-all-the-angles-all-the-time-and-when-you-need-it-news broadcasts of the house, the doorstep, the driveway, the neighborhood that he was loathe to visit and probably should, though the cameras and reporters might have scared him off. Everyone wants to help, and everyone's a coward.

"The hospice called," he said. "They were concerned."

"And you aren't?"

"I don't know if you understand what it is I do," Mr. Onderdonk said. "I work with families in crisis. I—"

"What makes you think my family is in crisis?" I asked, and since I am no actress, I assumed Greg Onderdonk could understand my sarcasm. "My family's just fine, thank you; I mean, my husband and daughter, they're in New York, every-thing's great there. Here, there's only the two of us, me and my sister; the rest of the family is gone, dead, buried; that crisis is finished, you missed it. So there's no family here; no family, no crisis. Except for the world's crises. Over Jasmine, this whole Jasmine thing. Can't you do anything about that?"

"Well—"

"Well excuse me for thinking so," I said, and I wish I could have fired him, but he was not my conservator to fire. Only my sister could have done that, but she was in no state to fire anyone. Perhaps he could have fired himself, but I didn't think he was honest enough to do it. He probably wouldn't get paid until once Barb's estate was settled—not until she was dead. So he was going to hang on.

"But maybe you could come up here and act as my sister's representative. You are her representative, right?"

I think I heard Greg Onderdonk breathing over the phone.

"Maybe you could give a statement to the press, tell them to leave, tell them to leave us alone? And talk to our neighbors, and tell them we're sorry, we've lost control of events, but you're going to fix it. You're going to fix it with the cops and get rid of this circus."

"Miss," he said, and I knew this was a bad sign; when someone calls you "Miss," they're reminding you of your place in the world, and how determined they are that you do not escape from it. "This is my business. I could tell you stories—"

But I didn't want to hear his stories. I was already in the midst of one I'd probably spend the rest of my life telling. I still don't know where to start; there were so many beginnings of the end for my sister. This had to have been the beginning of the end of some part of it—maybe all the money she had spent years saving for reasons that had come to seem useless? Of all those beginnings, I still can't say what must have been the worst: when she met the people she loved or when she realized they could not love her back? Was it when she began to hate them and they could not be bothered with her? When she took her first drink with those people, and she liked it? Or the moment anorexia let itself loose through her system, and she began starving herself?

Anorexia may have been worse than the cancer diagnosis for Helen, because she had to live with anorexia and see it through to the end. As for the denouement of the cancer diagnosis, Helen always knew she wasn't going to be there. She wasn't going to have to witness it. Barbara's cancer was real enough to our mother, but she knew she could run away from it. I thought of the burn you get in your eyes from looking directly into the spotlights, the first few times you are up on stage. You think you can close your eyes and those black, flashing spots will disappear, but you still see them. You see the entire machinery of the eye as if it were startled by the light; you see the curving of the retina and the connection of the optic nerve, like a stem pulled up and out of its roots. You see the pulse of your blood and the black spots vibrating. Helen knew that for her the burn would eventually heal, or she'd become numb to it. She did not have to consider how those black spots consume whatever was originally there in your vision. For her the cancer was a bit theoretical, and whatever abyss it would open was going to be after her time. She needn't worry about its implications.

"Now I said I would contact the police, and I will. The rest is just noise—"

"You think Barbara can't hear all that noise?" I asked. "They say she can hear everything; you know—the television, the people outside, the traffic, the neighbors."

"Yes, I know," he said, though rather noncommittedly. "Now you tell her I'm going to take care of it. I'll be in touch," he said and hung up on me a second time. I thought of calling him again, but rage can be so exhausting. Greg Onderdonk must have been counting on that.

IN THE BEDROOM, I WAS SO TIRED, I wanted to get in bed with Barb, like when we were kids. But I knew it wouldn't fly. When we were kids and school was off for the day, we'd get into the bed as soon as our parents got out of it, and we'd stay there all morning, watching cartoons or reruns. In the afternoon, when the shows were over, we'd jump on the bed like it was a trampoline until Helen told us to stop. She was always afraid we would break the bed frame. On Saturdays I was at ballet class and Barb was in some gifted enrichment program, so on Sunday we'd try to reconvene, but Irv's sports were on television.

When Barb had anorexia, the object was to keep her out of the bed. Otherwise she would have laid down and died. The starvation was secondary. It was merely a method. Lying down and dying was what she really wanted. So the object became to keep her occupied. Keep her upright in a chair or standing or kneeling in some way, scrubbing floors or doing some gardening. We had a vegetable garden that summer, the only one we ever had; the doctor said Barb's activities should have nothing to do with food, but we had a strip of soil and not enough to do during all those waking hours, so we promised we really didn't intend to eat the stuff we grew. So we planted pumpkins, beets, and green and yellow zucchini. We thought we could give them to friends. We did puzzles and played cards; I was awful at cards; so I built card houses while Helen and Barb played gin. I was a little better at Monopoly and board games we had as kids. Helen did everything she could to make the Monopoly games epic. She bought more play money at the store and added it to the bank; sometimes we'd have two bankers to see which one would fail first. Or she'd pay us to play more than one piece, and we'd be playing against ourselves. I could play Monopoly at least; I mean, I knew the rules. But the games would be so confusing I could never tell who really won. There never seemed to be a single jackpot to grab, and, in the end, even the winner was exhausted.

Ionie knew how to keep herself busy with the dust rags. She ran them over the window sills, the lamps and the dresser, the dials of the television. Maria was stationed at the sliding glass window that opened onto the patio, monitoring the flow of visitors. She must have read my face when I came in, because she put her hands up in front of the glass, like she was saying, "stop" for an instant. I was tempted to have her send them all home, though I didn't see what that would have accomplished for anyone.

"You can keep them coming," I said as I walked past her.

"It's getting late," Maria said.

"What does Barb want to do?" I asked the room. I sat on the edge of the bed at Barb's feet and saw that her eyes were open. Then she yawned, but morphine makes people do that, I'd learned. Her eyes were still open afterward. "What do you want to do?" I asked her directly.

"She wants to know, were you on the telephone about Jasmine?" Ionie said, in that way of hers. It was an unnecessary remark, because by now Ionie knew everything there was to know about Barb and about Jasmine; that everything had been about Jasmine long before Ionie ever got here, and it would be about Jasmine for a long time coming. Barb told us, when she had anorexia, that she was not sick over Jasmine, and that one thing might have made anorexia worse than this cancer.

Because cancer doesn't have one singular cause you can just cut out or stopper up, and anorexia did; we could see it. Helen and I would have banned Jasmine from Earth if we could have. We would have made Jasmine illegal. But we couldn't.

"Jasmine," Barb said. The name could have randomly spilled out of her mouth, or it could have been in her throat at her tonsils for hours waiting to be pronounced. I could not tell.

"No, no Jasmine today," I said, and it felt like a declaration as I said it, if not an enthusiastic one. I was resigned to saying it and to validating the presence of Jasmine in Barb's mind for another day.

"What do you mean, no Jasmine?" Barb asked, and I thought I saw her shoulders tense, like she was trying to lift herself off the pillow and work herself into a fit.

"She's not here," I said. "Remember?"

The shoulders relaxed; or at least they let go of whatever momentum they had worked up. Barb fell back into the pillow in a slight, almost invisible way.

"She means the telephone call," Ionie explained. "You were on the telephone about Jasmine?"

"No," I said. "Not really." Barb was yawning again. "I was talking to the conservator," I said to Barb directly. "He's going to take care of some more things around here."

I thought I saw Barb nod, although that could have been wishful thinking; that's another thing that happens—to the living, that is, as they watch over someone who's dying. They intuit, they make stuff up; they make assumptions or decisions that aren't theirs to make. They tell themselves stories about what the dying are thinking. The hospice pamphlets instructed that the dying are thinking. The dying are very much alive until the very end.

And that was another thing that made anorexia worse than cancer; we didn't know what was going to happen. We didn't know whether Barb was going to die or whether she was going to come out on some other end. We didn't know whether she'd be forever changed, like disabled or have a different personality. We couldn't tell what she was thinking, whether she was planning to outsmart us somehow. She could run to the bathroom and throw up everything we put inside her. She could throw out her food when we weren't looking or pop some kind of laxative or a diuretic if we turned our backs for a minute. How did she get the pills? Was someone on the inside of the clinic helping her? We didn't know. We knew only that she wasn't to be trusted about anything coming into or going out of her system. She still operated under her own power with anorexia, and that is what made it worse.

Anorexia was worse than cancer, I decided that afternoon, because we knew exactly what Barb was trying to do. She hadn't decided to get cancer, of course; and she hadn't decided to get anorexia either. But cancer seems so much more aimless than anorexia. It's unfair and random. Anorexia at least gave us something to watch out for. Anorexia was trying to make her disappear; so we had to watch her to keep her visible. We had to watch her as she tried to make herself microscopic; we had to make sure she remained life-sized, an adult and not a child, not even a teenager; and we had to make sure she couldn't fall into the background and be consumed by the bed and bed sheets, making her impossible to find in the morning. The doctors told us that anorexia was a lot like alcoholism; it wasn't something that could be cured. It would always be there, to a degree, a chronic condition. Barb would have to learn to live with it and control it; we'd all have to learn how to control it or it would control her.

"He's going to take care of what?" Ionie said, and she must have felt threatened: she was still the head nurse, even if she was supervising only Maria.

"What he's supposed to be taking care of," I said. I had thought of telling Ionie directly, but the less she knew, the better for all of us.

"I told everyone to go home, come back tomorrow," Maria announced; I thought of something else that made anorexia worse than cancer—that no one visited. No one. No one knew what was happening or perhaps no one cared, or it might have been that Barb's so-called friends knew and cared but only because they thought she was getting what she deserved. That was what Barb said or theorized; we told her that was nuts, but Barb was insistent. She said that her friends were so eager to erase her that they couldn't wait around long enough for her to finish the job. Then don't play into their hands, I argued, but this was when Barb was down to 80 pounds, and she had prac-tically forfeited control over her body. The doctors warned that her body would soon belong to the disease, and the dis-ease could rush in and take a deeper bite, or it could slowly feed, like a mosquito. Anorexia would make a mockery of her attempts at control, they said. She'd get the exact opposite of what she wanted.

That she wanted anorexia—or the doctors tried to make us believe that—was another thing that made anorexia worse than cancer. There was nothing to want about it. Maria was pulling on a pair of surgical gloves, telling Ionie to get a pair. It was time to check Barb's pain patch, the port in her chest, the diaper, and the towel underneath it. It was almost time for the shift change, and the day shift had to leave the patient better than they had found her in the morning. At least with cancer, this was possible. With anorexia, it was always the same thing, and it was always invisible.

Barb shut her eyes and let Maria and Ionie raise her into a sitting position. She let them check under her pajamas and prod at her openings. She let them lower her back onto the pillow and mattress once they were satisfied there were no blockages, no leaks or blisters, and no sores nor other signs of friction; and no signs of approaching death by accident or by something unanticipated, something that they could be blamed for—but I tried not to think of it that way. It was another way cancer was better. With anorexia, we had nothing visible to check for, and if we missed something—if Barbara died—it would be on us, and only us. There were no nurses or home health aides to take care of Barbara; there were only doctors, distant and cryptic. They told us nothing, except what to be scared of: all of the things we could not see—the process of her body digesting itself.

We knew if we did not keep watching her, and that if she was not indeed processing the food we gave her, that her hunger would move to her heart muscle like it was a big block of candy, impenetrable like a jawbreaker or a large lollipop. And there were forces—we did not know them beyond being forces—that took quiet licks of her heart muscle, a slow savoring of a layer of sugar, one layer after another, until it felt confident enough about taking a bite, chewing what was left into nothingness. But we could not imagine how this would have appeared on the outside, on her skin, her hair, and the eyebrows and eyelashes that occasionally threatened to fall out. We did not know whether she was plucking them out, like a kind of punishment, or whether it was a natural response to the starvation.

Ionie filled out Barb's chart for the next shift. She had to ask Maria whether all of the protocols had been met before she could check them off. Together they went through all of the tasks that had to be performed and updated so that Barb would not die of unintended consequences: infection, sepsis, or less than sterile circumstances. Then Barb's death would be on them, which was another thing that made cancer better than anorexia. This predictability and guarantee of result if certain actions were taken. We could not see the germs, microbes, bacteria, and viruses that threatened to take Barb down a side path to her end. But we knew what to do to keep them away from her so she'd be comfortable in her final days. So that as she was dying, she would not be distracted by some nuisance on her skin or pain unrelated to the tumors; she could concentrate on the lack of oxygen to her lungs or blood to her heart. So we'd all know the cause without a doubt: that it wasn't some fault in the care she received or the treatment she withstood and that it had taken her too soon.

We would all be serene in knowing she was taken by something bigger than ourselves. So much better than dying from anorexia, which had started as something so petty, even ordinary; something that everyone must go through at some time: disappointment and a broken heart. These things are not supposed to be fatal; certainly, they weren't for me, or I'd be dead a thousand times over. More dead than Barb could have ever been, even now. And then there is the size of anorexia, how small it is in the early stages, a sickness you should be able to cut off before it bores a hole through the psyche and through the protective fat. Cancers can take years to make themselves known in the form of tumors, doctors have told us. It can't be caught early; that does nothing for chances of survival, they said. It's all a myth, cancer is. Anorexia is a fact, like gravity, talent, or the public's taste at any given moment. It all depends on what you do with it.

Barb was asleep. She'd be in and out of consciousness for the night. Anorexia was worse because Barb did not sleep at night. She was up, wandering through the house, and we were following her, from her room to the bathroom, to the living room where she might watch television—but we had to be careful. The TV could lull us into relaxing, into complacency and the sleep of the complacent. This would give Barb a chance to take off for the toilet and vomit. Or she might get on the scale and bend over with her ass in the air, where she could force farts out, or she might try to pull her feces out, which was something she tried, we were told by the anorexia clinic. But the staff there were able to stop her because she was so weak, and they knew what she was doing; they'd seen other girls do it. It was easy for them to spot. They wrapped her hands up in tape and gauze, until she'd claw it off. Then we—Helen and me, and sometimes Irv—would be at a loss; so we had to watch her in shifts, like the nurses do now. We could not take our eyes off her for a second.

Barb did make it easier for us in one way, though, because she talked. Or anorexia talked. It had an answer for everything. We asked her why she was doing this to herself, and anorexia said she was doing nothing. We asked her how she felt, and anorexia said she felt nothing. Irv asked her if she knew what she was doing to Helen. I asked it, too, over and over again. Anorexia said she wasn't doing anything. She wasn't sleeping, playing music, or running around with a bad element. She wasn't exercising, burning calories, or counting them. She wasn't exhausting herself. She wasn't eating. When Irv asked her a second time, she said she wasn't doing anything she couldn't stop doing. I thought this was a way in.

"So you're not doing it, your body's doing it," I said.

"Are you saying I have no control over my body?" she accused.

"No. No. That's not what I'm saying. I'm saying that people can't help it when they're sick, but they've got to listen to the doctor, take their medicine, follow the instructions."

"You're saying I don't know what I'm doing," she said.

"No," I said. "Stop putting words in my mouth."

"I don't put anything in anybody's mouth, not even my own. Isn't that the problem?"

"I don't know what the problem is," I admitted.

"If you don't know what the problem is, why are you even talking about it?" Barbara said, and her voice jumped, scaled the walls, and swung from the ceiling, like it had been caged for years and only now was getting the fresh air it needed. "You're saying I can't take care of myself, that I'm just some immature kid who'll never grow up, like you have?"

"No, I—"

"You think because you moved away and have your career and your apartment and a whole bunch of new friends we've never seen and probably never will that you're better than me, that you can tell me how to live and what I should do because you know everything."

"Uncle! Uncle!" I said, or I believe I did, because I said it so many times when Barb had anorexia, to get her to stop talking, because the talking was sometimes worse than anorexia. Helen was able to explain to Barb that I was trying to speak her language—logic, like math or science—but I didn't have the ability that she did. Helen told her that everyone, me included, wanted her to listen to the doctor because she had to get stronger, better, to go to college in the fall, and that she and Irv would make sure she got her own place, an apartment, if she could get herself back into the swing of school and studying again.

This is what we had to go through, Irv, Helen, Barb and me, and then the disease would start talking again. We knew it was the disease because of what it said. The disease said Barb wasn't sick; it said she had never been sick. She was experimenting; weight loss, hair loss, insomnia, and the smell were all side effects. If she starved herself more, perhaps those side effects would disappear. If she could control what went into her body, she could control what came off it and what came out of it: everything. She wanted to measure her impact on the economy and the environment, and she wanted that impact to be nothing.

"Endometriosis," she said. "Really thin people get it. Why don't you have it?"

"I don't know, and no thanks, whatever it is," I said.

"It's when you menstruate, but you don't, because the menstrual tissue is all over your body. There's no place for the blood to go. It stays inside of you."

"That sounds awful," I said.

"Does it," she said flatly. "Isn't it worse to leave your shit everywhere and your skin and your hair and all your waste, your tampons and blood and kids with diapers—"

"Okay, I get it," I said. "I actually don't get it, but okay."

"Endometriosis. That's what's going to solve all the problems."

"That's not going to solve anything, and I don't even know what it is," I said.

"Then how can you even talk about it?" she asked.

"Because I just know it's not going to solve your problems. It's not going to make you better or get you into college and all that."

"So all I have to do is go to college, and I'll be better? This will be over, and you can all go back to whatever you were doing before that was so important?" she asked, and I remember the size of her eyes as her voice rose, like she had discovered something explosive and knew how she could light it, set it off, and even add gasoline, burning herself in the process. "Do you think I'm faking so I don't have to go to college? If I don't go to college, you can't go back to New York and your dancing, your own apartment. Do you think I'm faking so that I can ruin your career—your dreams—because I ruined mine? Do you think I'm faking so I can bring everyone down to my level? Or maybe you think I'm faking so I don't have to do any more homework."

"No," I said. I had to admit it: I was stunned by the scope and ferocity of her ranting. "I never said you were faking."

"No, you didn't. But you might as well have said that. You might as well. Because I wasn't talking about college or your little career. I was talking about endometriosis, and you brought up college and getting better. Like that's the only way to get better, is to go to college. Like that's the only thing I was ever meant to do, go to college, be a good little girl and go to college."

"What I said was," I began, and I began this way so I would slow down, not sail into a full course scream like she was doing, "Getting another disease, endometri-whatever-it-is, isn't going to help you. It isn't going to make you better, so you can... get on with your life. Instead of sitting here and arguing with me, or Mom and Dad, all the time."

"Is that why I have to go to college—so you guys don't have to talk to me? So you don't have to fight with me? Well at least someone's finally admitted it. Just shuffle me along to the next grade, right? Keep me busy so I don't get into any more trouble?"

"You have to go to college because you're smart," I said, although I knew immediately it came out the wrong way, with a finality that was threatening.

"And you get to be an artist because you're stupid," she said. She seemed stunned by what she had said, though a little pleased with herself. Like she didn't know she had the ability to say things like that. "That's right," she said. "I said it."

"I never said I was smart like you," I reminded her.

"So if I'm so smart, how come I can't do what I want to do? How come you get to do what you want to do? How come I have to go to college, stay clean and healthy, while you get to wreck your body and you don't even know what endometriosis is—you could be having the symptoms right now, and you wouldn't even know it? You'd think it was a muscle cramp, something normal, something you'd expect, you wouldn't pay any attention to it. You don't have the slightest idea about what's going on in your body right now or when you're dancing; you don't know the difference between the body in exertion and the body at rest—you know nothing, and you're the one who gets to be an artist because you're stupid. I have to suffer because I'm the smart one. I'm going to college, and I can't do anything else."

"You can do anything you want," I said, because she had beaten me to a bloody pulp; she had dragged me down and finished me off. I wanted to tear my hair and eyes out but I couldn't, of course. She was the sick one. She was going to make us all sick before she was finished. There was always the possibility, though, that this was the disease talking again: I had to remind myself, so that she wouldn't think we had given up on her. But I wanted to give up. I wanted to give up so many times then. That's what made anorexia worse and cancer better; with cancer, we had already given up from the beginning.

Anorexia was worse because of conversations I didn't tell my mother about. Conversations when Barb would interrogate me about exactly how I got to be a dancer: how burning was my desire, what was my motivation, and what did I expect to get out of it? It didn't matter what my answers were, because she said they were too simple. No one becomes an artist because they enjoy making art, she said. Artists have to make art. It is their responsibility and their destiny. "It's not fair," was how she would usually begin, because it wasn't fair that I just fell into dancing and that I took my career for granted. Nothing was fair: I knew so much more about anorexia, but she had anorexia when someone like me was more likely to get it. It wasn't fair that I could talk about anorexia when she was the one experiencing it.

"I bet those dancers are more dedicated than you are," she said.

"Which dancers?"

"The ones with anorexia," she said. "They believe in what they're doing. You're copying."

"I'm not copying anyone," I said.

"But you want to copy me," she said.

"I don't want anorexia," I said. "They throw you out if they find out you have it."

"I knew it," she said. "You don't know anything. Maybe you've seen a few girls with it, but you don't know anything."

"I know what it looks like, when it's next to me at the *barre*, at the costume fittings. It's awful."

"It's enlightening," she said.

"No, it's not," I said. "It's a dead end. Think of all the time and effort that gets wasted because some girl gets it. All the years she practiced, all the auditions she went on, all those lessons. You get anorexia, and it's career ending. "

"You don't know anything," she said. "You're trying to crowd me out of my own disease. But you can't do that. This is my possession. This is my disease," she said, although it might have been anorexia stepping in for her voice, which was flying, diving, and bouncing off the walls like the air was no longer good enough for it. Her voice needed something more—to knock down walls and destroy the ceiling. "Why are you trying to take it away from me, the only thing that's ever been mine? The only thing that makes me different, that makes me special, because otherwise I'm just like everybody else, with nothing to offer, just another fan who can only take and take and take?"

"Okay," I said.

"Do you know how hard it is when no one notices you, but you notice them? When you've spent your life noticing other people, and they don't see you because they think you're average or boring or ordinary, compared to whoever they're hot for or in love with or the person who can do the most for them?"

"Okay," I said. "I get it." Because I did get it. Because there was always a chance that I might not be noticed, that I'd be in the *corps* forever, that all my years of training and all the practice and work would amount to nothing. When Barb had anorexia I was young enough to think that I'd beat the odds. I would rise above. My talent and determination would make me. I was going to be a soloist in a few years, then a principal dancer. I would be a prima ballerina because that is what you went for; it was the whole point of being in a company. But there was always that chance that it wouldn't work out, that I'd burn out, be passed over, get pregnant, or get injured—I couldn't imagine anything worse than getting injured, other than being ignored. I did not want to entertain that scenario, but Barb forced me. She might even have planted a seed on that day.

"No, you don't," she said, "because if you did, you wouldn't be a dancer. You wouldn't make the effort. Because you know there's no way to get noticed when there's always somebody out there ahead of you, someone who's got connections or is beautiful or knows where to get the drugs you want, the liquor you can't buy because you're too young."

"This isn't helping," I said, because I remember that as being something Helen would say when we were children. If we had a fit about not getting what we wanted—an ice cream or in my case, a dress I wanted, or a toy and we were somewhere out in public.

"I don't care if it's not helping," Barb went on. "Who's it supposed to help? Me? You? You always have to be the center of everything."

"Okay," I said. I screamed it. I admit it. I was trying to keep up with her, but I snapped. "You can be Barb, the anorexic. Great! We'll put it on your tombstone for you. All right?"

That shut her up for a while. And I felt like I had won. That was the thing about anorexia: I was always angry at Barb. Or if I wasn't angry, she'd make me angry. I was furious with her that entire summer. I learned how not to be angry at her, but it took years or maybe my marriage and the birth of my daughter. I had to learn that it didn't matter whether she thought everything I knew or could find out was stupid, a lie, and it didn't matter that I couldn't defend myself. I had to learn that while she was brilliant, she did not know anything about my life, and I told her so: she knew nothing about paying bills, living on a budget, and the discipline that was required to keep my place in the company even though it did not pay my bills and actually busted my budget. She did not know anything about the sacrifices I was making or the sacrifices of all the people in the company.

"My art is original," she said. "It's relevant. It's engaged."

"Okay," I said.

"I'm not part of the problem, like you are," she said. "I'm not doing the same thing over and over that hasn't worked. I'm not doing the safe thing that never got anyone in trouble. I'm trying to make a difference. I'm trying to change things. You're just going along with whatever's happened before."

"Yep," I said, though I knew such a quick answer might not fool her into thinking I was agreeing with everything she said.

"Those ballerina stories, where do they come from? Women as princesses, women as swans, women as naïve country maidens: do you know where that crap comes from? It comes from the patriarchy. Do you know what you're doing when you dance those parts? You're perpetuating the worst kind of patriarchal, misogynic, regressive stereotypes of women. You're keeping them alive to poison another generation. You're making it harder for all the other women who are trying to make it in this world. You're part of the problem."

"Okay," I said.

"Real art changes things. That's why real artists are remembered," she said.

"You're right," I said.

She was stunned. "Do you think you're going to be remembered with what you do?"

"I don't know," I said. "I haven't gotten that far. Maybe. If I'm lucky."

"Then what are you doing it for?"

I think the problem with my answer that day was that it came too easily to me. If I had struggled with it, Barb might have believed that I was being honest. But I knew why I was dancing. I had been dancing since I was six years old, and I had made it into the *corps* at a New York City company. I was in my third year, and three, four, five, ten years in the *corps* did not seem unreasonable to me. Nothing about dance seemed unreasonable to me. "It's a way of life for me, dancing," I said. "And that's about all the art I can handle."

"That's too comfortable," Barb declared, but she was only revving up. Once she launched that voice, there'd be no holding back. "That's cowardly," she said. "And lazy. So vague, like you're afraid of really saying something, standing for something. That's empty and easy. I'm talking about making an impact, changing the way people think and feel. How they feel about art, about girls making it, how they treat people. I'm talking about changing the way people live."

"I'm too wrapped up in figuring out my own life to do that," I said. Because that's how I felt about it then if not now. Because that's how I wanted to feel. I was strong. I was a quick learner. I was generous in my dancing—occasionally. That is what people said about me. I had been dancing since I was six years old because all the girls in the neighborhood took dancing lessons. They dropped out but I stayed. I stayed because I couldn't do anything else as well. I couldn't play sports, flirt with boys, or do schoolwork that well, but I could dance. And

Barb knew this. I couldn't understand why she needed so desperately to fight with me about it.

"Then you're a sellout. You just do what they tell you to and smile and collect a paycheck," she said. "You look like you're making art, but you're only making more of the same— what everyone thinks they want, what's expected—and when you burn out no one's going to think twice about you. No one's going to remember your so-called art. Jasmine: people are going to remember her. And Jack and Nicky. Not me, though. They took me down to your level. You're just like me now; how do you feel about that? You're nothing...."

I knew she didn't mean all this. Or maybe she only meant some of it. The parts about Jasmine, Jaqueline, and Nicole: they were going to be famous and rich, too. She wasn't jealous of them. It was much worse. Their fame and riches were erasing her, she said. Did they know they were doing this? Did they care? That didn't matter. The job was practically finished; she was helping them accomplish it. I wanted to make her realize what she was doing. But I couldn't, because she was jealous of me. Jealousy must be more insidious than erasing someone. It must be more insidious than anorexia. Because that jealously is what took over every conversation we had that summer. Jealousy is why I couldn't get through to her.

"Okay, so I'm nothing, okay?" I wanted to use her logic— or anorexia's logic—against her. "I'm nothing, I admit it, and we can be nothing together. Is that what you want? I can stay here with you forever, and we'll be nothing together. We'll live here and be mad and bitter and scare all the neighborhood children, and then you won't have to worry about what I'm doing, because I'll do whatever you tell me to."

"So you can blame everything on me?" she said. "That's what you really want to do. You're using my anorexia as an excuse not to—not to—not to—"

"Not to do what?" I said, and I was tempted to tell her what I had given up staying with her that summer. But I knew not to do that. I knew that whatever sacrifice I was making to be with her that summer, it had nothing on whatever she had lost. My dancing and the ideas I tried to attach to it weren't real to her. I couldn't tell her that simply doing the thing, the steps, the practice, and the constant, incessant need for movement, was the point of my dancing. Because I made my art by testing my limits. I knew what I was and who I was. I had been told who and what I was for so long: by my parents, the teachers I had all through school, the choreographers who had turned me down for parts, and even the ballet mistress. I was too strict with myself on stage; I was someone who needed to work until dance was second nature to me. My first nature, my natural self, wasn't quite ready for the roles I aspired to. I had to prove my toughness.

"I'm not going to let you destroy me," I said. "I've got enough problems already."

"This isn't about you and your problems," she said.

"I know that," I said. "Do you?"

This is what made anorexia worse, because cancer was all about Barbara. How could it not be, with her lying in bed, whipped by disease, and made helpless by narcotics? The problem with anorexia is it didn't do enough to Barbara. It didn't do enough to us, the rest of the nuclear family, and we continued with our lives while hers was ending. The world had stopped spinning for Barbara. Whatever happened between her and Jasmine, between her and Jacqueline and Nicole, had punched her in the gut, ripped out her insides, made her look at herself in a way she couldn't handle, or didn't want to. I could never say, and I still can't, because she never would tell me when I asked her about it. She never could make it real for me, I guess. We were sisters who could not get through to each other.

It was a long time ago Barb and I had this conversation, the one that convinced me how different we were; or perhaps that's what I wanted to take away from the conversation, because I didn't want to end up like that. I didn't want to end up at the end of my rope before I had a chance to realize how long or short my rope was. Whenever something went wrong in my career—and there was a lot that went wrong—I tried not to think of this conversation. I tried not to think I had let any of the doubt or any of her predictions crawl inside of me and fester. Yet by not thinking about the doubt and all the things she said; all the things that my teachers and my parents had said to and about me; and all the things the ballet mistress, choreographer, or the other dancers had said about me; by pushing these things out of my mind and telling myself I could overcome the shredding of my ligaments, the tears in my tendons, all the sexual harassers, serial philanderers, and all the other obstacles I had come up against and finally had to quit, admit that I had lost, I was burned out and squashed like a bug; I had been beat at my own game. By not considering this conversation that I had indeed remembered perfectly (and that Barb had gotten under my skin like no one else did) is what made anorexia so much worse than cancer, worse than our parents' divorce, worse than my injuries, worse than anything I could or ever would know for myself. I had spent a lifetime trying to prove I was at least equal to my sister in what I could feel, think, or experience, but anorexia said no. I could never be. At least cancer did not say this.

CHAPTER 15

MAGIC IS MISDIRECTION. Hollywood magic, however, is magnification. Only those who can withstand magnification get to be famous. Or only those whose ability to misdirect, so that the magnification does not expose their flaws, get to be famous. I was never good at misdirection, only digression and disappearance, all the wrong methods. Because the music business is all Hollywood. Or the music business as it was presented to me is, as it rejected me. The music business does not want to admit this. Or the music business as I thought it was, when I was an aspiring musician, won't cop to this. The music business believes it is above Hollywood. But it is all Hollywood in all of its barbarous glory. You might be able to take the music business out of Hollywood: Jasmine did with the help of The Regent. Jack, Nicky, and any number of people I never knew and never wished to know did. But you can't take Hollywood out of the music business. That would make it too easy for people like me to get a foothold in it. That would wipe out the exclusivity and all its cachet.

If you looked too closely at Jasmine, in full magnification, you might see what I've seen. You might be heartbroken and disillusioned. Or you might be validated in your awe and admiration for the artist and the woman: Jasmine. She is unafraid, undaunted in her ambition to be not just the top selling, but

most influential vocalist, musician, and songwriter of her generation. At the very least, she is appealing on first glimpse,
sexually voracious if you manage to get a longer look, and
amoral if you spend too much time with her. In other words,
she is more than skilled at satisfying her needs. Those needs
are, after all, her first priority, despite whatever you have been
fed by the media. Those needs are central to who she is, why
she sings and plays, and what she writes about. In the music
business, her needs fuel her style and appearance. No smoke
and mirrors are necessary here, although she is not beyond
adding them, should she desire to enhance her mystique. But
I saw through it from the very first, which is why I had to be
erased. Otherwise I would muddy up the picture, accentuate
the flaws and blemishes, and watch the entire enterprise sink.

Jasmine is an enterprise. She has been one probably since
she could speak. I'm not saying she was coached or packaged
by the music business or, more specifically, by her parents.
I'm not saying she started out as some kind of bubblegum
commodity. But the Jasmine I would come to know was
always aware of the impression she was making and what that
impression might cost in gains, losses, standing, and opportunity. What you might judge as precociousness, rebellion,
or genuine teenage angst and curiosity was actually the cold-
blooded pursuit of success, whatever form it might come
in—as a punk rocker, a backing musician in power pop, or a
singer-songwriter with the liberation of her fans as her only
agenda. Jasmine went through all of these personas, but now,
like me, she has got to stop. No more reinvention, no more
dips in the collective subconscious to decide on her next incarnation, and no more fitting into previously untapped niches.
Her shapeshifting, mind-bending, hiding-in-plain-sight act is

finished. She is stuck forever, just as I have been for decades, except I did it while alive. I'll bet anything it's easier to do when you're dead.

If everyone saw Jasmine as I did, her career might never have gotten started. Or she might have wound up a studio musician or a scorer of television dramas; she could have been integral for someone's sound or mood, but still largely invisible to the public. I would have been satisfied with this: the most dispiriting of her characteristics laid bare before the public at the beginning, and the public making its decision. It's a chance I never had. The decision was made for me, though I'm not sure who made it. My parents, Jack and Nicky, Jasmine, or my sister: there must have been many decisions, some by people to whom I might not have given accurate credit that would culminate in my disappearance. Or, if not in my disappearance, in my waking death. I am not talking about now, as I am dying. I'm talking about all the years I've had to watch my tormentors go on with their lives to reach their fame or infamy to become what other people would let them be. No one would ever let me be anything other than what I was from the beginning.

I was the truth teller. I was the one who was honest. I thought this was what punk was all about. That's what I got out of it. That was my creed. Punk gave me license. I was on a mission even if no one else was. After progressive rock, dinosaur bands, string arrangements, synthesizers, and faux operas (the kind of stuff my sister listened to), there was punk to save me, to save us, and to save everybody. Put everyone on the same level by stripping down to the essentials, which was the noise. Concentrate on the noise. That's what people told me. Make everything fast and loud, memorable in three minutes. That's not too hard, they said. Could I handle it? No more love triangles or beauty pageants. Don't worry about costumes, makeup, who's butch, or who's the prettiest. Everyone is equal, and everyone is important.

No liars allowed, no deception or exploitative tactics. This was going to change the world, shift power, and redistribute attention and resources. This is what I was always told whenever I dared to ask what we were doing, hanging out in alleys drunk on Southern Comfort. We drank it because it was familiar, something we had in common from our childhoods: cough syrup—Robitussin. So sweet it was destructive. Boring a channel from our throats to our souls. The liquor made everything hot and loose, and I could talk to those girls. I could tell them not to get tangled up with Santorini and other outsiders, who only wanted to divide us. Set us against one another because they thought we were desperate. But we weren't desperate. We were in control. It was only the outsiders who made us seem that way, because they were projecting onto us, using us to play out their own little dramas.

Santorini had nothing but the grease in her hair and the stench on her skin. She was disgusting and possibly a sexual predator: we didn't have that descriptor for her back then. We had "pervert" and "deviant," but there were so many perverts and deviants; there was no way to distinguish their predilections and methods. Jack and Nicky wanted to be famous without having to work for it. They wanted it to be automatic. They wanted to take the easy way out when punk is not about that. Jasmine turned out to be the same way, selling one line but living the other. This is how these girls distracted me and how they betrayed me with my own doctrine.

My conservator knows everything. Whatever you want to know, he can tell you. The deposits and withdrawals, the sources of income, the charitable donations—no animals, I told my sister. And no artists. There are more important things in life. Or there should be. Like the homeless. I've left everything to the homeless, which should be quite a lot, considering that I started with half a million in cash before the hospice came in. I've always been good with my money. I've got investments. I've always done my own taxes. I don't need an accountant. I don't need anyone to tell me what to do with my money and how much of it there is, either tied up or liquid. I've got more than a mind for numbers, but also for their possibilities: compounded interest, capital gains, inflation, and market fluctuations. Go look at my taxes. That's my confession.

I never needed an accountant until I got sick enough for hospice. I can't read the numbers; they seem to jump and slide out of their boxes. It's as though my dyslexia has returned, and I have to chase after whatever is on a page—letters, numbers, and pictures. They don't want to be deciphered. Nothing is stable: the beat of my heart, the course of my bowels, and my two-dimensional perceptions. I know these nurses aren't giving me my medications. But when I look at the protocols, the amounts for the dosages, and the time of day they are to be administered, the charts squirm. The figures and times of day pour off of the paper. Notations change both shape and character, swinging between the familiar, estimations, and illegibility. If I manage to comprehend one drug's schedule, I've managed to forget it by the time I translate the next prescription's subtleties. In school they said I was smart because I could detect patterns, untangle their origins, and figure out their purpose and applicability. Now there are neither patterns nor principles, only the haze of instructions articulated too fast or too obscurely.

I had to hire the conservator to protect me from my sister. She's always been out for my money. Ask the conservator; he has everything. The passbooks and checkbooks, the certificates of deposit, the IRA, the 401K, the disability insurance policy, and the disability payments. I have a standing court date with the Social Security people because I have to prove, despite everything, that I am still disabled. If I fail to prove this, they cut off the allowance. One thousand, two hundred and sixty-five dollars each month: what my twenty-odd years of employment and paycheck withholdings have earned for me. I worked hard so I could be a regular Daddy Warbucks. I know my sister is after my money because of what she said when I told her I had written her out of my will. She said I should leave all my money to my niece, who happens to be her daughter, but I said no way, you'll squander it before she's an adult, before she has a chance to squander it herself.

I don't trust any of my friends either. My accounts are, frankly, just too tempting. I turned everything over to the conservator. I've authorized him to be completely honest. My life has always been an open book and so have my finances. I have nothing to hide, no secrets. I pay him to be honest, because I have no friends. Only associates—people I am forced to associate with because everyone fears my candidness. They know they have made compromises in their lives that I would never make. They say one thing and do its opposite. They take abuse at their jobs or from their spouses and in-laws, from their parents even, that they would never admit to, because it makes them look weak and obedient. And they are punk rockers—or they were, in a past life. Or they wanted to be. Because punks don't take shit from anybody. I found out, though, that punks can be just as self-serving, obsequious, and frightened of running out of money, getting kicked out of their house, or being fired or friendless as any guy in the street, and that's why I'm leaving everything to the homeless.

I tried to take a homeless man to the emergency room once. He approached me at a bus stop. The other people at the bus stop backed away and hid their faces, but I wanted to see—I needed to see—his deformity. I wanted to see what made him imperfect, whether it was physical or economic, what life had done to him that made him grotesque in the eyes of the others; what made him other from us, we docile, patient, consumers of public transportation in car-mad Los Angeles. He raised his hand to my eyes and unwrapped the sordid bandage that barely contained his hand and exposed a deep cut on the dorsal side. The cut ran widthwise, as though it were some kind of industrial accident, not something you would deliberately do to yourself, no matter how desperate your situation.

I tried to look into the cut, but his flesh was so bloated; his body had long since gone to work to close up the wound and protect against infection. I could not see much, but I could guess at the depth of the cut and the amount of exertion likely applied to whatever sharp object had exacted it. What I could not see were the layers of skin, muscle, and connective tissue that had been violated, but still the injury was impressive, monumental. I could tell from the swelling and the devastation it wrought. I knew the man would lose his hand and his livelihood, regardless of whether he worked with his hands, though it was clear he was not trapped in any humane or white-collar profession. He had a jacket but only a T-shirt underneath, and his blue jeans were as fecund as his bandage. But if he lost his hand there'd be no reentry into polite society because a missing hand is the end of an acceptable appearance.

He'd be a freak, a mutant, and irredeemably homeless. I told the man he'd get sepsis if he kept playing with the bandage. He grunted.

I told him how the skin would turn green and begin to peel; his fingers would go numb and the entire appendage would break off as though it belonged to a hollow, papier-mâché puppet. That he'd be lucky with only that, because the sickness might travel in the other direction, up his arm, and render it dead and contagious. I told him he needed antibiotics and clean dressings, but he said, "I'm hungry." There was a convenience store down the block, and I tried to take him by his other hand, swollen with dirt and callouses, but he shook me off and headed in the direction of the store.

His voice was too vague in volume, barely intelligible, but he knew what he wanted. Nuts and beef jerky: I bought as much as he could carry, and a bottle of whiskey, so he could disinfect the cut—that was as close as I was going to get him to medical attention, besides the other twenty bucks I slid into his jacket sleeve before he walked me back to the bus stop. That's when I decided all my money was going to the homeless. I wasn't sick then. I had beaten everything my body had thrown at me, every habit and every weakness. I kept to a diet and exercise after working on all those cancer studies. I knew the odds and the causes. I knew what to avoid, in which contexts, and the amounts I could conceivably tolerate. I was keeping to all the limits. My decision had nothing to do with redemption or making a name for myself. It was as pure an act as I will ever carry out. Now that I'm dying, I can be assured of my legacy.

I had a lot more money when I made my decision. I had a lot more money when I was healthy. Cash, certificates of deposit, T-bills, mutual funds, and the stock that our grand-parents had purchased for us at birth, although my sister squandered hers. AT&T, thousands of shares, purchased for nothing and now worth five figures at least. Our grandparents wanted us to have old money, stable money, money that just multiplied upon itself like a disease to inoculate ourselves with. They wanted to ensure we would never be hungry and never be homeless. As long as we owned a piece of corporate America, they figured, we wouldn't have to resort to shoplifting or prostitution. My grandparents had faith—more than I had. I kept only so much money in my cash accounts so that I'd be covered by the FDIC. Hadn't they learned anything from the Depression? Wasn't the stock market volatile and irrational on occasion, a finicky barometer for the health of the economy? Perhaps they remained naïve about money. But stock became respectable again. Or it became an acceptable risk. It separated the potentially marginal from the completely naked. Perhaps they thought they could buy the next generation out of vene-real diseases and public shame. That's what they must have thought when we were born and when we were still babies.

Once they died, we were free to spend that money. My sister squandered her stock. She sold it for rent money, for plane tickets, for affecting the kind of luxury that is merely temporary: facials, massages, and experimental treatments on her tired muscles. I imagine there must have been some clothes, evening gowns, as if she were going to the Academy Awards and sitting in the front row with the biggest stars, sure to be on camera. She must have burned right through that money as if she were a club kid. I know about dancers. I know they're all cokeheads. My sister and I never talked about money until I got sick, and I had to write a will. I told her she wasn't going to be in it. She said she was fine with that, but she wanted me to leave something to my niece, her daughter. She did not say what or how much.

I thought, for a while, this might be a good idea. Generous, practical, rational in the eyes of our friends and what is left of our family. My sister and her husband, who called himself a musician but never played a concert or composed anything, certainly couldn't provide for my niece. They were hustlers, though in New York I suspect there was some prestige to this. Lining up gigs, going on auditions, bartering their services for babysitters or preschool fees. They were artists. If they hadn't been artists, though, they would have been losers: the unskilled, undereducated people who hung on to their dreams too long; adolescents in their forties, nearing fifties, without pots to piss in. And this includes their rent-controlled apartment. But if you put "artist" before or after someone's name, it changes everything. She's got carte blanche with museums, banquets, lectures, and universities. My sister and her husband, another artist, are not poor. They are dedicated and self-sacrificing. Their friends will stage a benefit—they'll put on a show in a donated concert hall or a dormant Broadway stage—if they get sick or when they have to retire because of age or infirmity. My sister said of course she wanted her daughter to go to college; she didn't want her to lead the life that she had. But who was going to pay for it?

Not me. Because I knew what leaving money to my niece meant: making my sister a trustee. Putting her in charge of whatever I willed to my niece. The money would be gone before she could spend it. Or before they could spend it on her education. A private school, a summer camp, or piano or guitar lessons: no. It would have disappeared, turned into vapors, by the time my niece was old enough to understand that she'd been given an inheritance. By the time she could decide what she wanted to do with it. If her mother ever bothered to tell her that it existed. There was one other possibility, leaving my sister's husband in charge. I could have made him executor of the estate. He could have drawn a salary. And he could have been my niece's trustee. I would have done it even though technically he's a pianist like Jasmine was though he had been classically trained and still practiced relentlessly. Then I remembered overhearing something he said about my acts of charity. He said they were nowhere near as random as I thought they were, and they were too showy and too much about me. I should have realized this would come from the man who had chosen to marry my sister. She exacted a pull on him that could only have been doubled on my niece, and I said no. No to all three of them. No to the remains of my family.

I have to pay a percentage to the conservator, but the homeless are getting whatever is left. I can't keep track. Already I've given away so much: to the man with the swollen hand, a woman named Flora, the shingles lady, and Jimmy Stixx and his girlfriend, Leesa. He had a girlfriend, but he couldn't live with her, or the landlord might find out, raise the rent, and then she'd also be homeless. And homelessness is not for unmarried couples, Leesa said. It's only for wives, mothers, and maybe old ladies, because they're either already owned, or they can't be. The competition for possessions, the human kind, is just too savage.

Leesa told me all about it when I wrote the check out to her, because Jimmy couldn't take a check. He had no identification. The homeless are not big on identification to begin with. They've renounced their driver's licenses and their insurance cards and trashed their report cards and tax records, if they ever had any tax records. The papers that make us citizens—birth certificates and vaccination charts—what makes us whole, valid participants, equals, or something other than wax figurines placed between the bright and beautiful so they might have to watch their steps, not trip over the scenery—all of that stuff had been burned, immolated for these people. The commitment to homelessness is total.

The homeless prefer aliases. They're big on aliases and the things that happen to their bodies: teeth that crack or barely cling to the gums, their fractured ribs, their jaundiced skin, and their diseased blood. They're very big on dermatological conditions. Swarms of fungi, scabies, and impetigo. It's in the blankets and mattresses at the shelters, or they pick up these scourges from encampments, tarps shared as bed covers, or cardboard for living quarters. Water pools on their sunken tents, and they wash their faces in it. I've seen trench foot, particularly among men. They always manage to find that one damp spot in Los Angeles, a toxic oasis in the stucco desert. The dampness turns their feet to paper, then to pulp, then dust vaguely organized with hair and nails.

The homeless live in a reverse world, or the opposite of everything that is Los Angeles. They've stopped caring about appearances, associates, the neighborhoods they came from, the people they grew up with; they've stopped caring about food. They assume they'll go hungry. They plan on it. This is their power, the core of their resistance. I took Flora to a steakhouse and she wanted a hot dog. I took her to Carney's on the Sunset Strip, and she wanted steak. I bought her a steak sandwich at a deli, but she was afraid her teeth would fall out if she tried to bite into it. The only meal she ever enjoyed with me came with a Bloody Mary she didn't drink; it was the celery that amazed her, cold and crunchy at the back of her mouth. The homeless don't dream of heat and hot water in their dreams, the reveries of the infamous. They dream about refrigeration, creating their weather. Or maybe celery doesn't keep well in Dumpsters.

The shingles lady: the first time I saw her, it was in the parking lot of a grocery store. The next time, she was panhandling a few blocks west in front of a restaurant. The restaurant let me bring her inside because they'd never seen her before, but they said we had to leave her bags at the coat check. They never let us back in again after that. The shingles lady shuffled between several locations. I couldn't always keep track of them. They changed without notice, from the Valley to West Hollywood. She got around somehow, without my help: I never let a homeless person in my car. I never drove them anywhere. I never approached the teenagers I saw if they were alone. There were always witnesses. I wasn't stupid, though I was unaware, incapable of anticipating how fickle they could be in their tastes, needs, and modus operandi. The shingles lady switched up her outfits, from a cowboy hat and boots to gloves and a snood. In winter she wore skirts and T-shirts as if she were a hippie; in summer a bomber's jacket she occasionally wore inside out. What she feared most was being recognized. Recognition is the last thing the homeless want.

I didn't have to do what I did. I didn't have to buy the shingles lady tampons, but I knew they were what she wanted; so she could wear underwear again and pants, too. I didn't have to buy Flora a raincoat, but she said she could make it into a lean-to if necessary; so it worked double duty. I could have volunteered at a soup kitchen or made donations. But then the homeless would have just been numbers to me, like the tumors I counted on one of my research projects. Count, or be counted, it turns out. Some people count more than others. The ones who appear on our televisions, in our magazines, and in the movies: they count the most. They are more than numbers; they are points of aspiration. We are confronted by them so often, in so many different contexts, that we have no choice but to inculcate them into our minds and our subconscious. From there they tell us how well we measure up and how deep and depraved are our failures. We—the no-talent, overfed, and underappreciated; we—the statistics, combed through on the census tracks, whose numbers never rise high enough for any Gallup poll; those of us without box office takes, Nielsen ratings, or a spot on the Billboard Hot 100. The homeless, meanwhile, number in the hundreds or the thousands, in amounts no one can count accurately as if they were stars, infinite galaxies, or the mutations cancer cells are capable of. They live on the edge of the great insatiable pit of loneliness, and they make no secret of it. They are done acting cool, knowing what is hip, being on the up and up or in the loop; they are finished acquiring possessions, positions, Brownie points, or star stickers. They are done getting and spending, fucking, and stargazing. Now that's punk if you're asking. That's authentic and authentic suffering.

The homeless are my people, though I am forced to admit I am not one of them. I know this because I will be counted at least twice when I die, which is more than any homeless person is counted. I know this because of how I used to count cancers, breast by breast, always totaling into an odd number. When I found an even number of cancers, I knew I had done something wrong or that a woman was struck twice; perhaps in the same breast, perhaps in both of them. I'd have to go back to the documentation, research other databases, and figure out whether someone's cancer had already been previously recorded in another epidemiological study. Once when I was counting, I discovered someone I knew, the mother of one of my sister's ballet friends. She was an actress and then a photographer. Her entire life was there for me to summarize and record for posterity, as if getting cancer were her only accomplishment. Certainly it will be that way for me, several times over.

I will be counted once for my breast, and one or more times for this jungle of metastases: the right hipbone, lungs, spleen, brain, and liver. Whether each incidence of cancer will get its due recognition is up to the doctors and who wants to be responsible for what. Some of my cancers have already been registered through scans, biopsies, studies, and that last, formal declaration of surrender: the tumors were inoperable. At the end the medical examiner will take out these organs, weigh them, and find them hollow. The cancer may not have fully consumed them, but their innards have been chewed, as if sampled, then spit out. The cancer is always looking for something more to its taste, complex and succulent.

When I told Jimmy Stixx I wouldn't be seeing him anymore because I was sick, because I was dying, he didn't say what everybody else said. He didn't say he was sorry or I shouldn't talk that way, that attitude was everything, or that I could extend my life in precious days and months if I got myself right with the world. He didn't say that I should think about all that time I had left, and all the wonderful things I'd be able to fill it with. "What can I do?" is what he said. He gave me his girlfriend's telephone number; so I could call if

I needed him. He almost gave me his denim jacket, the one with the Rolling Stones logo with Charlie Watt's autograph ripped into it. That jacket was what he had managed to preserve of his past life as a drummer and roadie. He worked on the Stones' tours of '72, '75, and '78, or so he said, although the condition of the jacket spoke in his favor. He had the autograph embroidered over so it wouldn't fade, but the sleeves were white threads, insubstantial, skeletal from what they had been thirty years earlier. A lot like my own bones must be, I imagined. I wanted to take it from him, but I couldn't. I also thought there might be other things he could do for me later. Much later if I remembered to ask him.

CHAPTER 16

THE REPORTERS WANTED TO KNOW how we felt about the arrest. We hadn't heard about the arrest; we kept the television off that night. Barb seemed to rest better without it. But we knew what to do when the doorbell went off and the telephone rang. We knew to ignore the sound of the doorframe inhaling as someone was trying to push the door in, thinking we'd just leave it unlocked and they were welcome to come in at any time. Maria and Ionie came in through the back door behind the house, where they could avoid the gauntlet of microphones and cameras set up by the front steps. There were Barb's charts to update, and the night nurses had to be consulted. Barb had to be bathed; her patches and port had to be checked. The sheets had to be changed, and the diaper and the towel Barb slept on in case of accidents; there was the medicine to administer. I don't know exactly how much morphine Barb was on by then, though the dosages seemed more frequent to me. Her breathing thickened, or the effort needed to complete a breath increased. Her feet shuffled, like she was running in her dreams.

We managed to get through all of the morning routine—although it was taking longer, because Barb's joints and muscles had stiffened, like she was braced for something—until Ionie had to take the sheets to the washing machine. On her way past the window beside the front door, she saw them: the reporters, drawing closer together, and the camera and microphone crews lining up behind them.

"Who are they expecting to come out now?" she said upon returning to the bedroom. "Like we have nothing better to do than be interviewed."

"Something must have happened," I said. "Some new development." I realized how much I must have sounded just like them; that I was living from one big moment to the next, strung along by the suspense. "Turn the TV on," I said and noticed how Maria was grimacing. "Low. For just a minute."

On the screen, there was a police officer, the front left of his uniform overtaken with badges, bars, and other decorations, talking about closure and justice. He was complimenting his colleagues and reassuring the public because the killer had been apprehended. The police official was certain they had the right man. A vagrant, a homeless man, a hobo: the police officer didn't have much trouble coming up with ways to describe who this man was. A bum, a transient, a street person; a threat to the health and safety of the community that the LAPD is proud to have taken care of, through hard work, a lot of hours, and determination and grit. The police officer also thanked Jasmine's neighbors, who had cooperated with the investigation, although they had identified this man as a gentle soul. They could not imagine his hurting anyone. He was the neighborhood mascot, a beggar in front of the local grocery-convenience store. He ate garbage out of the Dumpsters and panhandled in the parking lot.

The screen switched to a man being led in handcuffs by two other police officers. These were ready-for-TV cops, their faces like their boss's, like the news anchors', and the reporters' standing outside the house: sharp and compelling. Los Angeles is a city of faces, I was beginning to understand as my sister was dying. Not like in New York, which has plenty of its share of celebrities. I'd seen them in Central Park with their kids, sometimes at the 68th Street sandboxes or the water parks along the river. Kelly Ripa, B. D. Wong, and Ethan Hawke: they all looked tired, temporarily relieved that they had found a way to keep their kids occupied. They almost looked normal, like any other parents. Not like the type you were lucky to spot in Los Angeles. It wasn't in the shape or color of their eyes or anything about their hair, nothing so simple. It wasn't even in how the placement of their features adhered to the golden mean—I heard that somewhere: beauty is all about proportion—but in their complexions. Their cheeks, chins, and forehead were scoured and scrubbed until light seemed to emanate directly out of their pores: so you would know how difficult it was to be that good looking; so you could appreciate the pain that went into the making of their appearance.

James H. Stevic Jr. did not look like this. His hair was parted on the side and swooped down over his forehead: so no one could see enough of him to say what he looked like. He might have been blond at one time, his hair could have darkened with age, or it may have been the consequences of his living arrangements. His features looked as though they had been smeared on, an afterthought to the rest of him. There was no planning in his face out to the last symmetrical measurement. Everything was random and haphazard, like the face I had and that Barb had, the kind Maria and Ionie had, and everyone else who melts away when compared to the beauties and exotics—the kind of kids Barb and I grew up around and competed against. I in ballet, and Barbara in her band. I thought punk rock wasn't about being pretty, but have you ever seen an ugly ballerina do the mad scene from *Giselle*? Didn't think so.

The screen switched again to the driveway; I felt myself take a step back from the screen once I recognized it, flattened and flickering in the sick room. A reporter was talking into the camera about the many questions that still revolved around James H. Stevic Jr. "You saw him wearing that jacket in the clip we have, but actually he was shirtless underneath," the reporter said. "Police found him at what best can be described as his camp site in the hills, and his belongings, such as they are, were scattered all over the place, I was told. Those belongings included memorabilia from Jasmine's career, raising the possibility that Stevic is a deranged fan, but we still don't know for sure."

"Does it mean this is over now?" Ionie said.

"Are you kidding?" Maria said to Ionie. "This is just the beginning. Remember O. J.?"

"How many cases did I watch that one through?" Ionie sighed.

"Another puppet show," Maria said. "You'd better call that conservator again," Maria said to me.

"Am I the head nurse here?" Ionie said. "Call the conservator," she instructed as she walked down the hall toward the front door. I was plugging the telephone back into the wall when I saw Barb shuffling her feet, like she wanted to run after Ionie, or make her own appearance before the cameras.

"Don't worry," Maria said. "I'm watching her." Suddenly, Ionie was on the television screen, shaking her head, or the camera was unsteady, like there had been a scuffle. The voices of the reporters gushed over one another, and the picture went out of focus, then switched onto the ground, the feet, ankles, and legs of the crowd, before it flew up to Ionie's face. She was shaking her head as she spoke.

"What do you think is going on here?" Ionie was saying. "Do you think we're planning a party and the like?" Maria smiled. I had one ear to the telephone, listening to the telephone ring in the conservator's office. "Don't you know we still have a patient inside, lots of work for us? If you will excuse." She went for the door as the reporters shouted out more questions. No one was answering at the conservator's. Maria stood and applauded. Barb's feet shuffled again, like she was trying to sand her way through the mattress.

"A sign," Maria said.

"Of what?"

"The limbs, involuntary movement," Maria said—though not to me. She was talking to Ionie, who understood even if I did not.

"Isn't her color still good yet?" Ionie said, looking over Barbara. "I don't know." To me she said, "Didn't you get him, the conservator? Won't he have plenty reason to come this time, finish up the job?"

"What?" I asked.

WE WROTE A STATEMENT—meaning me and Greg Onderdonk—to give to the media while Maria and Ionie kept an eye on Barbara. I know that Ionie always considered me a nuisance, but it seemed as we waited for Greg Onderdonk to call us back that Maria had begun to feel that way, too. She handed me a brochure on "end of life care," which was what I thought we had been doing. I had only to open my mouth, or look at either nurse, to have them resort to the hand signals for calming me down and shutting me up, remaining quiet while their surveillance of Barb took in her entire body. The blankets had suddenly become an impediment, but without them Barb shivered badly.

They seemed glad when I left the room to sit with Greg Onderdonk and write the statement. We had to sit in the dining room and write at the dining room table, because the kitchen felt too close to the reporters on the other side of the door. They hovered over the driveway, it seemed; I thought I could hear them occasionally test out the stairs, like they had to remind us of their presence. I tried to ignore them, but Greg Onderdonk was anxious to get everything out of the way, and he had a series of phrases he wanted to use, because they were familiar and unsurprising.

"Give them what they expect, and they won't pay too much attention," he said. So we strung the phrases together—our hopes for closure for Jasmine's family, our thanks to supporters, our request for privacy so Barb could die with dignity. I was quickly learning there is neither much privacy nor dignity when you are stranded on a mattress with your friends, relatives, and nurses fretting over your every last bodily function. But I did not bring this up with Greg Onderdonk because he likely already knew that. This was his business after all.

"I don't see why we have to give them anything," I said.

"Then why did you call?" he asked, and I was furious. This was a fine time for him to decide to demonstrate his super competence, when for the rest of Barb's illness he had practically been missing in action.

"The nurses told me to," I said, though I knew that was a poor answer.

"Just get in, get out, and don't look back once you're done reading," he said.

"I'm not reading this out there," I said. "You're her representative."

"Not to them," he said. "You want them to leave you alone, you've got to give them something. Just enough to break up the pace. Not too much. Just a little.

"This is what you pay me for—this kind of advice," he said.

"I'm not paying you," I said.

"You know what I mean," he said. "Don't you?"

Before I went in front of the cameras, Greg Onderdonk ran the statement by his employees and officials from the hospice, since both of their businesses were at risk; it comes from associating with a known former murder suspect, I guess. That they were taking Barb's money apparently didn't count for much. "Let's get this over with," he said. At least he walked out the door with me, standing slightly behind me as I made apologies for my appearance and Barb's condition and read our official plea to be left alone, finally, into the gathering of microphones. I assume my voice was awful, shaky, and too rapid, like it always is. But there was also a strange, unnatural quiet as I read, a quiet that I had forgotten about and that had always intrigued me about stage work, but I could never enjoy whenever I encountered it.

I could hear the film rolling through the television cameras as I spoke; and the shutters of still cameras opening and closing, or so I thought. I assume that there was no actual physical material in those devices since everything has been computerized, but I still heard those noises. I heard the muffled traffic of the streets in the neighborhood, from people taking detours likely because of the ruckus Barb's death was making. For a moment it felt as though the world that had been twisting at such a outrageous pace had slowed to a halt and was waiting for us; for me to stop protecting Barb so she could be done with it, die, and leave the planet, and I could begin mourning, however I was supposed to do it. I think this is what it means to be in a vacuum and isolated, moving about without the obstacles of water, air, or the ground that supports us; much like I felt when I could hear only the sounds of the box of my toe shoes against the stage, and the awe of the audience, as I made my turns, took my leaps, or posed for a moment so I'd have breath for the next bit of choreography. I used to live for moments like this, not so much for being the center of attention but for being able to command it, though it was made of silence, essentially. And Barb always felt she had to fill the vacuum, with noise, screaming, and shouting, because punk rock abhors a vacuum. But she was becoming a vacuum herself then, if she hadn't already put herself in one, and for most of her adult life. For too much of it—for all of it. All of it ending.

I read the statement to shut everyone up essentially. But it didn't work. It only made for more questions. How did we hear about the arrest, what were we thinking, how did it feel, who was there with you, how did you tell Barbara? Have you told her anything? Greg Onderdonk stepped to the microphone and said, "No questions," but still they threw them at us: what is Barbara's condition? What were her exact words, what kind of relief did she express, what were your doubts, your expectations? Amid all the shouting, the spinning of gears, and my heart pumping like it was directly behind my teeth and flooding, there remained that undercurrent of quietness, like the air had been distilled. These were individual voices that normally sounded like a blur on the television, and their intentions were clear. They were not looking for the familiar or drama, or even details. They were trying to prove something: they had been right from the beginning; there had been a reason to camp out here and to distract the world with their broadcasts and breaking news updates; this exercise had not been in vain because there had been a story here. Or at least the ingredients of a story: a mystery, suspense, the deathbed where the confession was sure to come, and the sisterhood that was really more of a competition, but how could they have known that? Nevertheless they needed to prove there had been some kind of drama unfolding, and they had to be there in case it spilled out. They went only where the news was. It was not their fault the story hadn't panned out, because they had done their best. Sometimes your best just doesn't cut it; this I knew. I don't know whether they did.

"Thank you, thank you, everybody," Greg Onderdonk said, and I felt his hands on my shoulders, drawing me back toward the door. Back into the house, down the hall, and into the room where my sister was entering a new phase in her process. That's what the brochure Maria had given me called it, "her process," like death was designed especially for her. Like there had never been any other alternative for Barb's life. She was made for this kind of suffering.

"But did Barbara know this guy?" one man shouted from the crowd. I didn't know which guy he was talking about, and Greg Onderdonk continued to gently push me toward the door, as if I would not make it there without his guidance. "Your sister was a musician, wasn't she?" the voice persisted. "So is this guy, James Stevic. Your sister was in a band, right? California Youth Authority?" I hadn't heard that name since the summer of anorexia. That summer, California Youth Authority was like a bloody flag she'd wave in my face whenever I tried to talk to her about my dancing and how it had become a job once I joined the company. She didn't want to hear it.

"Come on, come on," Greg Onderdonk said into my ear. His breath that close was not bad, but tepid, like it had long ago been drained of anything pleasant.

"California Youth Authority," the man said again. "Your sister's band?"

"Yeah?" I answered. "What about it?"

"Maybe she knew this Stevic from the band? He's a musician, a drummer."

"Don't answer," Greg Onderdonk said.

I tried to see who the man was, whether there was any way to identify him, but the sun was in my eyes, or maybe it was only a reflection of the sun, an exaggerated light bouncing off the news camera equipment. It was already a hot morning, and the sun in my eyes reminded me how much worse it would get if I didn't get inside right away.

"That was thirty years ago," I shouted back at the reporter. "How would I know?"

"Will you ask her?" the reporter said, and to this I stepped inside the house and shut the door behind us, because how would I know who to give the answer to. Because I was a New Yorker, and in New York you don't go around asking after the names of homeless people. You especially didn't do that thirty years ago; you don't do that now; and how would Barb know any homeless people let alone this man. She might have gone to school with someone who grew up to be homeless; all those brilliant, tortured minds she was introduced to in the special gifted programs. Some of them were bound to go nuts, weren't they, with the burden of all those extra IQ points? I mean, Barb did. Not enough to wind up on the street, thank God. We used to worry about that sometimes, me and Helen. But it didn't happen. She never had to live under a bridge, on the fringes of a park, in a cardboard lean-to or a tent. So she probably didn't know him. She had no reason to. He could offer her nothing. And James H. Stevic Jr. was a young man, or so the television had told us; in his thirties—not our age. They said he was from somewhere else, not born here. There was no way she knew him. Maybe he knew her from some old recording or newspaper article, but there was no way she knew him.

"I told you not to tell them anything." Greg Onderdonk had grabbed me by the arm and held me back from going into the bedroom.

"I didn't," I said, and with that I retook possession of my arm to the point of nearly shoving Greg Onderdonk. It occurred to me that he was a small man, maybe my height, and his hair was ludicrous, curled under in a pageboy. He must have thought it still looked good, as it did when he first grew it out, like, maybe, forty years earlier? Who said I couldn't count? I was on a roll.

"I didn't say anything the guy didn't already know," I said to Greg "Herman's Hermits" Onderdonk.

"But now all the rest of them know. They won't let it rest. They'll—"

"That's not my problem," I said. "My problem is that my sister's dying, and I might never talk to her again."

Greg Onderdonk tried to straighten himself up and iron out his posture. He shrugged his shoulders like that was going to make him taller and enable him to look down on me. But it didn't work at least from my perspective.

"So you'll excuse me," I said.

CHAPTER 17

IF YOU WANT COMPETENCE, you have to pay for it. That is what I've learned in life—in Hollywood, in science, and in death—if I ever die. The nurses have put me on oxygen. I imagine that's what's happening. It's the only explanation I can come up with given the hissing in my ears, the rush of air up my nose, and the dryness at the back of my throat. Forced respiration and the push through the sinuses. They are giving me oxygen, but I had to pay for it. I thought oxygen was free or that air was. But in death you learn everything you thought you knew is actually upside down, or everything you thought you knew is being taken away from you. All your thoughts and principles become useless. There is no way for you to remain on Earth, so you die. Or you do not die so much as abdicate your position, the space you occupy. Make room for others, for the next big thing, or the trend that overtakes you. Death is like fashion in this respect; like Hollywood and celebrity, moving quickly, trying not to look back.

If you ask me more questions about the homeless and what I have left for them, it will cost you. Or it will cost me and then the homeless, because the conservator works like a lawyer. He bills for each hour, each second. He deducts it from the estate, and that means not as much will be left for my heirs, or the homeless, as I have already explained, as I have tried to make clear to you. I had to hire a conservator because I know what happens when people die: the grasping, the frenzy, and the fight for dominance among friends and relatives. Who knew her best, who is most affected by the death, who will inherit—if not the money, as I've made certain in my case— the power to define the dead person. In my case, it's my sister, I know. There's nothing I can do about it. She has been here through all of it. But the money—what I was best at, what I was better at than just about anybody I met, except for the pop stars I knew, mostly Jasmine but probably Jack and Nicky, too—the money is safe from my sister, because I'm paying that conservator. He knows what to do.

I told Jimmy Stixx he'd have to be able to prove who he was if I put him in my will. He told me to put Leesa in instead; it would be just as good, and it would work out just as well, but I wasn't going to risk it. I'd have to find another solution. I told Jimmy Stixx that I was dangerous. I was unpredictable. I could blow at any moment. That's what people said about me after I broke up with Jasmine. That's what people said about me when CYA broke up; when I asked people if I could join their bands and jam with them. But they said I was undependable; I couldn't be trusted. They said that I had no presence.

The last time I saw Jimmy Stixx, I told him about it. He asked me who was the greatest drummer in the history of rock 'n' roll, and I was supposed to say Charlie Watts; Charlie Watts was his hero. Jimmy Stixx said the Charlie Watts autograph on his jacket kept him strong, because Charlie Watts was clean. He wasn't a user, and he wasn't a womanizer. He was the only decent person in a cabal of thieves and addicts. He talked a lot about addicts, addictive personalities, and how people got hooked on one another as if they were substances; as if their presence, or lack of it, fulfilled some physical need, a hit on the pleasure center. That was why he was going solo, keeping himself away from other people. It was why he stayed homeless even though he had his girlfriend, Leesa. Even though he could move in with her if he wanted, except he couldn't. The landlord would raise the rent, and then they'd both be homeless. He didn't want to put her through that.

The problem, he said, is that people are poison. They're habit-forming. People were like cars, with built-in obsolescence. They got used up, they ran out of their humanity, or they got selfish with it and started hoarding it. The homeless are big on monologues that do not give away much information, and Jimmy Stixx had several, one about grooming. Grooming is what kept him out of the "criminalized" justice system. He'd shower at Leesa's and have her cut his hair and do his laundry. But he lived the way he liked in the hills around the Hollywood sign, away from people and their civilized living arrangements. People in apartments and people in houses: he did not want to become addicted again to drugs, to people, to roofs, to walls, or to indoor plumbing. Shelter was as seductive as any mind-altering substance. Shelter made him lazy. A mattress and hot water made him bored. Boredom made him hungry for a buzz, a trip, or a hit of whatever could take him out of himself, his body worn down by creature comforts. Before I told him I was sick and before I told him I was dying, he said I should head into the woods sometime. I could take my car, a tent, a stove, blankets, and anything I needed. But I had to go on a cleanse and weed out the human toxins. Get rid of the disappointment and paranoia of living where I did among other people in the Los Angeles suburbs.

I usually saw Jimmy Stixx when I went running in Beachwood Canyon, Jasmine's neighborhood. So when he asked me that last time who was the greatest percussionist in the world, I told him it was Jasmine's mother. Not Charlie Watts or some suitably respected studio musician, but the mother of my one and only obsession. I told him everything. I told him about Jack and Nicky, CYA, and why Jasmine and I split. The problem, everyone had agreed, was that I had no presence. I didn't understand what they meant; that night at the Whisky I proved I had stage presence. But it was presence of some other kind, some other method, that was lacking. Charlie Watts had no presence either, but it didn't matter for him, a man and a real musician. I asked Jack and Nicky, before they left for Chicago, whether I should speed up my playing, cut myself live on the stage with my guitar strings, or vomit into the audience. No, they said, it went deeper than that. I was insecure and too nervous. I talked too much. I interfered where I wasn't wanted. I'd never be in a band again unless I learned to mind my own business. I could be as honest as I wanted—with myself. With others I had to learn when honesty was necessary. I had to stop using honesty as a weapon. I had to stop lashing out.

I knew what this was all about. They were going off with Jasmine, and I wasn't. But still they were jealous, maybe of what Jasmine and I had, maybe because they knew they would never get close to her like that. Now they were her employees, underlings. She could tell them what to play, how to play it, and what to wear; she could tell them anything, and they'd have to do it. They said Jasmine didn't pick me to go to Chicago because my whole anger trip was inauthentic and because I was too good, with the homework, the school night curfew, and the college thing. Because of my parents, where I lived, and how I was raised. Because I was raised, curated, nurtured, and influenced, while the real punks had no parents and no addresses; they were feral, rejected creatures who knew how to look out for themselves. I still needed adults to pay tuition. All I could brag about was knowing how to balance a checkbook and write an essay to get into college. I was an honor student, and I had an honor student's self-righteousness. Jasmine needed musicians, not hall monitors. She needed street-smarts and seasoned professionals, not budding career girls.

Unlike Jack, Nicky, and even Jasmine, I can live with myself. I can look at myself in any mirror and be certain about what I see in the reflection. It's not some kind of act or simulation. It's real, unadulterated, unaltered, the true effect. I declined reconstructive surgery on my massacred breast. I declined after the surgeon said I wasn't serious enough about my disease. By then I had lost my hair without the tumors noticeably shrinking, but he said I wasn't serious enough about the mastectomy.

I had asked the surgeon for a double mastectomy, in fact, but he said I hadn't thought it through enough. Any woman who wants to part with a healthy breast has not considered all of the consequences. I told him I was single, childless, never married, and possibly asexual, though if anyone would give me a chance, my direction would be lesbian. But he looked at me and decided it wasn't possible—my cancer, my sexuality, and my diagnosis between Stage II and Stage III. The epidemiologists couldn't tell where to put me because I had three tumors, not just the one they were accustomed to categorizing. The surgeon must have looked at me and decided that I was not credible. Not because I had come to him with cancer that was so advanced, but because I was so blasé about parting with the last of my femininity. But he didn't know that I had never been considered that feminine to begin with.

I told Jimmy Stixx everything. He said he wanted to make everything better. Jack, Nicky, Jasmine, and the cancer. He said I'd saved his life, and now it was his turn to stand up and stick his neck out. He didn't believe in karmic debt though he was frequently in it. He could right things, even the score, level the playing field. I was tempted. I was tempted to tell him where Jack and Nicky lived and who Jasmine really was; I had been using pseudonyms for everyone to protect their privacy and their innocence. Their supposed innocence, because they had done everything I had accused them of. But I didn't want to be in karmic debt to anyone either. I didn't want to give those girls anything that they could hold against me in this life or the next. All I told Jimmy Stixx was that Jasmine's mother was the greatest female percussionist in the history of music, that it was possible that she lived nearby, and that I had gone to school with her daughter.

Jimmy Stixx said that I had presence. It may not have been the kind of presence my friends valued, but I had it. I could attract a crowd. I could hold it. I asked Jack and Nicky if I would have had presence if I were butch. If I came down definitively on one side of the divide, instead of skirting around it as I did. I was neither a femme nor a bull dyke. Where did I stand? What was my appeal, my need, and my talent? They said, if I wanted to have presence, I would have to forget all the crap that I was worried about. Presence was about being in the moment and not worrying about the future. Presence was giving it your all no matter the setting, not squirreling away time and attention so that you could finish your homework. Presence was about being committed, to being butch, a bull dyke, or a femme. Jack and Nicky said I was afraid to commit to anything beyond what my parents wanted for me, that I was

SISTERHOOD OF THE INFAMOUS

a coward, a spoiled kid afraid to come out with what she really was and what she really wanted.

If I had presence and if I were committed, I would have been able to get away with the things I did, the things I said, and the way I left Jasmine in the lurch after that last night we were all together for dinner at Jasmine's house. Jasmine's mother, the percussionist, and her father figure, the guitarist, were there and her brothers. We ate in the dining room, where Jasmine's parents had put instruments on the walls: guitars, tambourines, a Resonator, and bells. Her mother kept wind chimes in the windows. Anyone could have driven by the house and seen us that night, so jolly and convivial, but it was all fake. That's what I uncovered. It was all a show to gloss over the reality of lying. Jasmine was a liar about herself and her parents. I wonder whether she knew I would find out. I wonder whether she was, in her way, trying to prepare me for it.

Jasmine never called herself a punk. She said she was raised as a hippie, and hippies weren't nearly as bad as punks said they were. But she was no singing-songwriting flower child. She was doing her own thing, she said. She was evolving. This is what she was trying to convince me of, that last night, before dinner. Sure, her parents' hippie music could be stupid, overblown, and self-indulgent. But so was a lot of other stuff, including what we listened to—the mainstream artists, Blondie, and The Police. Not everybody could be The Jam. Jasmine was going to play keyboards and do backing vocals for The Regent, and she was taking Jack and Nicky with her.

The Regent was unclassifiable. He was ahead of his time. He was nostalgic and deferential. The Regent wasn't going to change music, but he was going to change the music business. He had his own label and his own studio, and he played all the instruments on his records. He made his own T-shirts and sold concert tickets through his own agency. He was signing artists and songwriters, putting them in charge, and building a collective. It was going to be like Motown, but for rock 'n' roll. A rock 'n' roll commune. Living off the land or the sound the land inspires. The Regent was kind of a hippie. Jasmine, Jack, and Nicky were going to help him.

So all the people I knew in the world were going to Chicago to become backup musicians for some pop star. Someone who wore costumes as if he were Elton John. Sequins and feathers and a lot of other distractions. He wrote ballads for other singers and anthems for other bands. In other words, he wrote songs for money, just like anyone else might have. But he dressed up what he did and who he was in rhinestones and velvet swatches. He tried to be that much more generous with rights and licensing and called his business a musical commonwealth, an homage to the planet and a humanistic enterprise—though it was a business. He put a price on creativity, love, rebellion, and whatever else he sang about. He toyed with his audience members. He snapped at their patience, squeezing the desperation out of them. He rendered them docile and compliant, and he kept collecting from them. Jasmine said she was going to Chicago because she might not get another chance like this. To live the musician's life and learn from someone other than her parents. Have an adventure: Chicago! Have the wind whipped out of her, live off deep-dish pizza, and immerse herself in the blues: what could she do there that couldn't be done in Los Angeles? I asked. She had to see whether she was beyond failure; now was her time to fail if she was going to. She'd be too old to fail in a few years. Too old to come crying home to her parents and start again. So much for punk, I said to her. So much for being a part of something larger than yourself. So much for trying to change people, what they value, getting rid of prejudice, materialism, snobbery, and—

Jasmine stopped me. She stopped me with a kiss, because she knew me. She knew how to play me and turn me on and off; she knew how to lie to me. Because I was so obvious. She said just like I had to go to college, this was her purpose; I would have remembered the speech she made word-for-word if it were not drowning in treacle, in crystals and cotton fabrics, the tapestries that hung from the walls in the house, the satin pillows, and the incense that burned in every room. Jasmine never grew up. She lived in a castle. She took me to the turret at the top of the third floor and showed me a view of all of Holly-wood and promised she'd come back and wouldn't forget me.

Jasmine liked her parents. She loved her brothers. They were musicians, too. They played in garage bands and in jam sessions. They were hippies like Jasmine's parents. The dining room had a Resonator guitar hanging from the wall, bells, *maracas,* a set of conga drums, and a Gibson steel acoustic. The wind chimes in the windows were her mother's idea; the chandelier had candles instead of light bulbs. The table was round rather than rectangular so that there was no head of the table, no one person in the family above all others. I wonder if I had been butch, whether I would have had the guts to say what I thought of all this adornment. I wonder whether I would have realized then what it must have been hiding, whom it was meant to fool, and how it must have warped Jasmine's mind, living in it.

I wonder if I had been butch, would the surgeon have believed me when I said I wanted a double mastectomy?

Would he have believed me when I came in with my file and asked me what was wrong? Lesbians are thought to have an increased risk for breast cancer based on their behaviors, their body types, their relatively low rate of pregnancies, and attending low rates of breastfeeding. But there are no percentages, as there are for ethnicities. There's only dread and assumptions—you know nothing of your own body because you've never used it properly. To the surgeon who said I wasn't serious about cancer, I ask now what would have happened if I had a nose ring, black lipstick, or had weighed more? Though those things may not have made any difference since I was deep into chemo by then, nauseated and afraid I might be back-sliding into anorexia. If I had that tough look and been built like a cop with a bulletproof vest, maybe people would have listened to me. They would have known I meant business; I wasn't lashing out like a little kid. They would have registered the extent of my muscle and my willingness to use it. They would have intuited that I was more than my words and that I followed through on my intentions. If I had been a different kind of lesbian, I would have had my double mastectomy, and I might be still living, rather than nearly dead.

I began telling people I was asexual after Jasmine. I was never attracted to anyone again, and no one was attracted to me. I wondered if I had been butch, would I have attracted somebody, because then it would have been clear what I was, what I wanted, and how I would get it; and I wondered whether any of that mattered, aside from my own satisfaction. My needs would be paramount. I'd be the alpha, the omega, the director, and producer. I would have been everything Hollywood needs. If I had been butch, then Jasmine would have expected something like the stunt I pulled; her parents would have been prepared for it; all of us would have been. But I wasn't butch. Because I was afraid to be. I was raised to be afraid of most things, and I was afraid to cut my hair so it would be like my father's, a Sergeant Carter crew cut, scalded, practically bald, and authoritarian. I was afraid to be anything than what my body said I was, small, sweet, and a genuine star-struck fan girl. Butch never would have worked for me. I was a rookie lesbian on my first relationship. I was in the thick of my first great awakening. I would make mistakes, blow etiquette, indulge in all the self-pity and cruelties straight kids get locked up in with their dramas, but in the end, wouldn't I be forgiven? Everyone else is.

I went for the Resonator in the dining room. You could eat, you could play, or you could do both, Jasmine said. Her father was playing a Stratocaster at low volume, and Jasmine's brothers sat opposite him, one on a Gibson steel acoustic and the other on acoustic bass. A power trio with Jasmine's father in the lead; his sons played rhythm for his background, and they followed their father as if he were giving chase. I couldn't keep up with them and just tried to keep in tune, figuring out how the Resonator worked with its twang and echo. Jasmine's father: no one called him "Dad" or "Father." They called him by his first name, as though he were the cool music teacher or a celebrity of international stature. His name was wrong for that—Herb—his name did not dazzle. But in the years to come he would be called a legend, an underappreciated artist who had to wait for recognition; thank God it came before he died while he could still enjoy it.

Herb wore a Grand Funk Railroad T-shirt, which I thought was supposed to be ironic. But Herb kept leading everyone in easy songs, stuff everyone knows, like the Beatles and the

Stones; so maybe it wasn't an ironic statement he was making. He was a hit maker after all. He knew what was golden. He wore John Lennon glasses and socks with his sandals. A Grand Funk Railroad T-shirt was his motto. He nodded at me as he noticed I was having trouble. Jasmine's mother had already brought out dinner, and Herb told me to eat; I didn't have to play. If I had been butch, he never would have made that offer.

If I had been butch, I would have seen what was going on. How Jasmine and her brothers called their mother what she was—"Mom" or "Momma"—but not Herb, who was not their father. Not even their stepfather, but their uncle or their father's cousin, probably any male relation with the right name to match the children's and cohabit with their mother. Herb raised Jasmine and her brothers as though they were his own, so long as it remained clear who he was, and was not. This I read in an interview even more years later. I wondered if I had been butch, whether they all would have come out and told me outright, so that I wouldn't have had to feel as though bowing and scraping to Herb was required.

If I had been butch when I asked if we could play some Bowie, something with a little more heft to it, he wouldn't have asked me, "Why?" He would have found something substantial to play, something pertinent and real. If I had been butch, Herb may have shown me more respect. Or he might have understood what was already apparent about Jasmine; he wouldn't have been shocked or speechless when the big reveal that was in store actually happened. If I had been butch, maybe people would have been nicer to me, because they would have known from the shape of my body that I was headed for death young. I was a perfect candidate for cancer. Something about metabolic syndrome, the hormones generated by abdominal fat, though we don't really know that. It's just a correlation between body type and the propensity for breast cancer. Breast cancer moves most often to the hip, the brain, the liver, and bone. I know I am speaking out of turn here; that I am predicting morbidities and mortalities without the proper backup, but I have dispensed with scientific discipline. This is the story of how I outed my girlfriend to her parents.

"Jasmine told me about you," Herb said to me, after I asked if we could play some Bowie. Jasmine moaned, or it sounded like a moan, whatever came from her mouth. It might have been a word, one that adolescent girls use to address their fathers, with the vowel elongated. But Jasmine couldn't have said that, because Jasmine and her brothers didn't have a father. They had a father figure. So they had to use his one-note name and stretch it into two notes—"Her-rb," they might have said—though I wasn't paying attention; I was more worried about what I would do next. But I'm pretty sure she did say this, "Her-rb," because the next thing that happened was Herb, the man, the myth, the rock 'n' roll legend, said Jasmine's name in the same way, all rhymey-sing-songy, but flat and indignant, as though we were living in a situation comedy, written for the lowest common denominator. We were all acting our parts with a set of musical instruments, the fabrics, candles, and incense as if this were an extraordinary home with an extraordinary family. The rules and the relationships were supposed to be different here: open, honest, and fair. People were supposed to be enlightened, accepting, and incapable of being shocked by the modern world and how its inhabitants related to one another.

"Do you know who Woody Guthrie is?" Herb asked. His eyes were on me, drawing me into a box, a corner, where he had unilaterally decided I belonged. I had been captured; I had fallen into a trap. I might as well have been a toddler back in the pigeon-toed brace; I couldn't answer because he already knew the answer—of course I had no idea who Woody Guthrie was. And now I was going to suffer for it. I didn't know who Woody Guthrie was because I was 17-years-old, I had been raised by wolves, and I didn't know anything. All I knew were numbers and perhaps how to manipulate them. I was a genius, though, but Jasmine hadn't told him that. She hadn't told him anything. At least nothing about us, who I was, and what I was capable of. She should have told him, but she didn't.

"Woody Guthrie said there's no such thing as bad music," Herb said. He may not have been a father in the technical sense, but he knew how to do what fathers do, lecture. Music was like food, he said; music was about communion and connections; not about people connecting to the music, but people connecting to people. Drums and percussion: that was the first music, he said. It didn't have words or messages, only desire, a primal need to find union with other beings, other humans.

"But if you're not part of the solution, you're part of the problem," I said, because if music was only about what Herb said it was, then he could justify anything in the name of music. Misogyny, for one thing: that was the central message of the Stones, Led Zeppelin, any number of stadium bands, the blues, and even some female artists whose names escape me at that moment, but punk was kicking them all in the groin and clearing out the sewer that was male superiority, arrogance, and hatred.

"Punk is the solution," I told him, because I wasn't going to be part of the problem, like Herb was, and like how I could see Jasmine was going to be. I think I repeated it, problem and solution, problem and resolution, because that is how you present an abstract when you're writing an article or delivering your dissertation. At least Bowie held out possibility for those of us, like me, Jasmine, Jack, and Nicky, of another way of being. If I had been butch, maybe my citing of this line would have been credible. But I wasn't butch, and he thought this little girl he had "raised" was like all the other little girls, hanging onto every deed and word of their patriarchal betters. He thought this woman he had shepherded through grade school, music lessons, into junior high, on from there into high school, and into pre-stardom was just like every other little girl who dreamed only of fame, glamour, and most of all the man who would supply it to her, without question. But Jasmine wasn't like that. She was nothing like that. She had promised me I would get beyond all of that and together we would make our own world, where girls didn't get shoved into categories, careers, bathroom stalls, or braces, and we could do it with our music and the way we played it, with a record deal so that everyone could know what we were saying and what was possible.

But I was not butch. I was not impressive. I was less than five feet tall, and I had no vocal range; my voice cracked on high notes and it weakened, turning sharp and sour when I had to reach the low notes. My voice was untrained and erratic. And I told Herb it didn't matter that Woody Guthrie was the first punk or what he said. It didn't matter because Jasmine knew my music, liked it, respected it, and knew what I was going for because Jasmine wasn't the little girl that he'd known since she was born or was five or six or whatever. He didn't know Jasmine like I did; he didn't know who she really was or what she had to hide from their family because she was afraid of them, just like I was afraid of my family if they found out we were lesbians. We knew families were a joke, and they were a trap; families are people you get thrown in with, and we were going to break out of them. I was breaking out of mine, and Jasmine needed to break out of hers if she was going to stop this game and be honest with herself.

"You, all of you, are part of the problem," I said. "You call yourselves musicians. You call yourselves a family. But you have no idea what Jasmine's music is really all about, what Jasmine's all about. What me and Jasmine are all about."

"What's that?" Herb asked.

"Don't you know? Isn't it obvious? Or are you ignoring it on purpose, because it would spoil the little perfect picture you have of your daughter and what she's been saying to you, to the world."

Jasmine said, "Don't, Barbara," because she knew what was coming. Or she pretended that she did. It normally trailed behind her, like a scent, though now it hovered all about her, as if it were a film that kept people from seeing what she truly was. She was a hypocrite for standing behind that film and for embracing it as though it could protect her from everything.

"God, can't you taste the duplicity in this room?" I said to their faces. Jasmine grabbed onto my thigh and squeezed, with every inch of her being. I was supposed to scream from the pain. "Do you know how it can destroy you, being willfully blind, ignorant, refusing to see?"

Jasmine said through her teeth, "Barbara, shut the fuck up," and just as quickly smiled casually to the rest, "Don't listen to her; she gets this way sometimes."

"Get which way, honest? Truthful? Telling it like it is? Your daughter's as gay as I am. She's a lesbian. Behind your back she's fucking girls, fucking the patriarchy. She knows all this is a farce. So much for—"

"I'll get the dishes," Jasmine's mother interrupted, and Herb told "his" boys to leave the room. Jack and Nicky had rushed to Jasmine's side. She could not look up from her lap even though I was calling her name, "Jasmine, Jasmine, look at me, you know it's true," but she couldn't bring herself to say it, not in front of Herb and her mother, who like all the other mothers in this world was a ghost, a disappearing act, with nothing to say other than what the *paterfamilias* deemed acceptable to say. Here I had sprung all of the cages; I had liberated myself and Jasmine (Jack and Nicky, too), and yet none of us was moving. The adults were doing all the talking as if they could beat us back down again.

If I had been butch, this would have all turned out differently. I could have stood up from my chair and told them what's what. They were shouting at me as though I were their daughter, their little girl, their property. They demanded Jasmine get rid of me, show me the door, and never see me again, but she kept her head down. She was speechless once exposed. If I had been butch I would have told her mother and Herb that they were the ones who were ingrates; they were the ones who were rude, but I realized that if I was the pure, truthful, faithfully righteous person I knew myself to be, I had to get out of there. I had to run as fast as I could. If I had been butch I might have been able to defend myself; I might have been able to take all that abuse. Had I known that my genes and environment interacted in such a way that I would experience the outcome forecasted for the butch body type, I would have stood my ground. I would have grabbed Jasmine and rescued her.

That's what I should have done since I was butch—I am butch in terms of my morbidity. I am dying as though I am any other butch lesbian with breast cancer, side effects of chemo and radiation notwithstanding. Beyond loss of hair, vomiting, and the end of fertility or menstrual cycle, the side effects of the treatment can be more individual. But the correlation between being overweight and exhibiting a cylindrical-shaped, perpetually wearing a bulletproof vest type of body is one that can't be ignored. Perhaps it is the cruel joke of estrogen, at higher levels in the less feminine bodies because of the fat cells gathered around the middle, or perhaps it is the higher levels of insulin that trigger the disease. We don't know. And I don't know for myself, since I was always too scared to go butch. I was scared of what my parents would think if I sawed off my long hair, if I let my waist go, widened and rounded it. My father always said I took the path of least resistance, which is the real reason why I went to college and went into mathematics; if I had really wanted to be a musician, I wouldn't have let what he or anyone else thought get in my way. I could have taken lessons; I could have majored in music; I could have run away and joined a different circus if the one Jasmine, Jack, and Nicky were running off to wouldn't take me. But my father never knew the effort it took not to become butch, not to give in to my body's instincts. And now my body has betrayed me.

Perhaps there was one night when it did not betray me, and it was that night at Jasmine's. Jack eventually asked me, years later, what was I thinking that night, and I don't know. I don't remember. But I do remember having Jasmine's attention that night, knowing that I was losing it and that I may never get it again. And her family, so perfect and chummy, was fake, or Jasmine was fake. I had to see which was which. I had to show them that I could see right through their deception: Herb's medieval fiefdom, his vanity project, and the rhythm section/ensemble he had filling out his mediocre jamming. I could see right through Jasmine, and Jack and Nicky, too, leaving punk to become backing musicians in a pop act that would probably fizzle before the decade was finished. But I would have been in this forever—music and punk rock—if I had been given the chance Jasmine, Jack, and Nicky got. If I could have commanded an audience like they did; so I showed them. I showed them I really could have. I did.

CHAPTER 18

THE COPS CAME BACK. I was in my pajamas when they came on the weekend. It had to have been a weekend since Dorothy and Marion were there. Finally, they came. They came on a Friday night and put a sign on the door: "Patient in Hospice: No Admittance Without Prior Approval," and the number of the hospice office to call. The sign was no bigger than the "CAUTION: OXYGEN IN USE" sticker in the window, but it was more effective. Dorothy and Marion put an end to the crowds. Or maybe people stopped showing up when that reporter did his story on the television about the possible ties Barb had to accused murderer James H. Stevic Jr.

I felt bleary with exhaustion, incompetent, and useless since Dorothy and Marion had arrived to take charge. They hugged the nurses, asked after their families, brought them chocolates and gift baskets with teas and bubble baths—for all the shifts. Days, nights, and weekends. They brought a special cream to use on Barb's feet and hands, and they gave the nurses samples of it. In other words, Dorothy and Marion were prepared. They took steps, had strategies, and knew to think about things I hadn't thought about. I was the one from New York, where you tip and gift so you don't have to cajole and beg. Clearly, I hadn't learned anything.

When Dorothy and Marion had called me, I threw some clothes in a suitcase and used my husband's credit card to pay for my flight. He told me not to worry about the babysitting; that he'd take care of everything—the groceries, our daughter's play dates, and her lessons—so I could concentrate on Barbara. It had been a week since I'd last seen them, and I don't know how long since I last talked to them. I was becoming disoriented; I was unsure how much of the past week had actually happened and how much had I dreamed; and I wondered whether I was dreaming when the knocking at the door began. I tried to blot it out and dismiss it as something Dorothy and Marion could handle; something they would prefer to handle without me. But I couldn't get that sound out of my head, the pounding that alternated with the doorbell, like the games of my childhood youth coming back to haunt me.

"I know this is a bad time," Greg Onderdonk said. He was standing in front of the cops but without any confidence. I thought maybe the cops had made him do it—front their latest invasion—by how tentatively he stood, like he couldn't wait to run away and let Simpson and W-Y-R-E-C-K-A take over for him.

"Only the worst," I said, although I knew it wasn't true. Things would get much worse once Dorothy and Marion left after the weekend.

"There's been a new development," Greg "Herman's Hermits" Onderdonk said.

"What?" I asked, but I knew. We all did.

"Could we come in, ma'am?" W-Y-R-E-C-K-A asked softly, but I wasn't buying his timid act. I had seen how he moved and how he held himself.

"You need prior approval," I said, pointing at the sign.

"You don't want to do this out on the street," the detective-sergeant said. He stepped up and gently moved The Hermit aside. The detective-sergeant was carrying a notebook and opened it, like he was about to read something official and damning.

"All right," I said.

They knew where to go, this trio. Into the kitchen, standing around the table. Not sitting down, because they were all business. The business of arresting me or Dorothy and Marion. They were going to arrest somebody, it looked like. But it couldn't be Barbara. They hadn't brought in a stretcher. Her death was the only thing saving her, apparently.

"I told you not to say anything to the press," The Hermit said.

"You came all the way up here to tell me that?"

"No, not exactly," The Hermit said, and I was surprised to see him march in place for a moment. He had been lifeless, practically, when I had needed him and suddenly he was jumpy, unnerved by the situation he had avoided. "But if you hadn't said anything to that reporter—"

"I didn't say anything to that reporter," I said. "All I did was the math."

"What?" The Hermit asked, like he was outraged.

"All right, all right," the detective-sergeant said, and he put out his arms, like he was trying to keep the peace and break up a fight. "What Mr. Onderdonk is trying to get at here—"

"If you hadn't said anything—" The Hermit was bouncing up and down on his toes, like he was trying to be taller but couldn't hold the pose right. Like whatever he was saying was supposed to elevate him in his own estimation; or that it should have elevated him in the cops' minds. "—they wouldn't—"

"We would have figured it out," the detective-sergeant said, and he patted the notebook with pride. It must have been all in there, the story of Barb's life twisted to satisfy the needs of the cops, the grieving public. "Eventually."

"You've exposed your sister to all kinds of liability," The Hermit said.

"What?" I said.

"Liability. Do you know what that means?"

"I know what liability means," I said, although I wasn't sure just how it applied in this situation.

"Do you know the standard of proof in a liability case is less than in a criminal trial?" The Hermit's curls were bobbing around his chin, ears, and neck, like he was in a slow-motion shampoo commercial. It was all he could do to keep his kinetic energy in his head and face, keep it from traveling through the rest of his body. "Do you have any idea what a civil suit will cost; what it will do to my business?"

"We're sorry, ma'am," W-Y-R-E-C-K-A began.

"You're sorry? That I'm ruining this man's business? You're going to arrest me for that?" I knew my voice was too loud, but I didn't care. I needed Dorothy, Marion and the weekend nurses to know what was happening, because I couldn't deal with the absurdity myself.

"We're not here to arrest you," Simpson assured me. "Or anybody," he said to The Hermit. "We just need to talk."

"To Barbara? She's really not up for it," I said.

"Look," Simpson said, and he looked tired, washed out. This must have been his day off; it was not only on his face, but in how he stood, in a slack, lackluster pose. "James H. Stevic: he knew your sister. Or she knew him. We haven't worked out the nature of their relationship."

"You opened the door to this," The Hermit said to me. His face was shining, although there was no perspiration or tears. Maybe he was melting. "There will be lawsuits—"

"That's not the issue here—" Simpson began.

"As executor of this estate, for me it's the only issue. I have to know what I'm dealing with—"

"Mr. Onderdonk made a deal with us," Simpson said in a kind of sing-songy apology. "He'd tell us what he knows, and he could accompany us here to see what you know. What anybody knows. That's the first step. Before we start talking liability and wrongful death suits, we have to nail down some things. The money trail still zigs and zags. But it's all headed in one direction."

"I don't know what you're talking about," I said.

"Justice, justice demands," Simpson said, and when he looked down at the floor, like he was gathering his most profound vocabulary, I was afraid he would launch into a soliloquy. "We have to try, for the record. We have to try one last time. We have Mr. Onderdonk's permission, that's all we need, legally," he declared. "Unless you want to stop us, and then you'd be interfering with our investigation."

"You'd be an accessory," W-Y-R-E-C-K-A advised me, like he was doing me a favor. "We could take you downtown, process you—"

"You said you weren't going to arrest me," I said to Simpson.

"You're right. You're right," the detective-sergeant conceded, and he might have winked at his partner, but I couldn't tell. He was adjusting his hat over his eyes by pulling on the brim. "If you let us talk to your sister this one last time—" he began, but he did not finish. He stepped in front of The Hermit with a wide gait, like he was expecting to tower over him. But they were both short men, shorter than I would have been if I were still dancing. That did not mean I could persuade them that a nearly comatose woman wouldn't have much to say to them; she'd have to be dead for them to let up, and she was still alive, or somewhere in between, somewhere inaccessible to us, and the gold-digging, grasping folk who were going to sue her over Jasmine's death. So it didn't matter, I thought.

"Sure," I said. "Sure, go ahead. You know the way," I said, and I made what I hoped they'd interpret as a grand gesture, something cooperative and selfless, in stepping away from the kitchen door, so their path to it was clear. "Do whatever you need because far be it from me to stand in the way of justice. Ca-ching ca-ching!" It was my turn to sing then, and I pumped my left arm to emphasize the "ca-ching" I had pulled somewhere out of my memory. "Go ahead because afterward I bet you'll be able to make a bundle off this one. I mean, Mr. Onderdonk's worried about money, you're probably worried about money—book and movie rights for the cop who unravels the Jasmine conspiracy. Maybe they'll make it a mini-series. Or a documentary. That would be better. More prestigious, right? They have a longer shelf life. The offers for you to consult will come pouring in, I bet. Who are you going to get to play Barb, huh? She should know before she dies. She deserves that much, doesn't she? I mean, since you've decided you know all about her, what she lived for, even what she's living for now, why she's fighting—"

"Why are you still protecting her?" The Hermit asked.

"Why aren't you? I mean, that's your job, right?" I asked, because I thought it would buy me some time. I needed a few more seconds to put everything together, make it logical, and give it an arc, like the rising and falling action of a drama.

My sister the murderer. Or at least she planned it out and hired a guy to do it. My sister, the murder broker. I did not necessarily believe this, but I did not necessarily disbelieve it, because of who I understood my sister to be in her worst moments. In my worst moments. When I thought about all the resentments and jealousies that had engulfed us, the competition that I was winning anyway because I'd still be alive when this was over. I was winning: that's what made me think how improbable it was for Barb to kill anybody. For years I had tried not to feel anything for Barb, just as she felt even less for me. But I couldn't help it. I couldn't help all the time I had with her—if not the memories and then the effect of those memories.

"I don't need to protect her from anything," I said, and I was proud of my answer, because it gave away nothing. Or nothing that would get them any closer to what they needed. They knew who killed Jasmine, but they wanted the why; if not the reason, because there was no reason to kill someone, then the excuse and how it made sense to the people doing it. They might as well have been searching for the reason Barb got breast cancer, why she did not get to be famous like she wanted so much, or even why I was a failure, or maybe not more of a success. Some things are random, I thought whenever I tried to console myself. But some things are not. I grew up in Hollywood. I lived in New York. I knew how these things went, who gets to be famous or infamous. I never imagined there would be so much variety or so many gradations on the scale in my own family and in my tidy but expanding universe.

"Just go right in," I said. "Now's your chance—I wouldn't want you to miss it. There you go, you remember, right down this way. There you go. Knock yourself out. Have a ball."

I don't know if they heard all of this speech, the mighty triumvirate of The Hermit, Detective-Sergeant Simpson, and his big boy wonder who brought up the rear. I don't know because they walked out as soon as I showed them which way to go. I didn't trail behind them as they set out like they were tackling some long, arduous journey. I didn't pad along behind them because I knew what they would find there at the end of their journey. The Hermit would have known what was waiting for him there, too, if he had any brains. I guess he didn't, and this was the proof positive that Barb, always so worried someone was going to take her money, had hired an idiot to guard her life's savings.

I listened for the cops' footsteps and how they would end when they entered the bedroom whose atmosphere had progressed from reverential to hellish. The sound that oxygen tanks make was unnerving, the alternating inhaling and hiss. I wondered how anyone, let alone the cops, would hear what Barb was saying with that mask on her face, her mouth covered in a fog from the cold oxygen hitting her hot exhalations. That's if the cops ever got close enough to ask the questions, with Dorothy and Marion there confronting them. They would have stood up as soon as they saw they had visitors they hadn't previously met, although they knew The Hermit, if not by that sobriquet. They wouldn't pay attention to him. Then they would have winked and nodded to the weekend nurses and had them surround the cops, an ambush of polite concern. Dorothy and Marion went to the same schools as I did and grew up with the same people, and yet they were able to handle these kinds of situations, while I obviously could not. It must be another one of those IQ things.

This was how they went about protecting Barbara. Not like how I did it, spontaneously running interference. Barb had a habit of asking me to "be my big sister" whenever she wanted a favor. Usually this involved my calling a plumber or electrician when something at the house needed fixing. Occasionally I had to call my mother's doctor when my mother was out of town and the doctor was calling with test results. Once, while my mother was traveling, a supposed cousin dropped in on Barbara and wouldn't leave. I had to phone the police and the cousin's parents (they were related to Irv, I think) and get them to remove the houseguest. I was a pretty good big sister from a distance.

For the up-close jobs, though, only Dorothy and Marion could cut it. Only they could stop the snapping of the fingers in Barbara's face, the clapping of hands to her ears, or the shouting of her name like doors would be broken down if there were no answer. The Hermit and the cops would not get any closer to my sister than I had gotten to the post of principal dancer in my career. Barb was over everything at that point—pain, sensation, people, and circumstances. Morphine was no longer administered by mouth, but through tube and needle; the drip constant. The drug ran through a machine that sounded like a heartbeat, although it was neither measuring out life nor confirming its existence.

Dorothy and Marion must have worked this out. They must have had insight into the abomination Barbara's last days were bound to become. They must have realized at the beginning of hospice; not that Jasmine would be murdered, of course, but that there would be trouble; that Barb wouldn't be allowed to go in peace because she had never had peace in her life. They had plotted it out, assigned roles and tasks; they had played out every scenario possible in their heads, collected their wits, and steeled themselves for any possibility. They knew Barb would not go, or could not go, quietly, like the rest of us. The world didn't treat Barb like that, or Barb wouldn't have had it; she had to have the last word, the "goodbye, cruel world" moment that would be impossible to pry from everyone's recollections of her. If she did not go out screaming, then she would have someone else scream farewell to her.

My husband said something interesting to me when all of this began; by "this," I mean the cops, the investigation, and the ensuing three-ring nightmare, especially my bravado performance as the aggrieved sibling. Those were my fifteen minutes, I suppose. I'm glad I got them out of the way so I don't have to wait for them any longer. But my husband was watching the same pageants of police action, fans grieving, cable television's breathless rerun of every piece of film they could find of Jasmine; and he came to a conclusion. "Your sister did not kill Jasmine," he said, "but she wants everyone to believe that she could have done it." He said this calmly, I thought, objectively, considering all the crap she had thrown at him over the years. Then again, she had something to say to all of my boyfriends. It wasn't that she didn't like them or him. It was just her way of establishing dominance, I was realizing. When she told him he wasn't a real musician—that he was a copyist, a robot, a Muzak machine, and a functionary—she was letting him know how superior she was: untouchable and unattainable. That was how she saw herself, like she was the real prize even though she had taken herself out of the competition. I was the consolation gift and the participation trophy.

"Your sister could never see something like this through," my husband said. "She hurts people but her insults are never original. A real crime like this would take too much out of her. She couldn't even conceive of it." Over the years my husband had said many things about Barb, some I nodded to, and others I understood to be the result of her dismissive treatment of him. I wondered why he never hit back; why he listened when she'd go on about the music business and play when she asked him to on the piano she kept in the living room at the house only to interrupt him with criticisms. I didn't ask him because I didn't want to upset the balance. He was outthinking her all this time, I suppose, and if he could be certain she hadn't done anything, I could be too. I wondered where Dorothy and Marion had gotten their stores of faith, although Barb had been far nicer, I assumed, to their spouses than to my own.

So by my husband's estimation no one had anything to worry about—except the cops, since Barb had them pegged like she had everyone else. They were fools, potentially harmless, but they still had to be dealt with. Maybe Barb explained this to Dorothy and Marion somehow, told them directly how she had set it up—to be blamed for something she didn't do but still have all roads leading back to her so she'd be at the center of whatever it was—a natural disaster or financial scandal. I expected she would have had an easier time making the stock market tank by summoning fire, flood, or earthquake to overtake the house. A murder had to be different, though. A murder would require prophecy. Prophets usually wind up as martyrs, and people already saw Barb that way: Dorothy, Marion, and everyone who had come to the house did. Everyone who knew her story with Jasmine and without Jasmine, and how Barb lived the rest of her life like a recluse as she mourned her youth, or Jasmine, or some higher principle that always got mixed up with Hollywood fandom or star-fucking.

My sister the martyr, and I wasn't following. I still don't know how I feel about that and all of the doubts I harbored.

The Hermit and the cops were in there for a while, longer than I expected. The detective-sergeant must have been interrogating Dorothy and Marion about what they knew. As Simpson spoke, W-Y-R-E-C-K-A would be handing them photos, mug shots, I guess, to see if James H. Stevic Jr. looked familiar; if they had ever spotted him with Barb. Maybe he'd been at a concert they all attended together, or once he was panhandling somewhere, and Barb had given him twenty dollars. Barb could be generous, particularly with strangers, most likely because there were no strings attached with strangers. Maybe James H. Stevic Jr. had been stalking Barbara: did anyone ever consider that? He'd found himself a benefactor, a sugar momma, a mark, and he'd been milking her for years. Maybe he killed Jasmine to get Barb's attention or to scare her. This was perfectly plausible, as far as I could figure out; I could run into the room and explain it, and Dorothy and Marion might believe it. The Hermit might write it down to prepare for his future testimony. But to the cops it would lack legitimacy because of who it came from, me, the sister. Of course I'd find another way to put it all together. Another way out of the randomness.

When neither Dorothy nor Marion could identify James H. Stevic Jr., The Hermit must have jumped in his shoes or made a victory fist in his pocket. If no one could tie James H. Stevic Jr. to Barbara Ross, then all those theories of how a frustrated criminal mastermind got away with the biggest murder in 21st century Hollywood would dissolve like so much fog, the low clouds that hugged the hills here in the mornings. The Hermit would then be able to collect on everything—Barb's cash, the house, her possessions, the record and memorabilia collections, the car—without having to worry about liability. He would have struck it rich with a minimum amount of effort. I assume his mouth was watering during this exchange, the apparent windfall so close and yet so tenuous. He did not dare taste it because its flavor would be so sweet and welcoming, its loss would be something he wouldn't recover from. Like losing a member of the family. Plus, losing all that money would be bad for his business and his reputation. To be associated with infamy like that: it's something that never goes away. I mean, look at Barb and what became of her and of me.

Finally, I bet, Simpson and his minions must have asked Dorothy and Marion how much time Barbara had left. That was the more pressing question. The Hermit and the cops must have realized this when they saw the state Barbara was in. She was nothing more than blankets attached to oxygen tanks. The bed must have become a map, a relief of her organs, though it had to be inaccurate in places, because she had no more organs. No stomach or kidneys since she wasn't eating or drinking; her lungs were in shreds from the tumors that had taken it over. Whether The Hermit and the cops were capable of seeing what was becoming of Barbara, I don't know. And yet I knew they had experience with dying; with dying bodies specifically. They had to have had, given their jobs. They must have understood how Barbara was eroding, like a stone that's been hit by other stones too many times. She was surrendering.

Or she might have been straining in every way she could have. She could have been wrestling with the oxygen hovering at her lips and nose; she could have been jerking her chest to shove the air in and jostle it out. The rhythm of her lungs could have tricked her heart so it kept beating. She could have engineered it, the mechanics of her respiration, goading the heart muscle, despite what all the other organs said. She would have used her will through thinking. When it was over, everyone said it was peaceful, but that is wishful thinking. That's what people say when they don't know the person. Or they didn't know my sister like I did. I mean I knew what Dorothy and Marion did not, what nobody else could have known, what Barbara herself couldn't remember. I've always known how uncomfortable Barbara must have been ever since my parents strapped her into that bed brace to straighten out her pigeon-toes. Something like that has got to leave a trace, an impression. She'd been struggling to get out of herself all her life; she'd been struggling to escape. She wasn't going to give up when she was this close to doing it, this close to vanishing.

CHAPTER 19

I KNOW MY IMPACT. I CAN MEASURE IT. My sister can't do this. Most people can't, without cheating. The cheating is probably worse here in Los Angeles, but they cheat in New York; they cheat everywhere there are people and resources, and one is not enough to satisfy the other: a shortage in attention spans, speaking parts, and entertainment dollars. Money, recognition, and follow-throughs: I can quantify each and come up with an equation. I can massage it in my favor. I can remain objective and swallow my own medicine. But if I were to do all this, my last service to humanity, no one would understand my premise, let alone apply the calculations.

Nothing in mathematics is useless, but people can be. They can be irrelevant, surplus, and excess; outnumbered with no power other than what can be derived through their purchases. There's a reason they call them "extras" in the movies, the crowds that make up the background, muttering "peas and carrots, peas and carrots." They appear to be having significant conversations, though they don't know how to construct on their own a truly pertinent dialogue. There's a reason why we can't all be stars. A dearth of intellect does not begin to cover the answer. There is the ability to love and be loved and to give off appearances while maintaining an image. There is gravitational pull, and there is presence. That I had none of these

I must account for, but I can no longer mourn them. I have only my body left, with its strange determination to keep pumping, keep producing wastes, and alter oxygen into carbon.

When I try to measure my impact, I get confused: is it a matter of evaporation or displacement? In the water, how many minerals and molecules did my body disrupt? If I had never been in the water, how many more life forms could have occupied my space? I wonder if I had not been inserted into a situation, how would it have been different—better, worse, farcical, serious, more efficient, less punk, or more mainstream? I should be able to zero in on particular moments and witness what my absence would have fueled, or how it would have gone unnoticed. I was either integral to the scene or I was extra, like curettage.

My sister took a short cut to all this. She used her body, which is what she's always done, her only option. She's made herself a daughter, and she attracted a husband. Presuming they outlive her of course. If they don't, she'll have nothing. But she can count on her issues, the depletion of her tendons and tears in her muscles, with her immune system and hormones that cannot keep up with the needs of her aging body. Her body is bent on its own destruction. But she has these two to remember her, to sit around and recall all the quirks, habits, aphorisms, and idiocies that made her their wife and mother, and no one can take that away from them, not even the gods that hated her, the nurses who neglected her, and the doctors who didn't know who she was. Perhaps her husband will write a sonata for her, a ballet or an opera that will be produced as a vanity project; I can't foresee how the material of her life would be suitable for a mass audience. Her daughter will do the same stupid things to her children as her mother did to her, and the cycle will be unbroken. Something will survive our family.

But that is the easy way, through the body: remembrance through proximity, forced intimacy, and the prison of relationships. I wanted something more than that. Or I was supposed to, with the expanse of my mind, or more accurately, my brain. The potential in a physical organ makes the body academic. And yet I had this body. I was forced to use it. I had to endure with it while my family didn't do anything. My parents and sister didn't need to build anything, like I did; they just had to exist in their bodies, and their bodies would have an impact on one another and on me. While I always had to be doing things, building things, creating villages and cities, and entire empires of accomplishments that led to more achievements. Their bodies could not be satisfied with what my body was able to give.

If I were to measure my impact solely based on my family's thoughts, I will always be a work-in-progress. They will always be waiting for promises to be met, the predictions of teachers, professors, and intelligence tests fulfilled. They did not understand that those numbers do not necessarily translate. There are other factors that tie in and that tie up the competition. You have to strike beyond family into the realm of the anonymous; go where people do not know you and may not want to know you, but you win them over; make them want more of you because there is never enough; and make them make you essential to their lives. A stranger who speaks or sings with their voice, addresses their fears, and celebrates their happiness. This is how Jasmine could be judged, by the number of households that bought her records. The number of times they were played, sung, memorized, and performed spontaneously. How often the words, the rhythm, and the melodies were cited. How much of each conversation around a dining table did she inspire. How often was she with them—at work, at play, and in the silence just as dreams break the first thing in the morning. How far did she go and how deep was the penetration.

I could measure these, or I could stick with a safer quantity: how much did she change the world, the music business, and the culture that had created her. The critics declared that she changed the focus of rock 'n' roll from male to female, from straight to gay, and from the formulaic to the experimental. There should be artists to follow in her footsteps, but there are none. So how much of a contribution could she be said to have made? It's not that she is matchless, but that she doesn't translate. CYA: we were a knock-off band, a copy of the Runaways, The Minors, and Suzi Quatro. We could barely keep up with ourselves. We did not get credit for trying. This is one way the music business demeans you, crushes your soul, and obliterates your vision; though people would say I don't know the music business. I was never in the music business. I was an outsider, a fanatic, a threat, and a consumer. Jasmine, Jack, and Nicky: they were in the thick of it. Nicky had children, I heard. Jack is out there somewhere, I've been told. Playing. Producing. Signing new acts, artists, and repertory. Jasmine *was* the music business, like The Regent. He taught her everything. I taught math to some kids—undergraduates, graduates, and the homeless. Jasmine was a pretty girl with an appealing voice. She was not a radical concept to begin with.

I had statistics and mortality studies, controls and experiments, zeroes and ones, the multiplicity of enzymes and hormones that push or dissolve illnesses, unquantifiable factors in the background, and the entire environment. When I could not make the numbers work on the high-tension power lines, I looked at magnetic fields and microwave ovens. But people were not dying fast enough. Children with leukemia and brain tumors. They persisted. They did not get diagnosed. They escaped my counting unlike the breast cancer victims. I could not prove causes, only correlations. But in my body, in the blood that will be drawn and the bones that will be burned; in my ashes spread on a field or dumped in the ocean, there will be answers. In the samples of my tumors, preserved, classified, and awaiting discovery in some registry of cancers that I used to count, that I gave permission to study my sickness; in how my niece remembers me, how she learned of my symptoms and illness, how I held on through various treatments, the hair I lost, and grew back again; I will hold this answer in code, why cells grow, go haywire, and must be killed because they will not return to their normal resting state. In the future I will be the source of all information. Prevention and immunotherapy, personalized medicine; if my life has not mattered, then my death will, unlike Jasmine's. Jasmine's death changes nothing. How she spends eternity is academic, whether she is burned, buried, or embalmed. Her body did not give the world a question or a dilemma. It lived, and it died. Its reasons for dying were clear and simple. Finally she has been denuded of all mystery.

This is my legacy.

CHAPTER 20

DOROTHY WANTED TO SPREAD BARBARA'S ASHES in the San Francisco Bay. Barb had some great times in San Francisco, Dorothy said. She showed me pictures of Barb at the Coit Tower, in Chinatown, and at the bottom of Lombard Street with her kids. So San Francisco it was. I did not know that Barb had ever been up north or that she had been anywhere besides the house and her job. Apparently I did not know what Barb was capable of. Dorothy filmed her kids pouring the ashes off a dock in some marina. They shouted "Go, Aunt Barbara, go!" when they turned the urn upside down. They could have rented a boat and had someone take them to a more appropriate location for spreading ashes. Three nautical miles offshore—I looked it up, to see what I would have been missing. But all that would have required permits, notifications, permissions, and of course money. Dorothy had none and was forced to improvise. I thought Barb would have been horrified by all the laws broken on her behalf. But perhaps she wouldn't have been bothered at all.

Dorothy brought the video of the ash spreading ceremony to the memorial at Barbara's house. She invited all the people, and she and Marion set up all the food and drinks. The only thing I did was argue with them over when the memorial should be planned. They wanted to wait until after Labor

Day, when more people would be available in town. But my daughter would have been in school by then, and playing hooky in New York is an entirely different matter than it ever was in Los Angeles. Dorothy and Marion complained I wasn't giving them, or Barb, enough time; the police and the press would still be interested in Barb, and they might send their contingents over. I told them Barb's niece had a right to say goodbye properly to her only aunt, and that won the day, if only temporarily. I made my husband come, too, because I had an idea of what I'd be dealing with if Barb's last week was any indication. And I wasn't going through all that a second time without him.

The Hermit, Onderdonk, gave Dorothy and Marion permission to hold the memorial in what had been renamed as "Barbara's estate," or in other words, his windfall. But my family and I were not allowed to stay there. That old liability issue again, although this time, his concerns were much more pedestrian. Broken china, nicked tables, or stained couches: this is what he fretted over, although I did not know how he'd avoid these mishaps if he allowed a memorial with 20 to 50 people in the house. I think he was probably more worried about my taking something from the "estate," a souvenir from my sister's vast belongings: vinyl records, concert T-shirts, I don't know. I told him this would be the first time my daughter could not stay in her grandmother's house, but he remained unimpressed. I could have asked Dorothy or Marion to put us up, but after our discussions on the timing of the event, I decided against it. We got a hotel, across the street from the high school where this whole thing got started. In Los Angeles the summer lasts forever, but you are not always welcome to enjoy it.

Dorothy and Marion were right: there were cameras, though the camera people and reporters mostly hung back, like they were being respectful. Or maybe they were afraid. Now they were dealing with the associates of a known conspirator. It didn't matter that Barb's case would never be taken to court and never proved definitively. Never disproved either, which is how this story will live on, as in, how it will never die. The news people did not ask us questions, but they must have wondered who we were, we dangerous, devoted few, who were coming to pay our respects to someone who had frustrated America's passion for justice and packaged endings. Going to the memorial made us conspirators, too, or so that was how we were nearly described on the late news that night. I didn't have a problem with that; I had already been branded, after all, as "the sister." Having my husband and daughter similarly named, however, was another matter. My daughter asked if news cameras showed up at every funeral.

The cops, meanwhile, stood on the side of the driveway opposite the cameras. Dorothy and Marion swore they did not call them, and none of the neighbors, like Mr. Silvers, came to the memorial; so I don't know why the cops thought their presence was needed. I suppose they had to keep tabs on the traffic or deter the morbidly curious from crashing the event. I looked for Simpson or W-Y-R-E-C-K-A as I rushed my husband and daughter through the gauntlet, but I didn't see them. After such a big case, working crowd control must have been beneath them. They got what they wanted, what everyone must want at some point. Maybe not to be famous in the way Barbara wanted, but to be considered good, hard working, and competent at what they do. Maybe just to matter. To count, when they're taking roll.

Inside the house, Dorothy and Marion had the video of the ash spreading ceremony playing on a loop. Next to the television they had an empty scrapbook, which they asked people to fill with their remembrances of Barb. There was room for pictures, too, and one woman brought a class picture from elementary school. Barb was in a dress—Irv demanded we wear dresses to school until our female teachers started showing up in pants—in the front row on the far left. She looked the same to me, smiling with her hands folded in her lap. Her legs were crossed like the other girls', and she wore knee socks and saddle shoes. Looking at that picture, I thought it was as though she had never aged. She could have died at age 7 or 8, for how exactly that picture captured her face, although there were other pictures. Her coworkers from her last job brought them in. They consisted of different angles of Barb sitting before multiple computer screens. In these she never smiled, but stared at either keyboard or screen in dire concentration. Dorothy and Marion said the scrapbook was for my daughter, and they'd send it to her. No sight of it so far.

I was surprised none of my mother's old friends came, though some of Barb's friends from the neighborhood and from elementary school were there. Like Leslie: she assumed I was inheriting the house and started asking questions. I told her to talk to Dorothy and Marion, who had populated the memorial with members of their own families. Such was the lack of dependable mourners. Maria came, at Dorothy and Marion's invitation, but the other hospice people were no shows. I wondered about Jacqueline and Nicole, but I was not disappointed they were also MIA. Barb's coworkers from the cancer studies came up to me to shake my hand and offer their apologies. Her coworkers from the last job were also polite. They seemed to know who my daughter was, and they told me how much Barb talked about and adored her. The food and drinks were also inside the house, but most people went outside into the backyard. There was no more competing over who knew her best or who was the most affected or the most sympathetic. Everyone either paced or sat around the patio or the surviving patch of grass, dumbfounded.

I wanted to tell my daughter how Helen used to water the lawn and spray the ivy with a hose whenever there was a fire in the hills. The backyard was supposed to be Irv's exclusive territory, but whenever there was a brush fire, it was our mother who was moved to defend the property. I had tried pointing out how the "CAUTION: OXYGEN IN USE" sticker was still up on the front window, because this house had always been about hazards, flammables, and the potential for disaster. I got her to take a brief look at the thickets below either side of our little hill; at the oaks, eucalyptus, Laurel, and sycamore. They must have been planted without regard for what was growing elsewhere. Over the years the desert air turned everything into chaparral. "No smoking in the canyon," said the signs on the road leading up to this place—at least when we were kids. I didn't see any on this last trip here, though I didn't think the danger had passed.

When we were kids, we got an occasional lesson from the local fire house about how dangerous the neighborhood was. The firemen would come to the auditorium where we'd all be sitting "Indian style," and they'd tell us not to play with matches, or even rub sticks together, so ripe were the conditions here. Native Americans used to call this the "City of Smoke," and the natural oils of leaves and stems were always primed. One spark could take down the entire canyon—and it did before any of us were born. Some of the older kids said they remembered it, but Barb said at dinner that night that it was impossible. She'd done the math, and those kids would have had to have been in their cribs at the time of the fire. But it made them famous, she said, to get to talk about it.

After the visit from the firemen, it seemed to me that fire was everywhere, although that's probably my mind crunching together many different events—earthquakes, mudslides, and the winds that knocked down trees and telephone poles, cutting the power. Those kinds of natural disasters don't seem to happen as often, or maybe they've been replaced in my mind by others, those of a more human variety. Like all the fights we had in the house, even when my daughter was visiting. We could never agree which way was the right way—to diaper a baby, treat a cold, bandage a cut, or comfort the dying.

I wanted to tell my daughter about how I used to watch her grandmother soak the grass, drown the ivy, douse any sparks that dared to land on our property. I wanted her to know how Barb and I, dressed in our bathing suits, used to point out the spots she supposedly missed, always near our toes in the muddy borders of Irv's lawn, so she'd turn the hose on us. It was supposed to protect us. If we hadn't been equally saturated there'd be complaints, then wails. One of us always had the advantage at the expense of the other.

To her credit, my daughter was none too interested in what I had to say. Maybe I should have told her on earlier visits to what had been her grandmother's house. But if I had told her then, she wouldn't have been old enough to retain any of it. Now that she was old enough, Dorothy's kids and the children of Barb's other friends—there were six kids altogether, enough for a gang—were far more enticing to my daughter.

She is an only child and will never know sibling rivalry. My husband and I did not really plan it that way, but I was so old when I finally got pregnant. I worry she'll feel orphaned once we're gone. She won't even have cousins. I wonder whether I've deprived her of something. The joys of sisterhood, even if Barbara and I missed out on them. I imagine sisterhood must be like assumptions about your history together—what is remembered and who did what and when. You don't have to talk about these things; they're understood. They're a foundation. You don't necessarily like them, but they are there, and you learn to live with them and not trip over them. Barb and I never had that. For us the background was always changing, or the ground beneath us was. Or maybe everything happened in a vacuum, and you couldn't count on what would be swept inside with you when you were pushed into it.

When both Barb and I were pretty young, Helen told me that no one but my sister would be as close to me because we were so much alike. I think this was before the elementary school declared Barb a genius, and I was declared not a genius. Once all that started, we didn't have any assumptions to make or any starting place to share. Maybe we didn't have enough time to build those things. Then our time was up, and we couldn't get it back.

There was something else that happened when we were young, when the school wanted Barb tested. There was no need to test me, of course, and as my parents explained it to me, they couldn't say why Barb was particularly worthy of all this attention, and I was not. People have different talents, they said. I would find mine, they said, and I suppose they were right. In the meantime, I was to remember that I was brought up with the same care and love they had applied to

Barbara. Whatever special attention they inadvertently lavished on Barbara, I was always standing to the left, or perhaps to the right, of her, and some must have rubbed off. A good dancer knows there's no difference between left and right; both must be developed equally, sharing in the strength that comes from diligence and practice. But of course my parents weren't dancers, and I was not even a good one. Helen and Irv also said we could spend a lifetime trying to figure it out, who she was, who she was going to be, why I was not like her and who I was, but that I shouldn't worry about it. So I didn't. At least I think I didn't. Now, it doesn't matter. Does it?

ACKNOWLEDGMENTS

THOUGH THIS BOOK WAS INSPIRED by the life and death of my sister, Susan Margaret "BR" Rosenberg, it should not be taken as a definitive biography. I have left out much of her humor and silliness and many of her accomplishments. She was generous to a fault, hyper-law-abiding, and incapable of hurting anyone. But what wounded her in her life hit so deeply she was never able to rise above it. She was traumatized by what she thought was love and therefore did everything she could never to again encounter it.

In the last months of her life, she was cared for by her friends Joyce Swenson and Shannon Wade under the supervision of Silverado Hospice. Silverado's administrative and nursing staffs displayed the forbearing of saints. I will be forever grateful to them and to Joyce and Shannon.

A residency at the Wellstone Center in the Redwoods was instrumental in the writing of this book. I want to thank the center's cofounders, Sarah Ringler and Steve Kettmann, and their daughters, for hosting me. While at Wellstone I met Jessica Hjarrand, Lisa Sardinas Baumann, Janice Cantieri, and Lara Rao. Their feedback, as well as my memory of their impressive talents and generosity, pushed me to do better. Thank you.

The first page of this novel appeared in the inaugural issue of *First Page*, a quarterly literary magazine based in Berlin. More information is available at www.firstpageliterature.com.

I never would have attempted to write this story if it hadn't been for a conversation with Barbara Tannenbaum. She helped me shape my approach and her enthusiasm was unwavering. The recollections of Melinda Johnson, Kent Johnson, and Kelly Blanscet were helpful and inspiring. I thank them for their time, for their forgiveness, for keeping the memory of my sister alive, and most of all, for always loving her. This book would never have been seen in the light of day if it wasn't for Cris Mazza, Alexandra Carides, and Christina Pitcher.

The nuts-and-bolts writing of this book was an especially solitary task. But I still want to note the writers and editors who sustained me, in one form or another, while I was hammering out these words. In no significant order, they are Jim Meirose, Chris Bowen, Cherrita Lee, Linda Lenhoff, Robbi Nester, and the Fiction Chicks (they know who they are). There are too many friends to name without forgetting someone and feeling awful about it, but you folks know who you are, too.

And for my husband Patrick and daughter Eva, I can never thank you enough for your love, your support, your inestimable tolerance, and for making my life worth living.

ABOUT THE AUTHOR

JANE ROSENBERG LAFORGE's poetry and short fiction have been nominated for the Pushcart Prize, the story South Million Writers Award, and the Best of the Net compilation. Her novel, *The Hawkman: A Fairy Tale of the Great War*, was a finalist in two categories in the 2019 Eric Hoffer awards. Born in Los Angeles, she has worked as a newspaper reporter and college English literature and composition instructor. She lives in New York with her husband, daughter, and two cats.

Made in the USA
Las Vegas, NV
26 April 2021

22082661R00184